R H

Candlelight Ecstasy Romance ®

SHE NEEDED TO BE ALONE YET HE INSISTED ON FOLLOWING HER . . .

She craved solitude to sort out these unexpected few minutes and put them into some kind of orderly perspective. There had been no one in her life since Warren. She didn't want anyone; it would only complicate her life again. Surely it was just a combination of fatigue, excitement, and too much wine that had caused the overwhelming physical reaction she had felt in his arms.

"Thank you for seeing me . . ." He stopped her words with an unexpected kiss, catching her trembling hand on the switch and bumping the door closed with his heel. His kiss deepened, drowning her in a dizzying rush of desire . . .

A CANDLELIGHT ECSTASY ROMANCE ®

114   LOVER FROM THE SEA, *Bonnie Drake*
115   IN THE ARMS OF LOVE, *Alexis Hill*
116   CAUGHT IN THE RAIN, *Shirley Hart*
117   WHEN NEXT WE LOVE, *Heather Graham*
118   TO HAVE AND TO HOLD, *Lori Herter*
119   HEART'S SHADOW, *Prudence Martin*
120   THAT CERTAIN SUMMER, *Emma Bennett*
121   DAWN'S PROMISE, *Jo Calloway*
122   A SILENT WONDER, *Samantha Hughes*
123   WILD RHAPSODY, *Shirley Hart*
124   AN AFFAIR TO REMEMBER, *Barbara Cameron*
125   TENDER TAMING, *Heather Graham*
126   LEGACY OF LOVE, *Tate McKenna*
127   THIS BITTERSWEET LOVE, *Barbara Andrews*
128   A GENTLE WHISPER, *Eleanor Woods*
129   LOVE ON ANY TERMS, *Nell Kincaid*
130   CONFLICT OF INTEREST, *Jayne Castle*
131   RUN BEFORE THE WIND, *Joellyn Carroll*
132   THE SILVER FOX, *Bonnie Drake*
133   WITH TIME AND TENDERNESS, *Tira Lacy*
134   PLAYING FOR KEEPS, *Lori Copeland*
135   BY PASSION BOUND, *Emma Bennett*
136   DANGEROUS EMBRACE, *Donna Kimel Vitek*
137   LOVE SONG, *Prudence Martin*
138   WHITE SAND, WILD SEA, *Diana Blayne*
139   RIVER ENCHANTMENT, *Emma Bennett*
140   PORTRAIT OF MY LOVE, *Emily Elliott*
141   LOVING EXILE, *Eleanor Woods*
142   KINDLE THE FIRES, *Tate McKenna*
143   PASSIONATE APPEAL, *Elise Randolph*
144   SURRENDER TO THE NIGHT, *Shirley Hart*
145   CACTUS ROSE, *Margaret Dobson*
146   PASSION AND ILLUSION, *Bonnie Drake*
147   LOVE'S UNVEILING, *Samantha Scott*
148   MOONLIGHT RAPTURE, *Prudence Martin*
149   WITH EVERY LOVING TOUCH, *Nell Kincaid*
150   ONE OF A KIND, *Jo Calloway*
151   PRIME TIME, *Rachel Ryan*
152   AUTUMN FIRES, *Jackie Black*
153   ON WINGS OF MAGIC, *Kay Hooper*

A FLIGHT OF SPLENDOR

Joellyn Carroll

A CANDLELIGHT ECSTASY ROMANCE ®

Published by
Dell Publishing Co., Inc.
1 Dag Hammarskjold Plaza
New York, New York 10017

ISBN: 0-440-12858-7

Printed in the United States of America
First printing—July 1983

To Our Readers:

We have been delighted with your enthusiastic response to Candlelight Ecstasy Romances®, and we thank you for the interest you have shown in this exciting series.

In the upcoming months we will continue to present the distinctive sensuous love stories you have come to expect only from Ecstasy. We look forward to bringing you many more books from your favorite authors and also the very finest work from new authors of contemporary romantic fiction.

As always, we are striving to present the unique, absorbing love stories that you enjoy most—books that are more than ordinary romance.

Your suggestions and comments are always welcome. Please write to us at the address below.

Sincerely,

The Editors
Candlelight Romances
1 Dag Hammarskjold Plaza
New York, New York 10017

CHAPTER ONE

"Well, what did you think of him, Lydia?" Thurston Kline asked enthusiastically. "I can see you were impressed," he added. The senator placed his hands on the massive mahogany desk, which was framed effectively by Old Glory and the white and blue of the Colorado state flag. He leaned forward, awaiting an answer.

"I promised him the money for his research," Lydia Wentworth replied obliquely, brushing at a stray wisp of black hair that still showed only a sprinkling of gray. "Isn't that what you wanted me to do, Thurston?" She smiled at her old friend. "He was really quite impressive." She nodded in agreement. "Sincere, direct . . ."

"He's a fine man and an excellent scientist," Thurston expanded.

"And what politician could turn down a request for funding a project dealing with the national symbol?" Lydia teased. "You know what a soft touch I am."

"Soft touch, my foot!" the senator snorted. "As I recall, your last two primary opponents are still licking their wounds. While we're on the subject," he sidetracked, stepping to the long narrow window behind him, "word has come down from the Appropriations Committee that you're giving our budget proposal rough sailing in conference."

"Oh, no you don't." Lydia held up a well-manicured hand. "We were not on the subject," she said, chuckling. "No business today. You invited me to meet your biologist and fund his eagle research. I've done that! I won't be flattered into discussing the budget compromise." Lydia's career in state and national politics spanned two decades, yet it could be matched twice over by her companion's forty years of public service. Thurston Kline,

7

"colorful conservative from the Color State," had been the thorn in the side of the liberals through seven administrations. And he was a treasured Wentworth family friend for many years.

"Very well, Representative Wentworth," Thurston intoned formally as he turned to view his guest with a fond eye. "We will speak only of Dr. Cade and his work." He returned to his seat in the high-backed leather chair that had suitably cowed his opponents and colleagues alike through four terms in the U.S. Senate. "His degrees and Ph.D. are from Cornell," he recited, ticking off the points on the fingers of one hand. "Specifically, his field of expertise is raptor biology, the maintenance and preservation of birds of prey—particularly the bald eagle. And of even more importance to me, personally," he said, leaning back in his chair and watching Lydia, "he saved my grandson's life."

"Saved his life?" Lydia echoed quietly, quick to read the emotion evident in his brown eyes.

"During the Vietnam conflict," Thurston related, smoothing his hair with both hands in a practiced gesture, "Todd's unit was pinned down in a firefight. Mitchell Cade took out a machine gun emplacement single-handed and saved them all. I owe him an eternal debt for that. I can never do enough to repay him."

"Of course not," she answered sincerely, understanding now why Thurston should be so concerned that she find Dr. Cade worthy of her largesse. He needn't have worried; the young man was sufficiently impressive on his own. A fleeting image of the tall, rugged-looking man they were discussing popped up before her mind's eye. So bravery too could be added to the list of his attributes. "He seemed a very hardworking, dedicated young man. I'm glad to be of help." She was certain that her friend felt a genuine debt to Mitchell Cade. Thurston was a staunch conservative and still wholeheartedly believed in his country's commitment to that disastrous war, yet nevertheless he had been torn apart when his own grandson was sent to fight.

"I'm only sorry he couldn't stay to meet Erin. I would have liked for her to get to know someone so sure of his direction in life," she mused reflectively. "Dr. Cade definitely knows what he wants to do. And does it."

Thurston looked up sharply at the subtle change in her tone.

8

"He's made out of a tough cut of cloth, all right," he agreed. "I think you'll appreciate his candor and his integrity; they're qualities you don't see much anymore. You'll be able to question him more thoroughly at the reception this evening."

"Yes, I'll do just that," she said, once again brisk and business-like, the pensive tone no longer noticeable in her speech. "I'm glad you will both be able to attend."

"Wouldn't miss one of your soirees for the world, Lydia," Thurston assured her and settled his bulk more comfortably into his chair. "Mitch is off to give a lecture at the Smithsonian, and then he's interviewing for a last-minute replacement for his staff. He'll have pretty tough sledding to find someone this late in the year. Not many graduate students can afford to work for peanuts, and the wilds of upper Michigan isn't exactly the most stimulating place to spend your summer."

"I suppose not, unless you're interested in bald eagles," Lydia said. "I plan to complete the paperwork for the grant this evening, and I do have more questions for Dr. Cade. I have to be back in committee at two o'clock," she murmured, pushing back the sleeve of her impeccably tailored navy-blue suit to read her slender gold watch. "I don't understand what's keeping Erin. She's usually not as late as this. I see so little of her these days, Thurston," she confessed. "Frankly, I'm worried about her. We've drifted so far apart these last few months."

"You worry more than is necessary, Lydia."

"But her outrageous decisions!" Even Thurston didn't know how terribly Erin's lack of confidence in her understanding and love hurt. When she closed her eyes, Lydia could still see her only grandchild, her face sculpted in inner torment as she turned with a heartbroken cry and rushed from the church door. Now, six months later, she had still not revealed the real reason for her refusal to marry Warren Markham. Lydia wanted Erin to confide in her so she could guide her, but she only drifted away, and the estrangement, though polite, was eating at them both.

Thurston nodded sympathetically, not even pretending to misunderstand her remark. "She wouldn't have been happy married to Markham. He's doing his dead-level best to move into the inner circle around here. He's a manipulator, a mover and a shaker, but deep down he's nothing but an influence peddler and

9

a first-rate snake oil salesman!" The pitch of his voice was evidence of the senator's dislike for Erin's ex-fiancé. "It's better that your headstrong granddaughter realized that when she did." He voiced his opinion aloud and watched with a hooded, piercing gaze as Lydia digested his remarks.

"But to have left him standing at the altar. Her only explanation to me was that she didn't know him well enough—after a two-year engagement." Lydia's lips tightened as she remembered the confusion and embarrassment Erin's flight from the church had caused in gossip-prone capital circles.

"She's young; she'll get her feet planted firmly on the ground again soon."

"I hope your prognosis for her future is correct," Lydia answered drily. "Perhaps I made a mistake not bringing her here directly after my daughter and son-in-law were killed?" Remembered pain darkened her eyes for a moment as she recalled the horrible fiery air crash that took her only daughter from her, but she gave her head an unconscious shake and went on. "Boarding school and college weren't enough preparation for this town. Washington is a pretty heady draft for a girl barely out of her teens. I wasn't pleased when she dropped out of college her senior year, even to help with my campaign. Less pleased when she decided to marry Markham, but she was nearly twenty-four at the time. Old enough to know her own mind, I thought."

"Don't be too hard on the girl," he repeated his cautions. "She's got the Wentworth temper if not the name." He chuckled delightedly at his own wit, but Lydia's answering smile was preoccupied.

"That's just the point, Thurston. She's not a girl anymore, she's a grown woman." Part of the problem, she admitted to herself, was that she and Erin were too much alike. Same dark abundant hair, snapping blue eyes, and finely molded features. Unfortunately, they also shared the same stubborn streak, and in addition Erin had inherited her late grandfather's famous temper.

As she gazed once again at her watch, an idea began forming in Lydia's fertile mind. The main difference between them now was that she, Lydia, had a lifetime of accomplishments to prove who she was, and all Erin had were shadows to live in. Her life was influenced by heroes, all the way down to her famous grandmother, one of the elite number of women elected to a seat in the Congress of the United States. Was that part of the problem in her relationship with Warren? Lydia surmised with a flash of insight. Did she see another strong will to eclipse her own? Or perhaps did she discover he wasn't strong enough to match her own high-spirited beauty and competence?

"You're up to something, Lydia," Thurston boomed, startling her from her cogitations. She refocused on his seamed face crowned by its luxuriant head of carefully groomed silver hair, a trademark recognized throughout the land.

"How could you possibly think that?" she answered evasively. "I was just speculating on the cause of Erin's delay." Erin's delay to enter the real business of living her life, she continued inwardly. Perhaps if she played her cards right she could push her granddaughter out of the shadows that dulled her outlook on the future and into the light of her own successes.

"Haven't been enough parking spaces around this building for forty years," Thurston complained obligingly, changing the subject as she wished him to do.

Lydia nodded absently, returning her rapidly calculating brain to the seed of a plan that was beginning to take root. They hadn't called the Wentworth clan robber barons for nothing, and some of that ruthlessness had rubbed off on Lydia as well. Erin was all the family she had left now, and she meant to do what was best for her, even if her granddaughter fought her tooth and nail.

Yes, it was a very good idea, Lydia concluded. Mitchell Cade's project was the perfect vehicle to pry Erin from the shallow, pleasure-seeking life she was rapidly adopting. Lydia came from sturdy hardworking stock, and Erin's aimless existence appalled and frightened her. She would have to play her cards right, but then she was an excellent poker player. The congresswoman smiled as details of the plan clicked into place like the tumblers of a combination lock. It amounted to genteel blackmail, and she would have to move very carefully to bring both Dr. Cade and Erin into her trap. But when all was said and done, she held the winning cards in this high stakes game. Securing Erin's future was worth the gamble.

* * *

"It's a beautiful sunny day in D.C., folks. All you hardworking civil servants brown-bagging it today will have perfect weather for lunch on the mall." The dulcet tones of the disc jockey bounded out of the dashboard speaker. Beautiful day! Erin McIntee scowled at the radio of her silver Corvette. Although only the middle of May it was midsummer on the banks of the Potomac, and Erin was thankful for her car's air conditioner. A few minutes shy of high noon it was already eighty degrees, and the humidity was definitely in the uncomfortable range, while heat waves danced from the capital city's massive expanse of marble and concrete.

She threaded the eye-catching little car through several lanes of heavy traffic, barely noticing the imposing edifices of the Supreme Court and the Library of Congress as she prepared to search for a parking space within reasonable distance of the Capitol building. She was already late for her meeting with her grandmother, and Lydia Wentworth was notoriously unsympathetic to people who upset her carefully orchestrated appointment schedule. If only she hadn't stayed so late and hadn't downed a foolish number of martinis at the Covingtons' cocktail party the night before. She would have arrived in plenty of time, without this dreadful pounding in her head, and there would have been one less sore point to smooth over with her grandmother. If only—if only—she repeated to the beat of the rock music on the radio. It was a phrase she was using too often this past winter and spring, she admitted as she whipped the Corvette into a space just milliseconds ahead of a Mercedes bearing diplomatic plates.

Slamming the door, she quickened her steps toward the east facade of the Capitol building. The sun was intense, escalating the pounding ache behind her sapphire blue eyes, and the heat from the pavement was already seeping through the thin soles of her chic high-heeled sandals.

Minutes later Erin whisked through the high-ceilinged corridors of the Capitol building, enjoying the dim coolness after the blinding brilliance of the noonday sun. She had entered through the huge bronze doors of the East Front, bypassing the public areas to follow a more private and direct route to her rendezvous in Senator Kline's sanctum on the second floor.

12

"There's a roll call vote in the Senate in twenty minutes, Ms. McIntee," John Whitney voiced in his usual nasal tone as he spotted her washing down a pain pill with water from a paper cup. He was eyeing her softly sheathed curves in the teal-blue sundress with distaste. She probably shouldn't have worn it today; the neckline was very revealing, and she resisted the urge to tug at it. Erin crumpled the container with unnecessary vigor and continued walking toward the small, monochromatic man with unhurried steps. She paused in the alcove outside the senator's outer office to face the legislative aide. Everything about John Whitney was gray; his hair, his skin, and the clothes he wore. He was the epitome of efficiency, performing his required duties and absorbing with no apparent difficulty those tasks which Erin had always considered her province. "You'd better hurry if you want to see your grandmother and Thurston together."

"I know I'm late," she said breezily, her hackles rising as they always did at the mere sound of his voice. "The traffic was incredible today."

"The tourist season is upon us," he said dispassionately, as though he were a seasoned veteran of capital life and not a newcomer to the Hill riding on the coattails of Lydia Wentworth's formidable reputation.

"Indeed," Erin answered in the bored tone that always brought a pinched look of disapproval to his bony features.

John had taken over the duties she usually performed for her grandmother the previous autumn when Warren decided she should devote her full time to the plans for their elaborate Christmas wedding. That was another warning sign she had overlooked, that imperceptible remolding of her life to fit Warren's design, whittling away, bit by bit, those areas that defined her as a unique human being, a person in her own right. Now it was too late, but it still hurt Erin that her grandmother had made no move to reinstate her on the staff.

She missed the many hours she had spent working on the Hill these last few years, missed them more than she liked to admit. When her grandmother began her campaign for reelection five years ago, Erin gladly left her classes at Colorado University, reaching with open arms for the excitement of D.C. She had been lonely since the death of her parents. Although the schools Lydia selected for her were comfortable, and the girls friendly, they were no substitute for the loving family atmosphere she had always known. When Lydia suggested she move to the capital she was delighted, feeling for the first time that she was doing something worthwhile with her life. She had been an able and competent research assistant, happily stumping whenever she could for the vibrant woman who was all that remained of her family. Abruptly Erin turned her back on John Whitney's sallow face and her own churning memories as she stepped into the private offices of Senator Thurston Kline.

"Go right on in, Miss McIntee," the senator's secretary invited with a merry smile as Erin swung into the room, closing the door with a decided snap. "The senator and Mrs. Wentworth are expecting you."

Erin made a wry face as the woman rose from her desk to hold open the carved door of the suite with its restful federal blue and buff walls. Erin's quick footsteps were muffled in the thick pile carpet. "I'm so sorry. I'm . . ." she began with a smile of apology as she sailed into the partially paneled room with her head high.

". . . late again, Erin," Lydia Wentworth finished for her errant protégé as her granddaughter emerged from Thurston's bearlike embrace.

"Yes, I'm afraid you are, my dear." He smiled, draping a long arm around her shoulders. "I'm due for a roll call vote. Those scoundrels are trying to rob us of a budget cut we've already got through by tacking it onto another proposal. They wouldn't know how to act if I wasn't there to get my two cents worth in." The silver-haired man chortled. "Damn, I've been around so long I'm finally back in style. Just like an old pair of shoes."

"A very comfortable pair, indeed," Lydia added, beaming at her friend.

"I must go, ladies," he said, catching his secretary's gesture to her watch as she entered the room. "Martha, try and track down the speaker for me later today. I'll see you two lovely ladies at the reception, my ornithologist in tow," he went on with a flourish, giving a nod to his secretary and a smile to Erin before he disappeared out the door.

"Yes. I have a great deal more to say to the good doctor before

14

I sign that check," Lydia reflected aloud, then waved a quick farewell to the senator, who was already gone from sight.

"Another Wentworth Fund Grant, Grandmother?" Erin asked curiously.

"Yes, dear. This man is doing excellent work banding and studying eagles in the wilds. He's a very determined and persuasive man. I'm sorry you missed him. You could learn a lot from a person like that. He, by the way, was early for his appointment," she added, giving her granddaughter a sidelong glance as they prepared to leave the office.

"I've invited him to the reception this evening. He's returning to Michigan tomorrow to continue his work. He lives there—in Paradise, he informed me. It's a very small town, but such a charming name."

"Speaking of paradise," Erin angled, wanting to test her grandmother's mood. "I have a wonderful invitation to spend several weeks at the Carsons' summer home in Hawaii."

"Several weeks? Good-bye, Martha." Lydia turned aside to bid the secretary farewell, and Erin added a hasty good-bye as they passed by her into the corridor.

"Just imagine, six weeks on a wonderful island paradise with nothing but flowers and palm trees. Berrie's parents are on a junket to China and Japan. She's still too upset over her divorce to spend the summer here alone," Erin informed her grandmother, watching her carefully rehearsed words drop onto the cool surface of Lydia's unchanging expression without causing a single ripple.

"Several weeks, or six weeks, Erin, which do you mean?" the congresswoman inquired. "What happened to your plans to return to school and finish your studies?"

"The university will still be here when I return," Erin quipped, dismayed that her grandmother should pounce so quickly on that subject.

"So you think you could afford to be away for—several weeks?" Lydia emphasized the words.

"Yes, of course. The House will recess soon, and John has most of the work caught up," Erin admitted with a bitter note, a dark naturally arched brow raised in derision of her successor. "You know how efficient he is."

15

"Indeed he is. Most reliable," Lydia answered repressively.

Uneasy at the turn the conversation was taking, Erin suggested lunch, and the older woman readily agreed. Heels clicking loudly on the tiled floors, they walked toward the representatives' dining room on the ground floor, following the low corridor covered with colorful patriotic murals that led to the restaurant. Once inside they were welcomed by several other members and their guests as they took their seats. Lydia was respected and well liked among the congressional delegations, and Erin was pleased by their reception. She admired her grandmother more than any person she knew.

"Erin, I want to discuss something of importance with you," Lydia remarked as they waited for their food and Erin toyed with the basket of crusty rolls the waitress had placed before her. Erin looked up quickly at the serious tone of Lydia's pronouncement, but the waitress returned at that moment and she said no more, remaining silent as they watched the serving of two Caesar salads and iced tea. Lydia engaged in a polite exchange of pleasantries with the smiling hostess while Erin waited as a growing feeling of dismay settled over her spirit.

"As you know," Lydia began again so suddenly that Erin jumped, "in two months the review of your trust will be due." Erin nodded, not testing her voice, and Lydia continued. "It is a sizeable amount of money that has been growing over the years, and at the present time I am the administrator of the trust." Lydia was choosing her words carefully, her attention fixed on the bowl of shining greens before her.

"Of course, Grandma," Erin said, slipping into the more familiar endearment. "Every ten years the trust is reviewed. I'm twenty-six now, not a teenager, so you'll be turning it over to me this year." That would be one less responsibility for her grandmother to handle, Erin pledged. At least she could prove that she was able to handle her own finances in a capable manner.

"That has always been my intention," Lydia said succinctly.

"What are you trying to say . . . ?" Erin faltered as the words her grandmother spoke began to penetrate.

"You are Erin Wentworth McIntee. You will someday be the heir to the Wentworth assets as well as your trust fund. I don't believe you are ready to handle such a responsibility when your

16

sole purpose in life seems to be to play tennis and vacation in the luxury spots of this world."

"Grandmother, please . . ." Erin implored, glancing about the room to see who might be in earshot of her grandmother's well-modulated voice.

"I had patience when you were dating that Markham person. You insisted he was the love of your life, even though I doubted his sincerity and told you so openly," Lydia reiterated. "You insisted on marrying him with all the pomp and ceremony my money could command. Then you run from the church in your wedding gown leaving that man at the altar and me with all the explanations!" Erin could tell her guardian was only warming to her theme of recalling past sins. "Leaving school and not returning. Leaving me in the midst of a fall session. Then refusing to marry the man that was the cause of it all. You've been playing at life for too long."

"You aren't going to turn the trust over to me? Is that what you're trying to say?" Erin gasped, too stunned to defend her actions concerning Warren Markham. She kept her voice deliberately low as the two pairs of sapphire eyes clashed across the expanse of cutlery and white linen.

"That is correct. You behave like a twenty-six-year-old child, and I must react accordingly. I cannot relinquish my duty with a clear conscience at this time." Lydia sat back in her chair, a flush darkening her carefully rouged cheeks as she searched the angry face before her. "You are a Wentworth. The last of the line. You spring from a family that has prided themselves on being men and women of action. They crossed an ocean and half a continent to carve a life from the frontier of a new land. They were determined, fiercely independent people. They made their own destinies."

"I can't cross the prairie in a covered wagon, Grandma," Erin snapped in disbelief, her pride reeling from this latest blow. Lydia had never spoken to her in this manner; not for as long as she could remember. Her mind raced furiously, proposing and rejecting arguments against her grandmother's attack. "The frontier was officially closed by an act of Congress over eighty years ago."

"You can start a difficult task and finish it," Lydia replied as

17

sharply. "I want you to prove to me that you are ready to handle your own life. I want you to show me the stuff you are made of."

Erin picked up her water goblet with a hand that shook as she tried to control the rush of angry frustration their altercation was producing. This couldn't be happening. Her own grandmother refusing to treat her as a responsible adult. Waves of humiliation swept over her nerves along with a tiny voice whispering that Lydia was right. What had she done in the past several years to earn her grandmother's good opinion?

"I want to see your fiber, Erin, and you have only two months in which to prove yourself. There will be a task for you to start, work to my standards of satisfaction, and complete," Lydia decreed with a martial light in her eye and her chin high.

"Grandmother, please . . . I . . ."

"We'll discuss the details later, Erin; your tardiness has thrown my schedule off by nearly thirty minutes."

"I refuse to be treated like this! You can't dangle my inheritance before me like a carrot on a string. It is rightfully mine." Her voice was rising, and she struggled to control it. "It's not fair," she sighed childishly, snapping her lips closed as she heard her own condemning words.

"You're right, Erin. I haven't been fair to you. Perhaps I have loved you too much, given you too much since your parents died. But now I have to know whether you can earn your own way." Lydia Wentworth was not giving an inch. "It is only fair to your forefathers and the children you may have that you be a worthy administrator of the responsibilities that will someday fall to you. Your ancestors fought drought, Indians, and plague to assemble the largest tract of land in Colorado. They have handed down a legacy of cattle, wheat, silver, coal, and land. It's going to be a huge burden for one person to handle. I know," she added a little sadly, and Erin knew she was missing her husband, the one man Lydia Wentworth had ever loved, "that one person is going to be you, Erin. After I'm gone you'll be responsible for it all."

"I don't want you to be gone," Erin said forcefully, a catch in her throat, as though by denying mortality she could erase it. She sighed helplessly as she studied her grandmother's features. She might as well save her arguments. When Lydia's mind was made up, few people could change it without a monumental battle. The pounding in Erin's head was communicating itself to her entire body. "You're going to live forever," she declared, reinforcing her own wish.

"No one lives forever, my love," Lydia said gently. "However, I've lived sixty-eight years on this earth, and I do not intend to vacate my space for some time yet. Certainly not before I have corrected my errors," she said bracingly with a smile at her unhappy granddaughter.

"I'm sorry I'm such a disappointment," Erin said, rising from the table as her hands tightened on the back of her chair, her spirit reasserting itself as quickly as it had deserted her.

"We will discuss the details further this evening," Lydia said in a controlled voice. Irate tears glittered in Erin's eyes, and she missed the look of love and pain that flashed across Lydia's face. Her voice trembled slightly, but her chin held its determined line. "I expect you at the party by eight thirty, Erin. Try to be on time."

Erin's head jerked up, the dejection on her face replaced by a haughty reserve. She examined her grandmother carefully for a long heated moment. What had transformed this loving, generous woman before her into a tyrant? She was unwilling to admit even to herself that her own flighty behavior of the past several years was the source of the rift between them. And the one thing that rankled Lydia the most, her rejection of Warren Markham, was the one act of defiance for which her reasoning was strong and true. But this was not the time or the place; she would not beg. Erin clung to the shreds of her dignity with stubborn pride. Without another word she spun and made a hasty exit from the crowded room—or was it a retreat—or was it an escape? Her cheeks burned with embarrassment and fury, and tears pushed at the corners of her eyes, but she held them back.

She can't do this, Erin thought in disbelief. I'm a grown woman. I should be allowed to handle my own affairs. How could she humiliate me in this way? Her angry steps carried her swiftly forward as she made her way blindly to more public areas of the great edifice. She suddenly found herself in a crowd of curious, gawking tourists in Statuary Hall, trapped and slowed by camera toters and rebellious children, and feeling the stares of the great

Americans sitting stonily on their pedestals as she waded through a troop of cub scouts and harried leaders. The dead, gray eyes of bygone leaders and heroes bore into her with unanimated cruelty, accusing her of a lack of purpose. But she knew it wasn't these stone figures who criticized her; it was herself.

It was true that her only claim to fame was her status as "Lydia Wentworth's granddaughter." She had done nothing of value on her own. Drifting—drifting like the frescoes on the ceiling of the Rotunda high above her. Drifting—drifting—drifting, her clicking heels repeated in her brain with every step she took. Never accomplishing anything on her own. She was always an extension of stronger, more gifted people. Wanting so much to be loved, to be a part of a happy family once again that she was even willing to subjugate her life to Warren's idea of the perfect wife and woman.

The humid heat of the Washington afternoon assailed her as she hurried down the marble steps to her car. Even as the frustrated anger welled up inside her, she conceded her grandmother's victory. She would do whatever it was Lydia had in mind, but no longer would she exist in someone else's shadow. She was Erin Wentworth McIntee, a human being in her own right. No longer would she allow someone stronger, more in control, to dominate her life. But first she'd do whatever was necessary to obtain her independence. Lydia was right on that point; she hadn't proved herself, and it was time she did just that!

CHAPTER TWO

Music floated softly on a gentle breeze to where Erin lingered in the shadows of the sheltered garden. Water whispered like a prayer over the rocks, splashing into the pool at the foot of the stone wall where she was sitting. Exotic scents from the herb garden mingled with the more easily recognized perfumes of roses and lavender. Erin sighed, smoothing the pleats of her lilac jersey gown with restless fingers as she glanced toward her grandmother's narrow white brick town-house, nestled in the wooded hills of Georgetown. Through half-opened French doors, light spilled out onto the slate terrace and reached out to her. Yet the rays fell short of Erin's secluded corner.

Hugging chilled arms around herself, Erin recalled the heated words she had exchanged with her grandmother. Sitting in the expectant calm before Lydia's guests arrived, Erin had finally given her word, as gracefully as she was able, to abide by Lydia's decision. Her grandmother nodded as she spoke, not retreating an inch from her earlier stand. On the subject of the task to be completed, she was unusually reticent, and Erin had by now reconciled herself to spending a summer in the humid heat of the city. Most likely she would be tracking down a mountain of dry, dusty, irrelevant facts and figures for some obscure proposal.

She sighed again, bending to trail her fingers in the cool water, listening with detachment to the plaintive rustle of the willow tree behind her and the night sounds of small frogs hidden in the reeds. Rising with a smooth graceful movement, Erin squared her shoulders and prepared to return to the party. She had been gone too long already, and for a moment she practiced a polished, happy expression, forcing her shapely mouth into a smile that would conceal her inner distress. Echoes of Lydia's accusations still revolved in her mind, evidence that their barbs carried the weight of truth.

Reluctant steps carried her toward the source of light and music and to her destiny as a Wentworth. She was entitled to her inheritance, she reasoned with her unconvinced self, but now she was determined to show her grandmother that she was also worthy. Blinking a little in the brightness, she stepped over the threshold into the crowded elegant room.

"Erin love, over here," Berita Carson caroled. "Where have you been? I've been looking everywhere for you. Did she change her mind?" the young woman asked, after Erin had crossed the room to greet her friend.

"No. I'm afraid not, Berrie," Erin apologized. "I really won't be able to get away. My grandmother needs me here."

Patent disbelief at the thinness of Erin's excuse showed on Berrie's exquisitely made-up face. "I simply can't go alone," she wailed, throwing out her hands and nearly toppling the wineglass on the gateleg table beside her chair. "I have to get away from this city. Certainly you can understand that." The attractive redhead retrieved her glass and took another sip of wine as her green eyes canvassed the room restlessly. "Always the same faces in the same places."

Erin knew Berita was right. It was a party like dozens of other parties. Strictly business, nothing social about any "social event" in the capital city. A few select cronies of her grandmother's were present along with several distinguished persons to whom an evening's entertainment was due, and the new breed, people on their way up the ladder or searching for the right commodity to catapult them into the political arena.

"I need to find someone other than a politician," Berita mourned, then came back to earth with a rush. "Lord, I've already tried that twice. I've had enough of that madness." She took another sip of her wine. "Well, you know how it was with Warren. . . ." She retreated slightly after slanting a glance at Erin's stiffened posture. "Really, honey, you're lucky you didn't go through with the wedding; trust me. Loving a man in politics is like swimming in a pool with a piranha; sooner or later it'll eat you alive. I guess I'm just old-fashioned, but I would like to try it with someone loving for a change."

Erin couldn't help but admire her friend's elasticity. The daughter of a career State Department official, Berrie, though still under thirty, was recently divorced for the second time. Yet she was still willing to try marriage once again. Erin applauded her bravery—or was it a bent toward self-destruction?—although she didn't share her friend's desire to rush into a serious relationship again. At any rate, after her near miss with Warren she wasn't ready to chance her freedom or her heart a second time. Someday, perhaps—but not yet. There were too many questions within herself that needed answers. Far too many.

"I did want you to come with me to Hawaii," Berrie pleaded, still hopeful. "Nothing to do in the islands but play tennis, swim, and lie in the sun for days on end." She sighed. "We might even meet someone special."

"Always the optimist. I'm sure you won't have any trouble finding someone to accompany you," Erin soothed when she saw Berrie's lips begin to quiver. "Lydia is going to be keeping me very busy for the next couple of months." She watched Berrie's straying green gaze slide toward a group of men with fond tolerance. Berrie was probably already realizing a pair of well-muscled shoulders to cry on would be much more therapeutic than Erin's. Shaking her head in resignation, Erin lowered herself into one of the spindly-legged chairs near her friend's and prepared herself for a long recital of real and imagined woes. She glanced quickly around the civilized room. Foam-green walls crowned with intricate wooden molding painted a delicate cream softened the effect of the brocade coverings on the warm cherry and mahogany Georgian furnishings. Brass fixtures glowed softly in the subdued light, and conversation was the main occupation of the guests around her. Noting that her grandmother's staff had everything functioning smoothly, she crossed one slender silk-covered ankle over the other, returning her attention to Berrie's animated soliloquy.

Berrie's back was turned to the archway leading to the dining room on the left. Erin could see couples dancing to music provided by the three musicians positioned at the room's far end. The area had been cleared of its Chippendale furnishings to provide space for the brightly dressed women and their partners to dance. The beautiful women in their expensive, very chic garments provided a pleasant, colorful diversion compared to the stark evening clothes of the men. A gripping twinge stiffened Erin's spine. Was it only the bitterness of her own experience speaking, or were women truly just a diversion in this city—an interlude, a fringe benefit of the power broker syndrome? This generation of politicians was a new breed—the Warren Markham type.

"Erin!" Berrie squealed, her feline attention directed over Erin's shoulder. "Who is that incredible man with Senator Kline?" she breathed. Her jade, feline eyes were fixed upon a point behind her friend, far across the crowded room.

"Very likely it's his ornithologist," Erin replied absently as she watched a recently appointed federal judge spill his martini on the muted jeweled tones of the oriental rug beneath his feet. "My grandmother is helping to fund his research with bald eagles. I believe he's here to complete the paperwork on the grant."

"An eagle man!" Berrie crooned in a throaty whisper, sitting up and forgetting to add the lanquid, heartbroken sigh that accompanied most of her observations these days. "He looks like a Greek god. I simply must meet him. My Lord, he's a giant," she rattled on while Erin experienced a curious sinking sensation in the pit of her stomach. Her expectations of a middle-aged, myopic scientist were evaporating even faster than the misty sadness in Berrie's eyes.

"What could they possibly be doing in the library?" Berrie questioned as she fidgeted in her chair. "Go on, Erin, find out who he is. I can't wait to meet him."

"Thurston is probably showing him Grandmother's paintings. He particularly enjoys the Winslow Homer. He's been trying to get it away from her for years."

"Erin, you must introduce me," Berrie implored. "Go get him. I'll wait here."

"I haven't met him myself," Erin pointed out, moving toward the paneled library with unconscious grace, the full skirt of her dress molding itself to rounded hips and whishing around slender thighs with each purposeful step. The light set blue-black highlights shimmering in her hair while diamond studs glittered in her ears and echoed in the fine chain lying against her throat.

"There you are, Erin," Thurston boomed, turning from the

empty fireplace and his familiar inspection of the coveted artwork. "I knew you would track me down sooner or later. My dear, may I introduce my friend Dr. Mitchell Cade." The man seated before her seemed to unfold from the wing-backed chair in sections, shoulders leading, followed by a trim waist tapering to narrow hips and long well-muscled legs. Erin had to tilt her head back slightly to meet his eyes, and she felt an odd, disturbing qualm at the purely masculine appraisal she encountered in his gold-flecked hazel eyes.

"How do you do, Dr. Cade," she mouthed, extending an elegant hand to be clasped by the warm brown hand he extended to her. "Welcome to Washington." He was over six feet with bold angular features and a mobile, smiling mouth. His nose was long and looked as if it had once been broken; his smile deepened as she continued her scrutiny, accenting the brushed leather lines around the hazel eyes. Her gaze traveled over his sensual face touching on the high cheekbones and wide forehead topped by an unruly shock of sunstreaked blond hair.

No wonder Berrie's description had taken such a lyrical bent; the silky white turtleneck and formal black jacket fit his athletic physique well, not disguising the muscled strength that pulsated beneath the fine fabric. Their eyes met and locked over the short distance that separated them; his, dancing with private mirth, and Erin's, mirroring the confusion that threaded through her thoughts as he continued to hold her hand in his. His touch was magnetic, and it was with an effort she broke the contact, surprised and disturbed by her immediate reaction to a complete stranger.

"Mitch is here on business from Paradise," Thurston chortled.

". . . Michigan," the man supplied. "My base camp is located near there, several miles from Lake Superior." He caught her gaze a second time, a marvelous knowing smile transforming his features. A smile that made her even more self-conscious of her own unrestrained study.

"He's here to see Lydia about funding for his eagle research," Thurston elaborated, thumping his companion on the shoulder with a blow that would have felled a smaller man. "He's an ornithologist, you know."

"And you're Erin . . . ?" Mitchell Cade prompted.

25

"McIntee," she supplied quietly, with more control of her shaky voice than she imagined possible. I must have been out in the sun too long, she scolded. But now she could understand her grandmother's preoccupation with this man. The term animal magnetism might have been invented just for him. Berrie had sensed it from across the room, and she was an expert. "Are you going to be in the capital long, Doctor?"

"I'm afraid not," he answered in a low, commanding voice. "I'm returning to my work tomorrow. Although I haven't regretted that necessity until now."

"Lydia is probably in her study," Thurston interjected, anxious to find his friend and conclude the business of formalizing the grant. "Let me find her for you, son. Erin, I'm sure I can count on you to entertain Mitch."

Erin was unable to answer, once again guilty of studying this fascinating male. He nodded in agreement as Thurston left the room, then turned to face Erin's silence.

"I hope I'm not taking you away from your friends." There was a hint of a question in the statement.

"No, of course not."

He nodded again, using the opportunity to resume his scrutiny of her. For a moment his gaze rested on her throat, then lowered to the hint of cleavage that gave a tantalizing glimpse of rounded breasts above the several open buttons at her neckline. Erin felt the touch of his eyes as though it was a physical caress, and a delicate flush tinted her skin.

He's only a man, she chided herself for her adolescent foolishness. He's no different from any other man, and he'll prove it in a few seconds by trying to make a pass, just like all the rest. For an instant she considered his possible approach. Would he be the suave man about town that would try to smooth talk her into his bed? Or the caveman type that she'd need to wrestle with in order to escape? She had become an expert at thwarting all kinds of advances over the years, but her heart was fluttering like the beating wings of a trapped bird.

"I think we should join the party," she said finally in an airy voice, stepping back, trying to lessen the pull of his vitality. He was blocking her path, his powerful anatomy becoming an obstacle to repel her, yet attracting her, too. He caught her arm gently

26

before she could react, and she was drawn into his sphere of strength. Not only was she held by his large strong hand, she was held by bands of subtle power, invisible to the eye, but clearly discernible to her heightened senses. She could feel her pulse pounding in the veins of her wrist under his firm grip, and was afraid he could feel it, too. Did this splendid golden stranger know how wildly her heart was racing? He held her still as he took a step toward her, abating her confused panic with his dark smiling eyes. He smelled clean and spicy, a refreshing scent that mingled naturally with the smells of leather and tobacco that permeated the atmosphere of the library.

They were both still images carved and silhouetted by the light from the room behind them. Music was plainly audible, and sounds of the party traveled clearly to them, yet it only increased Erin's wish to be isolated in this wonderful fantasy of a moment. She looked deep into changeable hazel eyes, catching a glimpse of the wild green land where he belonged. He returned her scrutiny, and she wondered what he was reading in her eyes. His regard fell like warming sunshine on the delicate, dewy roses of her lips, and he lowered his head, leaning toward her. She was fascinated by his mouth moving toward hers; her long fringe of lashes fluttered down, waiting an intense, seemingly endless moment for his kiss. She had an overwhelming desire to taste his mouth. Would his kiss be as clean and cool as the reflections in the depths of his eyes? A burst of raucous laughter broke the spell. He straightened abruptly and moved away, the fantasy diffusing, but still he studied her face as they both recovered their senses in the uncomfortable silence. Was it possible each was mourning the passage of the unrealized moment, perhaps both thinking he would be leaving in a few hours, heading for the forests and lakes of Michigan, knowing they would never meet again beyond the walls of this house? But after all he was only a man—she gave a mental shrug—not worth the heartache he would sooner or later cause.

"Could I ask a favor of you, Erin?" he requested seriously, continuing to hold her arm. Her heart sank. Here it comes; she braced for it—the big pass. The engraved invitation for the one-night stand—to warm the long, lonely night so far from

27

home. . . . She had heard all the lines and had burst them all like pastel bubbles floating on the wind.

"What would that be?" she answered suspiciously.

"I really don't feel that comfortable at these formal parties," he spoke honestly, sliding an index finger inside the neck of the sweater. "Could we . . . ?"

"No, I don't think so, Dr. Cade," she said shortly, forestalling his request, not wanting to completely relinquish the fantasy of a few moments ago. "Believe me, no one would ever detect a lack of confidence or discomfort on your part." Her tone was haughty and matched her aloofly arched brow and the chilling blue of her eyes. He released her abruptly, folding both arms across his chest, staring down at her with a curiously disappointed look on his face.

"I think you jump to conclusions too quickly, Miss McIntee," he drawled, raising a brow that nearly met a stray lock of sun-streaked hair. "I wasn't trying to make a pass. I thought perhaps after my business with Representative Wentworth is completed you might join me in viewing the Lincoln Memorial. I am, after all, a tourist, whose business has kept me tied up all day."

"Oh," she mouthed stupidly.

"Things aren't always what we expect," he stated flatly. A muscle danced along his clenched jaw, then his voice softened. "Sometimes surprise can be the best." He looked down at her with a hint of a smile that vanished like summer lightning. "But I can see you're anxious to get back to the party. Lead the way," he said with a broad sweep of his hand.

"Yes, I should be getting back," she said quietly, her round eyes dark and apologetic, but he had withdrawn that intangible aura of easy intimacy, and Erin didn't try to explain her rudeness. As they walked silently into the noise and laughter, her thoughts were bounding this way and that.

What surprised her most about Mitchell Cade was her own erratic response to him. In a matter of seconds he had run her through a gauntlet of emotions. She wanted to deny all those uncomfortable, dangerous feelings. She had sworn she wouldn't allow another man to stir her, make her forget how men could be. How they are! She knew how cruelly they could use a woman. Then why did she long for this man's kiss and embrace? She had learned her lesson well, but perhaps she had misjudged Dr. Cade, measured him by standards that did not apply in the world where he lived.

She stole a quick glance upwards as he walked beside her. His mouth was set in a determined line. Had he already forgotten her? Was he already thinking ahead to his interview with her grandmother? Or picking his next quarry? Berrie's slightly inebriated laughter rang across the room, and his eyes sought the source of the sound with swift accuracy. He was very definitely a man. A dangerous man was the resounding answer of her pounding heart. Watching his easy confident figure, she felt a tug of disappointment that he hadn't kissed her in the library. It would have been a kiss unlike any before; she was sure of that somehow. Stop it! She jerked at the raveled ends of her flighty imagination. For the last time you had better remember he's just a man like all the rest. She didn't have any more time for the luxury of such reflections; John Whitney was descending on them with righteous purpose.

"Dr. Cade, I presume?" He sniffed with a twitter.

"Yes," Cade answered, refusing to acknowledge John's lame attempt at humor, which pleased Erin.

"Representative Wentworth will see you now," he informed.

"Yes, of course." His businesslike response put John at ease. "May I have a dance later—just a dance," he clarified, sweeping her with glinting hazel eyes once again.

She couldn't resist giving him a delicious smile that lightened her cobalt eyes and erased the slight frown that was becoming a habit. "Certainly, Dr. Cade."

"If you'll follow me, sir," John prodded.

"Good luck with the grant," she said, unwilling for him to leave, but not really knowing why.

He nodded to her and turned to follow the pale figure of John Whitney, who led across the crowded rooms, reminding Erin of the doomed Ichabod Crane, frightened by the headless ghosts of his own imaginings. More fantasy, more fairy tales, she censured. She smiled in spite of herself, but as she watched Mitchell Cade's broad shoulders disappear through the doorway that led to Lydia's study, she regretted his imminent departure from her life.

* * *

"You're looking good, babe," Teddy Williams said, draping an arm around her with intimate familiarity. Erin evaded his arm with the skill of much practice, repressing the shiver of revulsion that the scent of his after-shave sent coursing through her. It was the same expensive cologne Warren always had used, musky and heavy, bringing to mind memories she had been trying to dissolve for nearly six months. "Where have you been hiding?" he chided as he escorted her to a group of friends and acquaintances. His choice of words nearly made her laugh out loud. When it came to Teddy Williams—a very junior partner in his father's law firm and a tennis partner of Warren's—she had indeed been hiding out.

Conversation ebbed and flowed as she sipped the drink Teddy brought her. She paid little attention to the talk around her. No one seemed to notice anyway; they were all too intent on talking, not listening. Teddy's insistent arm weighed on her shoulders. He was a small man barely an inch taller than Erin, and his thin brown hair was styled adroitly to cover a balding spot on the top of his head. She smiled and nodded, seemingly enjoying the group around her, but inwardly she was calculating the hours until she would be free to speak to her grandmother and resolve the impasse their stubborn natures had invented for them. Surely they could reach a compromise and regain the warm rapport they had always shared.

She was catching snatches of conversations going on around her, carried to her over the sounds of laughter and crystal chandeliers tinkling in a chance draft of air. ". . . consultants, that's the name of the game . . ." a buttoned-down climber was confiding to another seeker with long sad eyes, who countered with ". . . computer lists of constituents is the answer."

"Hell, all you really need is access," Teddy inserted. Erin was swept with a spine-tingling wave of déjà vu. Hadn't Warren said those exact words in this very room? ". . . we need to get into bed with the Bible Belt New Right," Teddy insisted. "That's the new power; Markham's right about that." Now she realized he was only parroting Warren's words. These political junkies always spoke of politics in sexual terms. It all seemed to go together in their minds—power, sex, politics.

30

"God, family, and the flag—how could we miss!" Warren had professed to believe the new conservative right was the power bloc of the future. He had told her many times in this room. "I share many of their credos," he insisted.

"What's the matter, Erin?" Teddy quipped, giving her shoulder a squeeze, "Your thoughts seem elsewhere."

"I'm afraid they were," she apologized. "What were you saying?"

"You're looking very fit," he repeated his observation. "Better than I've seen you since you and old Warren called it quits." His tone was sly, and Erin knew they all would give their eyeteeth to know the real reason behind her broken engagement to the socially prominent lawyer.

"I've been playing tennis with Berrie nearly every day," she said airily, her chin up.

"It sure makes a difference," Teddy commented with a friendly leer, sliding his hand down her arm to her waist.

"It certainly does. I no longer run around my backhand," she retorted, deliberately misunderstanding his intent and stepping away from his roving touch.

"Good heavens, we can't have you running around your backhand now, can we," he laughed, ignoring Erin's rebuff and leading her toward the dancing couples in the other room. She let him spin her energetically around the shining wood floor, giving only surface attention to his sophisticated, barbed comments on a variety of subjects. She could see Berrie in the arms of another refugee from the marital wars, a young lobbyist for an antigun group, and Erin hoped her impulsive friend wasn't already on the road to another heartbreak.

Teddy was smiling at her with gleaming white teeth, a smile that contrasted with his gray-brown skin. No one in Washington had the time or patience to get a tan from the sun, it seemed, but a tan was nevertheless considered a necessary status symbol. So Teddy, in addition to his perfect capped teeth, salon-styled hair, and expensive cologne, had the gray tone of a sunlamp tan. Warren, Teddy, and an army of others like them; by day scurrying like ants on the sidewalks and into the great buildings of the city, and by night haunting the exclusive parties of the influential. But always they remained the hucksters, hustlers, and influence peddlers.

"It's the man behind the man, that always stays in power," Warren had told her countless times with missionary zeal. "Give me a man with a little sex appeal, a little charisma, I can manufacture the rest and get him elected to anything from dogcatcher to president." She marveled over and over, with the clarity of hindsight, at how she could ever have fallen in love with Warren Markham. How could she have fallen for his lines? He was such a user . . . such a phony . . . such a piranha.

Glancing over Teddy's shoulder during their second dance, she became aware of Mitchell Cade, once again standing out in the crowd like a shaft of sunlight breaking through the clouds. He was standing next to a diplomat from South Korea and a junior congressman from Iowa, listening to their words with measured patience, but finishing the drink in his hand with one long agitated swallow. Erin smiled to herself; Lydia had evidently given him a bad thirty minutes. Erin wondered exactly what her grandmother had said to put that frown between his brows.

"Who's the blond gorilla that came with old man Kline tonight?" Teddy asked smugly, noticing Erin's straying line of sight. "All muscle and no brain. Another ballplayer trying to get elected to something, I suppose."

"That's Dr. Cade," she said with some satisfaction. "He's a dear friend of my grandmother's and Senator Kline. He's got all the political clout he needs," Erin fabricated, studying the handsome man again as he bent forward to answer a question posed to him by the South Korean.

He did look like a hero of another century, as Berrie had insisted, a man out of place, out of his time. Maybe it was this fantasy that perversely made him seem more true, more real to her eyes than the slick packaged young men of this city of political expediency and the cultivated hard sell. His gaze fell on her like a fresh breeze. Teddy spun her around once again, and the eagleman took flight. The song was dwindling to a quiet finish as Mitchell Cade's golden features loomed over Teddy, a heavy hand on his shoulder, breaking his grasp on Erin.

"I believe this dance is mine," Mitch said as the music started again after an embarrassing silence.

"Of course, old man." Teddy obliged, backing off the floor graciously as Mitch placed a sure hand on Erin's back. His casual touch ignited her nerve ends, and she shivered slightly but hoped he wouldn't notice.

"I thought he had monopolized enough of your time," he said, giving her the briefest of smiles, but it never quite reached his eyes as he pulled her into his arms.

His face was uncommunicative, and the tension of the muscled arms that held and guided her transferred itself to Erin. Again Berrie's fanciful description leaped into her unruly thoughts. He hardly fit her preconception of a bird-watcher, and he certainly didn't fit the mold of Capitol Hill. You would never see this man in a sweatsuit and forty-dollar running shoes, sweating and red-faced as he labored around the base of the Washington Monument on a lengthy lunch-hour run. He probably hadn't worked out a day in his life, Erin speculated. He probably didn't need to, she admitted as she felt the ripple of sinew and tendon under her hands.

She shivered again as the unbidden and unwanted memory of dancing in Warren's embrace crept into her mind. Her hands remembered the lax, persistent roll of flesh that always resided around the middle of his blockish body. Why should she recall his spongy contours now, when the body she was pressed so closely against didn't support a half pound of excess fat? The doctor's arms tightened around her, and she turned her head into his shoulder, oblivious to the world around her as she succumbed to the pure tactile pleasure of his embrace.

She felt small next to his rangy sturdiness, a completely foreign, but delicious feeling. Erin was five feet eight inches tall, her figure full and inviting, yet the top of her head only reached his chin. Most of the time she felt too well-rounded, too statuesque, hardly the shape for the eighties. Today everything was to be sleek and streamlined, including women's bodies. "You're Diana-like, dear," Lydia was fond of saying. "You were an early bloomer just like your mother." And to Erin's dismay she just kept blooming. "With your figure it's going to be very difficult to get anyone interested in your brain," Lydia would chortle. But tonight in this man's arms she felt a perfect size, perfectly alluring.

Her eyes wandered back to the eagleman, following the column of his neck along the strong jaw to the high cheekbones, then down the slightly divergent line of his nose. Unable to help herself, she continued her perusal of his chiseled features at last coming to rest on the strong, mobile line of his mouth, her pulses leaping with the recollection of the near touch of his lips. He smiled quickly as though he could read her thoughts and was taunting her with an enticing invitation. He pulled her closer, and she melted into his arms again, swaying gently to the music flowing around them.

He was a good dancer, guiding her with a knowing pressure on her back. He moved with the natural agility of a man completely comfortable with his own size and the physical power he controlled. Warren had been self-confident, brutally and arrogantly so. But he worked hard at it, insuring his self-importance by manipulating the lives of others—her life, as well as his current candidates.

Sensing her withdrawal, Mitchell Cade loosened his hold, and Erin came to her senses with a startled jerk. She looked up at the face above hers while the love song faded to a close. Her eyes were dark and liquid with remembered suffering, and she heard Mitchell Cade take a quick deep breath. Unheeding of the curious glances of the other couples migrating from the floor, they remained entwined and motionless as he bent his head leaning down to her. Suddenly he straightened and frowned, releasing her from his warm secure embrace, and she felt cheated again of the knowledge of his kiss. She was thinking too much about his kiss, she decided. She was thinking too much about this male entity, god or man, who was too full of surprises. For the first time in her life Erin wanted a man to make a pass at her, and Mitchell Cade stubbornly refused to oblige.

He was still frowning as he slid an agitated hand over his blond hair. However, he put a firm hand on her arm preventing her egress from the dance floor, still frowning as the music started again.

"Trouble in paradise?" she managed to get out, in a good imitation of flippancy. She was trying to hide her confusion at the sensations his nearness produced in her as his hand slid around her waist to rest on her back. The muscle along his prominent jawline flexed as his frown deepened.

"Not yet—but there will be," he said cryptically. He pulled her close once more as the music stirred to life. The volcanic riot of sound that erupted in her ears was only the beating of her heart, she realized ponderously as the blood coursed through her veins. He held her deftly while they moved with the sensual beat of the music.

"It seems Representative Wentworth has managed to ruffle your feathers," she tested, combating his sexual appeal with tiny stinging barbs.

"Spare me," he shot back. "I'm not in the mood for bird jokes. I've heard them all." Erin raised a delicately arched brow, pleased she had gotten under his skin at last. It made her feel slightly less vulnerable.

"A string has been attached to my grant," he went on darkly, "a very long, tangled string."

"Oh?" What was her grandmother up to now? Was she trying to bend Mitchell Cade to her wishes as she was Erin? But to what purpose?

"The grant is more or less a bribe," he said with a scowl for Teddy Williams, who was advancing on them. The other man backed off good-naturedly with an upraised hand at Mitchell Cade's show of ill will.

"She's becoming an expert at that lately," Erin agreed under her breath as they halted before a terrace door. "In Washington they call it 'compromise.'" He nodded with a grunt of dissatisfaction. Erin could see that John was making his way toward them now. Impulsively, she took hold of his large tanned hand and led the eagleman from the noise of the dining room through the narrow exit of escape onto the terrace. They moved silently into the cooling night until the biologist broke the silence.

"I'm to take a Wentworth family member to observe my work in the field. I explained to her that the work was strenuous and dangerous. She just smiled and said something about 'toughening fiber and building character.'" He looked aggrieved and a chill settled in Erin's stomach. "Hell, I'm not the leader of a boy scout troop!" He looked into her puzzled expression. "A granddaughter, no less," he grated. "I don't have time to coddle some

35

postadolescent female." His powerful hands clenched into fists. "I told her there are no separate facilities." He brushed a stray lock of dull gold hair that had fallen across his forehead. "I have her complete trust and confidence," he quoted, frowning even harder.

"Granddaughter!" Erin exhaled in disbelief, her unease at his earlier words erupting into cyclonic motion as she grasped the operative words. "Her granddaughter is going with you?" Her voice was rising as her anger sparked on the flint-sharp edges of her temper. She reeled away from him and began to pace the slate patio.

"I can't turn down the grant," he said more to himself than to her. "It's as simple as that, but I won't forget this," he vowed with complete sincerity. The blaze in his hazel eyes matched Erin's blue fire. "Being saddled with a moony, spoiled girl who's carrying a torch for some society lawyer is the last thing I need," he muttered wrathfully. "Unfortunately, what I do need is the money, and I can't afford to look elsewhere. I've got to get back to my work."

"So the eagleman is willing to eat a little crow in order to get his funding," Erin spiked, her chagrin at Lydia's machinations matching her wrath.

"Listen, only bald eagles can afford the luxury of pride, and their time is running out." He glared at her. "They can't afford to wait out any more delays, and neither can I. My research represents years of my own life as well as others. If some lovesick virgin wants to play in the woods, I'll put up with it."

"What makes you think she even wants to go?" Erin flared, his choice of words pricking her like a thorn.

She never heard his answer as a bony tap on her shoulder heralded the undetected arrival of John Whitney, his nasal tones honking through the animosity that hovered like a mist between the couple before him.

"She wants to talk to you," he ordered with a complacent smirk.

"She's not going to get away with this," Erin answered as she rounded on the abbreviated man. "Tell her it's blackmail. Tell her I'll do something drastic. I'll go streaking through this reception in the nude, if I have to, but I won't be sent to the back of

36

beyond with this . . . this . . ." Words failed her, and she took a shallow rapid breath. ". . . How would that look in the *Post?*" she threatened with finality. A crooked, wicked smile turned up the corner of her mouth as she saw the unflappable John Whitney blanch and sputter. "Give your employer that message," she finished with theatrical flare as Mitchell Cade's eyes narrowed and John Whitney made good his escape.

"What did you tell him that for?" the biologist demanded, a dawning of understanding on his face.

"Would you rather I told him you have a social disease acquired from close contact with wolves in your northern paradise?" she snarled, her anger instantly transferring from her grandmother to the man beside her. Why had Lydia seen fit to tell him of her private affairs? Would the humiliations of this wretched day never cease?

"Believe me. It's not *that* lonely in the U.P.," he ground out, controlling himself with obvious difficulty. Erin had one second of satisfaction at his show of emotion before he reached out, grabbing her by the upper arm and propelling her to the edge of the rose garden behind them. She went reluctantly, unable to loosen his hurting grip and already regretting her tirade. "It's you? You're the lovesick granddaughter?" he hurled at her in the privacy of the sweet-scented garden. "Since we are going to be stuck with each other, I suggest you learn some manners." He spoke threateningly, but he released her arm.

It was a mistake. Sparks flew from her sapphire eyes as she digested his remark, and she drew back her hand in rage, ready to slap the smiling superiority from his crooked mouth.

Catching her swinging forearm, he wrestled it down, the amusement dying out of his eyes. "Grandma didn't tell me you were a hot-tempered hellcat," he observed tightly. "What's the matter; couldn't your boyfriend stand the heat?"

"What happened between Warren Markham and myself is none of your business. . . ." she began in a jagged tone, all too aware of the granite strength of his hold on her arm.

"Warren?" he said with mocking interest. Her heart was pounding.

"It's none of your business," she repeated, lifting her chin with icy bravado, unwilling and much too vulnerable to allow her unruly response to show. "Let go of my arm!" She commanded with all the tactical calm of a general dispatching his troops, but she could feel a feverish heat building deep within her.

He smiled grimly, ignoring her command. He tugged gently on her wrist, apparently as a reminder of who held the strategic advantage in this skirmish. With his movement she jerked angrily against him, sending new waves of sensations coursing through her veins. The tension on her arm pushed her toward his muscular torso, deepening the enticing valley between her breasts and straining the dainty pearl buttons closing her dress. They both drew a quick breath, but she haughtily defied her feelings, arcing a defiant brow and feigning indifference. One tin soldier dueling the golden warrior in battle, yet she intended to be the one to ride away—alone and unscathed. But her woman's body betrayed her, responding to the man, who was regarding her with a visual caress that tingled through every nerve.

"I think Warren got out while the getting was good," he said raggedly, not making a move to retreat, his eyes filled with more than the obvious taunting amusement. "Unfortunately, I don't have that luxury."

"Would you please release me, Dr. Cade?" Her tone was thankfully clear and steady, sounding much more calm than her quivering center.

His strong hands were holding her relentlessly close to him. Too close; her heartbeat and breathing were racing, nearly tripping over each other. Panic swept through her, the cool confidence of the sophisticate diluting into rippling fear; she had used her best ammunition, guaranteed to stop any man in his tracks, that is any man but Mitchell Cade. He held her, unphased by the contact, not even a scratch to his proud ego or handsome exterior. She would be doomed to defeat if he knew how his body was affecting her. Maybe he already knew? He was a very dangerous man. She wriggled in his sensual entrapment, trying to escape his sexual magnetism as well as his powerful grasp, but he held her firm, admiring his victory.

"You can't do this!" she breathed. "If you don't have the courage to stand up to my grandmother, I do," she stated rashly, adrenaline pounding through her veins.

He slowly released her. She had finally drawn blood, pricking his pride with her desperate barb. He studied her angrily. She began rubbing the place where he had held her with soothing strokes, trying to busy her trembling hands. She remained silent, unable to think beyond the awareness of her dual emotions of attraction and fear. She was becoming aware of a sizzling displaced rage toward the large, self-assured man who was so easily capable of pushing her beyond her own control. He's no different than the rest, she lied to herself; Lydia's money is the most important thing in the world to him now. Even as the thoughts careened through her mind she recognized the illogic. He was being forced into a corner by Lydia's schemes as she was, yet their reactions to the strictures placed on them were as different as night and day. As different as an adult's acceptance of what they cannot change and a child's unguided rebellion.

Tears filled the sapphire pools of her eyes and threatened to spill over onto the softness of her heat-stained cheeks. She blinked them away. She couldn't bear to give her adversary the satisfaction of seeing her weakness as well as her temper. That would be the final straw. She couldn't spend a day with this arrogant man; she couldn't spend another minute alone with him. Raising her gaze, she could see him still breathing heavily, but as the tears receded and she refocused on his features, he relaxed his wary stance. He opened his mouth to speak, but Lydia's voice from the terrace decided him against whatever it was he had been going to say.

"Here you are," she called, gliding into the garden as Erin pivoted blindly away from the light. Her hands closed convulsively on a blood-red rose dyed burgundy by the night. A thorn dug into her palm, but she paid no heed to its sting, shredding the fragrant blossoms until the ground at her feet was littered with crushed spicy-scented petals.

"I'm glad you two are finding the time to get acquainted," she went on smoothly, noting her granddaughter's rigid back. "Since you'll be spending the next several weeks together—"

"Weeks?" they chorused in one voice as Erin swung around. Her dazed blue eyes flew instinctively to meet hazel agates.

"Yes, you are to assist Dr. Cade in his banding operation for as long as it takes. Approximately six weeks, am I not correct, Doctor?" she asked pointedly.

39

Mitchell Cade nodded, searching Lydia's face with his own gaze, apparently satisfied by something that Erin was unable to read in her grandmother's expression.

"Didn't John give you my message?" Erin interjected firmly.

"Yes," Lydia said, her own face calm and serene, only her clenched fingers betraying the effort she was expending to give just that impression. Erin was too preoccupied to notice the agitation, but Mitchell Cade's perceptive eyes were not so blind. "I'm sure John misunderstood you due to the noise and music," Lydia prevaricated.

"That's what happened, I'm sure," Mitchell Cade answered quickly, his glance challenging Erin to deny his words.

"Yes, of course that's what happened." Lydia's tone was grateful as she looked first in surprise at him and then squarely at Erin, addressing her solemnly. "I can safely say this will be the most important job of your life." Her eyes, so like Erin's own, left little doubt in the younger woman that this was the task set to obtain her inheritance.

"What are my duties to consist of?" Erin capitulated in a stiff voice, her eyes icy gems that glittered in the dim light.

Lydia frowned sadly at the antagonism in Erin's tone but went on in a businesslike way. "Dr. Cade is in need of an assistant, and I need a progress report of the work he is conducting for the Wentworth Fund. I'll need to know what is happening in order to determine whether to recommend the grant for automatic renewal." So that was the bribe Lydia had offered for the good doctor's cooperation, an automatic renewal of the funds. There was no use appealing to him on the grounds that neither of them would benefit from this plan. She bit her lip as Lydia continued speaking.

"Erin has some expertise in the research skills you are in need of, Dr. Cade. Is the arrangement satisfactory?" she queried, turning the full force of her charming smile on the man that towered even farther above her head than he did Erin's.

"I don't believe I have much choice. Am I correct?" he countered, meeting Lydia's steady blue gaze head-on.

"No, you do not," she agreed equitably, and unbelievably he smiled in return, his expression reflecting a curious mixture of emotion. He seemed to be acknowledging the elderly woman as

40

a worthy opponent, or as a powerful and conspiratorial ally. Erin couldn't decide which as he took Lydia's hand to seal the bargain they had made over her future.

"Then it's settled," Lydia announced to Erin's continued fulminating silence. "My dear, you have a great deal of packing to do tomorrow. The train leaves in the afternoon; your tickets are all arranged. By the way, Dr. Cade informs me it is still quite cool in Michigan at this time of year. Be sure to pack suitable clothing." Noting the telltale signs of another outburst of temper on her granddaughter's face, she wound up her speech. "I'll be looking forward to your first report, Erin. Are there any more points you wish clarified while Dr. Cade and I are both present?" she asked leadingly as Erin swept past her toward the lighthearted gaiety of the party.

What was there left for her to do? She felt cornered and alone, trapped by the closing of ranks between these two unlikely allies. She had given her word; if she rebelled now she would only prove Lydia's point and ruin her own chances of gaining control of her life. But this was the turning point; the child may be forced into the wilderness, but Erin McIntee the woman would return never to be manipulated by anyone—ever again. She would be independent—free—a whole person.

She halted, swinging around as the skirt of her lilac dress swirled about the soft curves of her waist and thigh. "No, grandmother. I intend to follow your orders to the letter. I'll accompany your paragon of industry and virtue to his north country stronghold," she announced, her scathing gaze raking the man offering his black-clad arm to the older woman. He lifted his eyes from Lydia to watch Erin's defiant figure with a gleam of answering challenge in their hazel depths. It was Erin whose look retreated first, but not before she had the last word. "I gave you my word, grandmother," she reaffirmed, "but God help us all!"

CHAPTER THREE

"Are you sure you can manage that yourself?" Mitchell Cade asked in a conversational tone as Erin wrestled the last of her bags onto the rack above the seats of the commuter train.

"I am perfectly capable of caring for myself," she huffed. He had been frowning in the same disapproving manner at her baggage since they had met thirty minutes ago.

"Good. I have neither the time nor the inclination to pamper you," he informed her pleasantly as he swung his one battered case onto the rack with no effort whatsoever. He edged past her and slid into the window seat as she continued to struggle with her dress bag. Erin's fierce glare terminated his enjoyable view of full breasts straining against her mauve silk blouse as she arranged her raspberry linen jacket triumphantly atop her luggage and settled down gratefully beside him.

"I certainly hope you packed something practical in all those bags," he observed, unabashed. A mocking smile just reached his eyes. "Warm and practical. It's still a long way from summer in the U.P."

Erin ignored his enlightening comments as she looked out over the nearly empty platform as casually as she could, hoping to see her grandmother's stately figure. But Lydia Wentworth was nowhere to be seen. Erin already regretted their stiff, formal good-byes earlier that day, yet she was determined not to allow her anger at Lydia's schemings to diminish.

A smiling conductor passed through the car, punching tickets, tipping his dark blue cap as he passed. Other travelers were settling into their seats as the sounds and activities around them took on the more hurried rhythms of departure. A tall distinguished woman advanced onto the platform, catching Erin's eye as they began to move away from the station. She leaned forward eagerly, but the smiling, gray-haired woman waving to an unseen late arrival was not Lydia Wentworth.

"She's probably tied up in a meeting and couldn't get away," Mitchell Cade said, correctly interpreting her action as the train began to gather speed.

"I really didn't expect her," Erin replied with a nonchalance she didn't feel. She brushed intently at an imaginary speck of dust on her white linen slacks, swallowing the growing lump of misery in her throat. She had never before parted from her grandmother in anger. Lydia had been her family since her parents' deaths nearly ten years ago. It was Lydia who came to tell her of the airliner crash that had killed her parents. It was Lydia who held her, who comforted her and tried very hard to make some kind of normal life for a heartbroken teenager. Now they had quarreled, and somehow Erin knew this man had figured in her grandmother's decision to make her prove her worth.

"This is my own personal trip to purgatory," Erin said harshly, her irritation transferring itself to the man she considered the current source of her exile. "Hopefully it will be a short one." She placed her handbag on the seat between them, delineating her territory and avoiding his examining gaze.

"Try to remember you're headed to Paradise," he said lightly, adding for her suspicious glance, "Paradise, Michigan, that is, via Detroit. In case we are separated en route," he added levelly, but his blue-flecked eyes danced with silent mirth. Erin blinked in surprise as her own eyes were drawn to his tanned face. Blue eyes today? He reached down to lift his worn leather attaché case from the floor, and Erin was once again released from the spell of his regard.

She watched surreptitiously as he sifted reflectively through typewritten pages, apparently easily able to dismiss her presence on the seat beside him. He worked quietly, jotting notes in the margins along the edges of the pages while chewing thoughtfully on the end of his short, stubby pencil. Following his lead, Erin reached into her bag and produced a paperback copy of a steamy best seller. The silence stretched out between them as she turned the pages by rote, retaining very little of the printed words. She resented the fact that his formidable presence was not so easily put from her own mind.

Occasionally when he shifted his position, his hard forearm would brush her arm as too-wide shoulders strained in the tight quarters. It made her electrically aware of his body close to her, and she gathered herself away from his incidental touch as though the evasive action could banish him altogether. It would work momentarily until a long hard thigh would nudge her and she would inch away, retreating further into her corner. Eventually she schooled herself to ignore the appeal of the vital man at her side and began to take a haphazard interest in her book. Mitchell Cade evidently didn't feel it would be necessary to speak a word during the entire trip to Grand Central Station, and that suited Erin's mood just fine.

The light linen jacket she was wearing felt comfortable in the cooler dark tunnels of the train station. Looking up from the porter's cart, she endured the satisfied look of a man who had successfully carried his point. Having imparted his lesson in self-sufficiency, Mitchell Cade had now unbent so far as to summon a porter to deal with their luggage. Pride insisted she carry her own bags, but after one look at the estimated miles of underground hallway reaching to the other track and the train they were racing to catch, she gave up custody of her luggage with becoming meekness. Threading their way through rushing travelers, the pungent odor of trapped diesel fumes stung her nose, and her ears were assaulted by the swoosh of releasing air brakes and the occasional blasts of an engine's horn echoing through the hollow cement caverns below the city.

Erin was lagging behind the long-legged strides of her companion as she entered the overwhelming, sprawling complex that was Grand Central Station. Although the rotunda of the station was huge and spacious, it had a darkness, perhaps old age. Seemingly, the only brightness was the sunlight filtering down from the large arched windows at one end of the ceiling, many stories above the floor. The few hundred people in the station seemed to wander and rattle around the massive room like loose change.

She tried to imagine the thronging crowds that passed this way in years gone by. Teary-eyed sweethearts and wives kissing departing soldiers farewell during the war years, before the overuse of airports, before the end of romance. Unable to resist the temptation of a nosegay of violets for her jacket lapel, Erin remained standing at the flower stand a few seconds, inhaling the delicate but assertive fragrance of the blooms, while Dr. Cade picked up a *Times* at the newsstand. Looking around her again, she was dismayed to see the commanding figure of her boss disappearing into another tunnel that led to their train. She hurried along on her heeled sandals, struggling to catch up with his long-legged stride.

Boss! The realization of her subservient position was crushing as she too mounted the metal treads of the train that growled steadily as it stood beside the platform. But she was determined to play her other role as the watchdog of the Wentworth Fund. He will rue the day I was put in his charge, she promised herself as she searched through the nearly full car ahead. Eventually, she found him tipping the porter who was depositing her luggage in a minuscule compartment in the middle of a long car of identical closed doors.

"Is this my compartment?" she asked as she made room for the grinning porter to pass in the corridor.

"This is it." Her employer's smile was already eroding her resolve. It was unfair for him to have such an effect on her.

She nodded, avoiding his gaze, slipping past the biologist as she stepped into the small room. Opening one of a pair of narrow closets, she gratefully relinquished her shoulder bag to a hook at the back with a relieved sigh. Her dress bag already hung suspended from a rod, and her cases fit snugly on a shelf below. "If you will leave I'll dress for dinner," she said a little breathlessly, whether from the long hurried walk or from the nearness of a being so overwhelmingly male she didn't know. He was standing at his full height, his eyes several inches above hers, and his proximity was disturbing. He was so close that it was impossible not to imagine what it would be like to be held in his arms, swept away by shared passion to a world where no one could follow, to be loved and cherished. But Warren had loved her in his way, she reminded herself sternly. He would have cherished her, in his fashion, and he would have shaped and molded her into a perfect copy of the beautifully dressed, expensively groomed consorts of the power brokers he most admired. And this man was even more dominating than Warren, his personality so strong, so overpowering, that if she surrendered to his charisma she would be lost forever, nothing left of Erin McIntee but an empty shell. Alarmed that he might read her thoughts, she cleared her throat and spoke again. "I'd like to freshen up and dress for dinner."

"Dress for dinner? I can tell it's going to be very difficult to treat you like any other gaboon." His voice carried an exasperated sigh.

"A gaboon?" Erin repeated, unsure whether or not to be offended by the simian-invoking word.

"It's a term we use to refer to anyone crazy enough to stay in the wilderness to work with birds of prey." His voice was intent and very near. As if to emphasize his statement, the train began to move with a jerk that swayed Erin toward him. He steadied her with a sure hand on her waist as she braced herself with an instinctive hand on his chest. For one moment of magic, intense blue eyes met his reflecting ones and the fragrance of violets mingled with cool spice. Erin was torn between wanting to push herself away and wishing to be surrounded by his arms.

"I think it would be best, Dr. Cade," she said barely above a whisper, regaining her balance and her senses, "if you continue to think of me as just another gaboon." But neither of them retreated.

"Of course." He dropped his hand abruptly, shattering the coupling dream whirling in Erin's mind. "After all, Mrs. Wentworth is counting on me," he said with a determined edge, stepping toward the door and scooping up his bag and case. He studied her for another long moment as Erin's breath caught in her throat. Her cheeks were flushed and the violets on her lapel were mirrored in her sapphire eyes. "From now on you're just one of the boys." He turned and disappeared through the open door.

"How many boys?" Erin managed to ask, but he was already heading down the car. Closing the door behind him, she began to realize how foreign and frightening the terrain of this new job would be—and that Dr. Mitchell Cade was her only guide. And he was only a man; how could he be trusted?

46

She turned to the window just as the train burst from its burrow into the hazy sunlight of New York. As it cut across the metropolis, the elevated tracks gave her a view of the teeming life at the back doors, alleys, and fire escapes of the Bronx, passing endless miles of streets and tangles of highway, flattening into industrial parks and warehouses, only to soar again with high-rise apartments, and finally dwindling into the eternal islands of the suburbs. The tempo of their speed was increasing, just as her desire to learn more about her job and the man responsible for it was increasing within her, causing a rising excitement and interest in the future despite her stern admonitions to beware.

Heads turned as Erin glided into the dining car. Her beauty was wrapped in a Givenchy day dress of fine oatmeal-colored linen. Its square sailor collar framed her face, while romantic cuffed sleeves softened the effect. She felt as if she had stepped back into a more gracious era and was glad she had given in to the temptation of the small, sophisticated accent of linen and net that perched jauntily on her glistening hair. She felt totally confident, and a smile lingered on her full red lips as she watched heads turn in approval from behind the illusion that sensuously veiled sparkling sapphire eyes.

Mitchell Cade rose from his seat at a table near the far end of the car. He was staring at her in astonishment, but there was approval and pleasure in his regard. Still dressed in the shirt and slacks she had seen him in earlier, he had added a tie and a light-colored corduroy jacket.

"Celebrating your last night in civilization, Erin?" he questioned, resuming his seat as the waiter assisted her with her chair and placed two menus on the table before moving off to accommodate his other charges. "Designer dresses have very little place in the scheme of things where we're headed."

"I'm well aware of that, Dr. Cade," she returned, not even attempting to hide her surprise at his accurate appraisal of her attire.

She bent her head to avoid his searching look and pretended to study her menu, but the words blurred before her eyes. Even casual conversation with this flagrantly male creature was be-

47

coming beyond her powers of concentration. Warren—no man she had ever known—was capable of causing this erratic flutter of her heart, this wayward functioning of her brain, this sudden sparking of steel on flint.

"I suggest we get down to business," he said pointedly as they surrendered their marked menus to the steward, who deposited the carafe of excellent Chardonnay they had agreed upon. He set two stemmed goblets of the pale wine before them and left the table. Erin's eyes had strayed to the darkening landscape beyond the window as it panned by in a collage of muted shades and hues.

Her lips tightened as she set her wineglass down with a click. "What do you wish to discuss? My qualifications for the job? I type very well. I file accurately."

"You did work in Washington," he stated flatly.

"As a research assistant . . ." she affirmed.

"To Warren? Did you work for Warren?" He was studying her with calculated interest. He continued his questions, watching her stunned face. "Do you take dictation?"

"No, I do not," she answered, surprised by the gratingly direct line of questioning.

"A lack you share with many Washington secretaries if the accounts one reads in the papers are true," he stated dryly, rearranging his silver flatware with a deft hand. "Did you work for Warren?" He asked a second time; his expression demanded an answer. She was now aware of the direction of his inquiry and was incensed with the insinuation that he could have a secretary and a bed companion all at the same time.

"*No.*" She spoke the single word defiantly, meeting his stare head-on with blue ice, hoping that her message was very clear. She was saving up for a blistering blast that would follow his expected lewd proposition. Damn this man!

"Good," he said succinctly, deflating the steaming rage building in her. He smiled and added into her unbelieving expression, "I don't want you suddenly to decide you can't live without your old boss and leave me high and dry—without an assistant."

"Dr. Cade, if we are both to survive this enforced intimacy, I suggest we keep our relationship on a professional level and get

48

a few things straight." Her tone was as repressive as she could make it. "I was a very efficient and competent assistant to my grandmother, to whom I will still be reporting. And I will continue that efficient job performance for you." She paused and cleared her throat, "And for the record, regardless of what you may think, I did not chase Warren Markham away. I was the one driven off." She was stunned that she would make such an admission to this aggravating man who had no business knowing anything about her private life and knew too much already. "Now could you describe my duties?" He ignored her direction.

"But if Markham starts to call and write you, begging you to return to his arms . . . ?"

"I doubt that very much, Dr. Cade," she ground out. "I left him standing on the church steps with five hundred guests already in the sanctuary. I do not anticipate ever hearing from him again in this life." She could feel the color leave her face, and she picked up the wineglass again, draining its contents as though she could wash the taste of Warren's name from her mouth.

"But you would like to? Hear from him, I mean?" He asked the question before finishing his wine, studying her over the rim of his glass.

"Never!" she said emphatically, perhaps too strongly, noting his skepticism as she glared at him. Erin's patience was already thin. She didn't have the will to explain complicated emotions to this impertinent man. She also didn't appreciate his backwoods psychology. The game was over. "Dr. Cade, just a simple job description will do."

"Naturally." His expression tightened in disappointment at her continued cool, businesslike demeanor. "Stated simply, you will accompany me into the field to observe and band eagles. You'll be expected to keep up, shut up, and take notes on procedures. And anything else I tell you to do—that's gabooning." He finished his statement, pouring more wine for himself and topping Erin's. "Is that clear?"

"Perfectly, Doctor." The words dropped like crystals of ice in the nearly frozen pool of silence between them.

"The hours are long, the work hard, and the conditions to your standards will be primitive. You'll be spending hours and days hiking, canoeing, and bouncing around in a jeep. Welcome to gabooning," he said, saluting her with his glass of wine before allowing the vintage to warm his throat. "We're stuck with each other, but I don't intend to inflict you on my staff." His eyes sparkled with victory as her lips tightened in an expression very much like her grandmother's. Damn the man; he was far too observant for his own good.

"How large is your staff, Dr. Cade?" she tried again, determined to be civil but distant. The waiter reappeared, served their entrees with smooth efficiency, refilled their water glasses, and glided away down the slightly swaying car before Mitchell Cade answered her last query.

"My assistant and friend Reuben Preston, a veterinarian Dr. Joe Jackson—and George, our cook and general handyman. For the next six weeks the five of us will be cataloging, banding, and observing approximately seventy nesting pairs of bald eagles." He spoke with such dogged precision she regretted her earlier hostility.

"And I'm to be your assistant," she said, sipping her wine. "Aren't you concerned you'll be upsetting the ecological balance of nature by introducing me into the wilderness?" She was relaxing a little in the quiet of the partially filled dining car. The lights had come up as they ate, dimming the view of dusky wooded hills stretching beyond the tracks.

"Some exotics flourish well when transplanted," he murmured, turning his attention to his food as if avoiding the lush foliage of her femininity.

She was toying with her entree, but the veal cordon bleu seemed to stick in her throat. She gave up the pretense and put her fork aside. "Dr. Cade," she began as the pause lengthened.

"Please, call me Mitch," he interrupted with a winning smile, showing straight white teeth. It altered his face, softening the planes and angles of prominent chin and high cheekbones. It reached all the way to his eyes, dissolving all his hostility and setting the blue flecks dancing in their depths. Already she knew it indicated true amusement. Warren's smile had never reached his eyes. It was a reaction as controlled and unemotional as every other aspect of his life.

"Mitch," she tried the name and liked it. "Tell me more about

Paradise," she said quickly, not wanting to fall prey to the lure of that smile too easily.

"It's a wide place in the road. The nearest town of any size is fifty miles away." He paused, becoming serious. "I know you really don't want this job. But I'm sure your grandmother won't keep you in the wilderness for long."

"Obviously Lydia feels I'll be in good hands." She instantly felt self-conscious about her choice of words.

"Absolutely." He smiled, replenishing her glass and his own. "The boy scouts, remember?" Erin nodded, returning his warmth, if not his confidence. "I'm sorry Lydia couldn't see you off at the station. I'm sure she cares about you very much, even though you may feel you're being punished or abandoned. I'm positive she has a logical reason for—"

Erin interrupted his speculations with a small cough. "Tell me about birds, Dr. Cade," Erin said, smiling, concealing her concern for how close he was coming to the truth of her situation. "I mean Mitch," she corrected.

"There are many different kinds of birds"—he raised a brow in surprise—"different types." He held his head to one side questioning for a moment and then relaxed, apparently finding the answer reflected in her eyes. He started to speak about birds. With his warming smile, the mellowing wine, and the soothing tone of his voice, Erin was lost and content, wishing never to be found. "I specialize in birds of prey."

"I'm afraid I've never considered birds seriously. They all have feathers and they fly, don't they?" she teased.

He couldn't help smiling. "The kind I'm interested in certainly do." He watched her with a pleased expression, either basking in her full attention or was it his birds? She couldn't be sure.

"Each type of bird has its own style of flight," he was saying. "Falcons are the acrobats. They cut through the air, using their wings like a seal uses his flippers in the water. While on the other hand the owl has no finesse at all. He muscles his way, beating down on the air to lift his body up, so he seems to bounce across the sky." She was enjoying the low sound of his voice and the images he created in her mind, along with the constant click of the metal wheels beating against the steel ribbon of track that

51

stretched into the countryside. He poured the wine and filled her with vivid imaginings.

"But eagles. They are the masters. They meet the wind, use it, and conquer it. There's nothing quite like watching an eagle hang in the sky—soaring and diving. It's beautiful."

"I can tell, you enjoy your work."

"Yes, I do," he said with frank satisfaction. "But I think I may even enjoy it more now." He was unapologetically studying her for every detail, concentrating on the curve of her mouth. There was a total void beyond the train; only the china and cutlery reflected in the dark mirror of the windows as the train streaked through the darkness. Her eyes magnetically returned to the powerful man across the table, but his unbroken study kept her speechless.

"Reuben is going to love you."

"Your friend?"

"He's a good-natured Texan with a heart as big as all outdoors. You'll have him wrapped around your little finger in no time. But just remember, you'll be assisting me." A hint of honest reminder slipped through the words.

"I'll remember." She smiled. His words swept away her voice, and he questioned her with an encompassing, mesmerizing gaze. She was succumbing to his charms, and that alarmed her. "It's getting late . . ." she finished lamely.

"It does look like the party's over," he agreed, referring to the waiters, who were clearing all the other tables to shut down the empty dining car for the evening.

Leaving the dining car, Mitch guided her through the luxurious club car, decorated to resemble its counterpart on a steam train of the last century. Erin would have liked to sit awhile in one of the plush red velvet chairs in the quaint, nostalgic setting, but the warm sure hand at her waist moved her steadily forward toward the sleeping car. Just outside her compartment a man hurrying along the corridor in the opposite direction excused himself and slipped by them. Cade made room for the man's passage by stepping closer to Erin, leaning lightly against her as he braced an arm on the wall. After the man passed, he made no effort to retreat, and his smoldering gaze wandered over the sheer, coy netting that covered her inquiring eyes. His study moved to her inviting lips, and with large square hands he carefully lifted her veil and folded it back. Erin's heart raced even faster than the faint click of metal that was the only sound of their speed through the night. She was hypnotized by his narcotic nearness and his slow deliberate movements. She raised her hands, curling them over his wide shoulders, her lips parting in pleasant anticipation.

His kiss was not unexpected, but his tenderness was. At first surprised by the gentle tasting caresses, then warmed by them, she leaned instinctively toward him as a flower bends toward the sun. His hands held her face lightly as his tongue began to seek entry to the sweetness of her mouth. She inched closer still to the source of her pleasure, returning the pressure of his lips, tasting the lingering traces of pale white wine.

Her arms stole around the tanned column of his neck and long fingers threaded through the soft, curling hair above the collar of his corduroy jacket. The gentle bondage of his fingers left her face, strong arms sliding down her ribs to draw her even closer as his kiss became deeper and more stimulating. She could feel herself being pulled into the vortex of his passion, her own body responding completely to the pull of his male magnetism. He lifted his head for an instant, watching her, as if delving into the emotions behind misty sapphire eyes.

Sensing her conflict, he gave her no time to chose between surrender or retreat. His mouth covered hers firmly once again, and his arms pulled her full against his powerful trunk. His straying hands moved down her back and slipped over the rounded fullness of her hips, increasing the intimate contact he had initiated. The hardness of his loins ignited suppressed desires, recalling to her resisting heart the awareness of her own hungry femininity. He pressed her closer, and the movement brought her back to the edges of reality.

"Please. . . ." she murmured in sudden panic as the steady vibration of the train reminded her that they were still standing in the corridor. "Someone might see us. . . ." Good heavens, was she blushing as hotly as she felt? He would think her a naive school girl. "I think we had better . . . say good night," she went on breathlessly as he bent to nuzzle her neck. Unbidden, her

53

hands returned to caress the hard muscles of his back and waist. He lifted his head from its persistent, sensuous exploration of the base of her throat. "I think we should say good night," she repeated more convincingly as a few inches of cool air lessened his magnetic attraction enough for her to control her voice. He reluctantly released her and moved aside, allowing her to turn toward the door.

"Erin, there's something I have to tell you," he said quickly before she could insert the key she was holding in a hand that trembled.

"Can't we discuss it in the morning?" she begged. She didn't know how much longer she could keep saying no.

"I don't think you understand what I mean. . . ." he began again, watching her fumbling. He took the key and turned it in the lock with one smooth movement.

"Please, Mitch." She needed to be alone, and he was following her into the compartment. She craved solitude to sort out these unexpected few minutes and put them into some kind of orderly perspective. There had been no one in her life since Warren. No one at all. She didn't want anyone; it would only complicate her life again. Surely it was just a combination of fatigue, excitement, and too much wine that had caused the overwhelming physical reaction she had felt in his arms. "Thank you for seeing me . . ." He stopped her words with an unexpected kiss, catching her trembling hand on the switch, and bumped the door closed with his heel. His kiss deepened, sending her plans for the next few minutes skyrocketing into oblivion.

Her hands were between them tracing the hard ridges of muscles below his collarbone. Iron bands tightened around her as his tongue grew bolder, seeking the inner recesses of her mouth, and she opened to its thrust, drinking in the pleasure of his intoxicating contact. He enveloped her in a rapturous embrace, her heart fluttering as his warm, firm touch caressed the corners of her mouth and his tongue returned to flick along the dewy freshness of her lips. She arched closer as his thirsty hands explored the oasis of her body, sending tingling waves of vibration along her vertebrae.

She followed his lead, letting her wandering hands roam where they would, learning the lines and angles of his torso, so hard on the surface, as her softer curves conformed to him as though they were two halves once again made whole.

Impatient fingers tangled in her fragrant curls, one palm holding her head as he discarded the hat. This task accomplished, he returned to kiss her waiting upturned lips once again. Soft, gentle kisses, their sensuous tenderness taking her breath away. As she melted deeper into his arms, her hands languidly slid beneath his jacket, tracing boldly over his ribs and spreading over his back to delight in the sheets of muscle and tendon beneath her hands.

In the darkness her mind whirled away in a wonderful myth flowing through her in a dizzying rush of desire. She felt herself being lifted up by this golden god and swept away on his magical embrace. One strong arm cradled her as they soared higher, and Erin's awareness of reality slipped away as his kisses deposited her on a soft, cool cloud. Even in the darkness she could see the gleam of his exciting eyes and visualize this golden man sweeping her off her feet and carrying her to a place where no other man could ever take her. She gloried in his kiss, returning it with equal fervor as the siren song crooned in her ears. Mitchell Cade hovered above her as his hand floated over her dress, sliding over the curves of her breasts, memorizing their round shape, while his demanding mouth teased the leaping pulse in the hollow of her throat. His mouth ravaged her lips again as an adroit hand teased the buds of her breasts, tempting the nipple beneath the fabric. She arched closer to the deity of love that transformed her mere body into an instrument of pleasure and passion. She reached with longing arms around his neck and kissed the mouth so close to hers, while tangling fingers in soft flaxen hair. His hands moved lower, caressing the silky material of her stockings, stroking in torturing patterns that circled higher and higher up the smooth surface of her inner thigh.

His body moved over hers and his weight was crushing her breasts, pushing her farther into the clutching softness of the mattress. Sanity returned to flare away her fantasy with the spreading fire of embarrassment as her spine locked in rigid shock. What was she allowing to happen here? How could his kisses cause her to forget so completely the heartaches of the last few months? How had she let the man induce her into bed, allow him to stroke her body like a lyre, coaxing a song from her that she had never heard before? "Please . . ." She pushed at his chest, her voice distant and low, being strummed out by the heavenly music. He was murmuring more of his spell as he nipped teasingly at the velvet skin of her throat, trailing up to her earlobe. His questing hand was returning to its maddening caresses of her thighs, the skirt of her dress twisted around her waist. She was totally confused, enchanted yet frightened by her raging desires, longing for fulfillment yet angry with herself and the man who had orchestrated this seduction with uncanny ease. She wriggled to her feet and lunged for the light switch, irrationally thinking the light would eliminate the harpies of desire that careened and swooped at her from out of the darkness. The light was blinding at first, but she focused on the shaken expression of the handsome man reclining on the bed. "I think you'd better go now," she breathed, her breast thrusting forward with each breath she took. She was amazed she could speak at all. His hair was tousled, and his breathing seemed as erratic as her own, but otherwise he was in complete control of himself.

"That's just it," he sighed, noting the kindling spark of anger in her eyes as she took in the once neatly made-up double berth and his attaché case and lone suitcase residing nearly at her feet. "We're sharing this compartment."

"That's impossible," she squeaked, coming down to earth with a thud that was almost a physical pain. Her face flamed as she realized the closeness of her escape. The golden god has feet of clay after all! Just when she was beginning to feel he might be different from the men she came into contact with every day of her life, he insisted on proving her wrong. "That's impossible," she emphasized, hiding her embarrassment and fear of her own weakness under an icy veneer. "I refuse to spend the night with you."

"You didn't seem to mind the prospect a few minutes ago," he pointed out with brutal honesty.

"That was strictly the wine . . . you took me by surprise," she stated with only partial honesty.

"By surprise?" His eyes darkened by their shared passion hardened as she watched. "You knew what was coming, and you took your share of enjoyment. Don't try to deny it."

She turned away, furious that she had no answer to his accusation. They both knew how easily he could elicit her response to his kisses. "I was merely carried away by the moment," she said coolly. "This is the nineteen eighties, Dr. Cade. Women are no longer passive chattels for your pleasure." She turned her back on his tense face, unwilling for him to see the hurt beneath her shell.

"I see." He issued the words with a voice dipped in cynicism.

"You had better ring for the porter and get this mistake taken care of before it gets any later," she offered, intimidated by his scowl but refusing to show it.

"There are no more compartments available."

"Surely something can be arranged. I won't stay here," she insisted.

"And I see no other solution unless you intend to sit up all night." He loosened the knot of his tie as he spoke. Erin watched, mesmerized, as he shed the corduroy jacket and began working on the buttons of his shirt. "I'm tired and we have a long day ahead of us. I'm going after what little sleep I'll get tonight." He ripped out of his shirt, his breathing still ragged. "I don't know what happened before, but your virtue is not in imminent danger now. You don't need to sit up all night in the club car, but it's up to you," he challenged, flinging his shirt disgustedly onto the berth. She tried to ignore his exposed upper body, but her eyes were riveted to the sculpted perfection of bone and sinew that only Michelangelo would have done justice to. She forcefully relegated her vision to his face as he spoke again. "Unless, of course, it's my virtue you feel is in danger," he mocked sarcastically, "being the liberated woman of the eighties that you are?"

He had turned on her with studied belligerence, and she hurled her answer contemptuously, giving him a scathing once over, trying to hide the effect his bold naked torso had on her senses. "You're just like every other man I've met, just out for what you can get!" She was beginning to lose her edge, and she started for the door. He flashed toward her, holding the door closed with a long, naked arm, blocking her exit from the room. When she spun to face him, her back against the door, she defiantly raised her chin, alarmed to find him taller, larger, and more hostile than before.

"It's not like that at all," he said, an expression crossing his features that she couldn't read.

"Not like what? Not like you arranging to have us sleep in the same compartment? Not like you planning to feed me, bed me, and God knows what else in that wilderness hideaway of yours. . . ."

"That's enough," he grated out, then corrected, "You've got me all wrong." He started to close the narrow space between them, the fine line of control evident in his furious hazel-shaded eyes.

"You're a man, aren't you?" Her question was redundant, as her traitorous body once again vibrated to his obvious maleness. He was a man, all right. The most dangerous man she had ever met. Her swirling mind was trying to come up with an answer that would explain the volatile chemistry between them, but there seemed to be no solution, only reaction. Overreaction was the key word, she decided. Overreaction, she repeated as he inched closer to her, his wide chest with its covering of fine curling gold hair thickening in his midsection and disappearing behind his waistband distracting her. She tried to flatten herself even closer against the door.

"I promise I can prove that I'm different than any other man you've ever met," he said, and there was no boasting in his tone, only truth. She knew inherently that he was right, but she fought against the knowledge, against his granite strength, trying futilely to get away. "I can prove it. . . ." He finished his statement by forcefully covering her mouth with his, holding her protesting body pinned to the wall, drawing away her life's breath with his kiss. She struggled silently, but his persuasive caress continued, sidestepping her haphazard defenses and invading her senses with demolishing accuracy. He raised his head, ending his deep penetration with such a devastatingly tender caress it shook her to her very core. "Please don't fight me . . . don't fight yourself anymore. . . ." he murmured.

She turned her head to the side, her ruffled curls and stained cheeks gave her a fiery, disheveled, totally sexy appearance. "You just want me to fall peacefully into your bed, is that it?" she gasped, attacking with words what she couldn't match in physical strength. She was praying for the stamina to deny his persistence, knowing that she wouldn't be able to spend a week with this man, not a day, not another minute.

"You're the most beautiful creature I've ever held. . . ." He bent his head to capture her cherry lips once more. Once again she felt herself becoming the craved possession, the prize for his long trip to Washington, the fringe benefit of his grant, and no one could convince her otherwise, not even a fair-haired god.

"Get out!" she yelled, her temper pushed past its low flash point by his comment. Pivoting out of his arms, she made a grab for his briefcase, holding it in front of her in a wary stance as she circled to face him.

"Easy now," he warned in a low quiet voice as though he were speaking to a frightened, defensive animal. She resented his confidence, the apparent ease with which he was handling their earthshaking encounter. She wound up, swinging the leather case in a vicious arc, aiming it directly at his arrogant head.

"Hold it!" he commanded, his stunned hazel eyes never leaving the missile, moving with striking force to intercept the weapon in mid-swing, wrestling it from her hands with ease.

"You are a hellcat," he swore briefly as she writhed against the confinement of his hands. "I only wanted to tell you how beautiful you are. Surely you've heard that before?" He was holding her hot twisting body at bay, as though he could no longer trust himself to have her in his arms. She stopped struggling; it only made her more aware of the superiority of his physical strength as the working muscles of his arms and his chest flexed so close to her vulnerable softness.

"Let me go," she repeated for what seemed the hundredth time. "I want to leave."

"I won't hurt you, Erin. You will be perfectly safe here."

She remained mutinously silent, and he gave an exasperated sigh, releasing her slowly and running a hand through his tousled hair. "It looks like you're going to be stubborn and sit up all night."

"I prefer to sleep elsewhere." Her voice held a tremor. It was the only concession she would make to his determined gaze and stubborn chin.

He looked as if he wished to speak again, but the words did not come. He smoothed a wisp of blue-black hair from her

59

forehead, and she stepped away from his touch. Pulling open the door, she sailed out into the corridor, slamming the thin partition behind her, exiling herself to an uncomfortable night in the coach car. But she knew she was really hurrying away from the very large threat to her heart that remained behind her in the small compartment.

CHAPTER FOUR

Mitchell Cade massaged the tensed muscles at the back of his neck with his free hand and relaxed into the cramped seat of his aging Piper Cub. His eyes flicked over the controls again; everything looked A-okay, just as the mechanic at Detroit Metro had assured him it would. Evidently the electrical malfunction that had forced him to continue his trip by train to Washington was a minor one. That was good; he couldn't afford any more delays. Or any more distractions like the one seated next to him.

A whiff of her floral scent drifted to him as she stirred and changed position. It brought to mind the first time he had seen her as she swept into the formal library of the Wentworth home, dark hair glistening like an eagle's feathers in the sun. She conveyed a calm serenity at odds with the youth and urgent energy in her blue eyes, boundless like a perfect cloudless sky. Her supple grace and refined features enhanced an innate sense of pride and dignity all wrapped in a beautiful body. Then as now he wanted to possess her, like some free and wonderful creature, keep her for himself alone.

And before the hour was through Lydia Wentworth had delivered her into his hands—with a look-but-don't-touch clause attached. He frowned. What trick of fate would drop this vision into his hands allowing him to be so close yet so far? Lydia trusted him; he remembered her words with a grimace. He glanced at Erin's reclining figure in the seat. Even the sight of her woman's body in the rose, western-cut shirt and designer jeans that molded to her every curve was enough to send a surge of pure lust charging through him. He must have been crazy, that hot Virginian night, to have accepted Lydia's stipulations. But he could never turn down a challenge. He smiled and took another look at the most capricious and sensual challenge of his life.

Her soft pink lips were parted, and there were shadows under the fringe of dark thick lashes lying on her cheek. Her head of careless dark curls rested on the back of the seat. What would she do if he kissed her again, now while she slept? Wake up scratching and clawing like last night? Damn, he'd never let any woman overrule his judgment like that before. Why this one? She was a walking contradiction with a siren's body and the lost seeking eyes of a wild animal caught in a trap. Outwardly pliant and conforming, but inwardly she was a fierce, no-holds-barred fighter, much like the birds he loved. She had the instincts and wit of a falcon, the tenacity of a hawk, and the talons of an eagle, accurate and deadly. She could cut a man to ribbons with a lift of her arched brow, banish him with a word, or dismiss him with an icy blue glare. But Mitchell Cade wasn't going to be so easy to dismiss, he promised. He was determined not to fall prey to her sophisticated aloofness or her street-brawling temper. He knew there was a loving soft woman beneath it all and he was determined to find her. He wasn't just another rarefied politician type; he knew how to value and respect so rare a treasure. He knew how to get what he wanted. Hell, this is crazy, he admonished inwardly. Just try to remember what you *do* want.

This grant is the opportunity you've been waiting for. And Erin McIntee was the kind of woman that he had dreamed of meeting one day, he argued obstinately. But she was definitely off limits. Representative Wentworth made that abundantly clear even before he knew the gorgeous woman was her granddaughter. How in hell had he let himself get in this fix? That was an easy one—money, of course. The automatic renewal of a generous grant, added to the funds he obtained from Thurston, would be enough to allow him to cancel the winter lecture tour that was his main source of financing; no more speeches to idealistic, young hotheaded environmentalists or sentimental blue-haired ladies at Audubon Society luncheons. It would give him months of freedom to start work on the book he'd promised himself to write ever since Nam. There was always a place for him to work back at Cornell. Or he might stay in Michigan; six

62

months of quiet and solitude, alone with the snow and wind, nothing to interrupt his writing.

It was a nice dream, but the reality was here in the plane with him. That had been his biggest mistake, allowing the congress-woman to outmaneuver him by dangling the possibility of freedom to complete his work in front of him, bribing him to bring Erin along. Lydia had hinted about Erin's possible future responsibilities and wealth, citing needed reflection as the purpose of the wilderness trek. She was probably hoping that all that reflection would make Erin realize her mistake for giving up a future of wealth and position with the society lawyer. But she obviously didn't want her only granddaughter mixed up with a pauper who studied birds when a wealthy society lawyer might still be waiting in the wings. But why send her away? Couldn't she have realized her mistake in leaving this Warren character at the altar just as well in the capital? He didn't know the reasons Erin bolted from her fiancé, but he wanted to find out. What did it matter? When Grandma decided she wanted her back, she would return to Washington without a backward glance.

Beneath them the cultivation of the Lower Peninsula was being replaced by the lakes and forests of the northern part of the state. His disturbingly attractive passenger stirred and opened gemstone eyes. She smiled at him, a sexy bedroom smile, as he watched her return from sleep. Mitch caught his breath, but the contented smile disappeared to be replaced by the cool anxiety that often marred her fine-boned features.

"We'll be landing in about forty minutes. Did you get enough sleep?" He hoped his voice was noncommittal, but the words were rough.

"Yes, I'm fine. Where are we?" She was frowning at his brusqueness. He was suddenly jealous of the smooth-talking lawyer she was running away from. That had to be it, he decided; her grandmother was sending her away to regain her senses. And he was stuck with the role of camp counselor.

"The Straits of Mackinac." He pointed down to the twin, ivory-colored concrete towers of the huge suspension bridge that spanned the five-mile gap of rolling water.

She nodded, saying little more, engrossed in the breathtaking view of architectural wonder and natural beauty spread out below the wings of their plane.

He gave himself a mental shake; if he wasn't watching her he was thinking about her. He hadn't done much else since they met. He'd studied and observed with the trained eye of a natural biologist, her every move, every expression and word. He had no doubt that he had seen desire in the blue sky of her eyes last night and heard it in the gentle husky tone of her voice. He was sure of it. It was whispered by the touch of her red tender lips and the beat of her heart and her soft breasts nestling against him as he held her in his arms. Longing strummed from her delicate velvet skin and sang from her body's curves as she molded to his length returning his kisses. Her passion unfolded with the fury of beating wings, fanning the embers of his own desire that skyrocketed like a flaming phoenix, taking flight into a wonderful fantasy that she seemed to share. They flew together, rising into the wind, higher and higher, like the mating flight of paired eagles, crisscrossing flight paths until they meet and join in the apex and spiral down—united—wings parallel and touching. Lovers mated, descending in a breathtaking aerial ballet, in free-fall, seemingly both willing to plunge to their death for just a few moments of shared ecstasy. He wanted to experience making love of that intensity with Erin McIntee, and he knew it would be ecstasy.

It was a wonderful fantasy, but the reality was that as soon as she could return to Washington she would go. She had erupted into an untamed fighter on the train, making it painfully clear she didn't want anyone possessing her, least of all Mitchell Cade. But he recognized the panic, guessing she had been captured and hurt before. Warren Markham must have hurt her. A secret resentment was gnawing away inside him as he vowed Markham wouldn't be allowed to hurt her again, not as long as she was under the protection of an infatuated birdman. Erin was like one of his captured birds, beautiful and wild. She would be with him for a while before he would set her free again. But while he could, he would care for her, heal and mend, and teach her to trust. Trust! On the train he had frightened her, backed her into a corner with his directness, stampeded her with his advances. She was used to the subtle, suave men of Washington, with their sophisticated prowess and witty conversations ripe with sexual innuendos.

If he ever held her in his arms again, all he could do would be to show her that he could be trusted. If he could hold her again . . .

Hell, man, you're thirty-five years old; stop daydreaming like a high school kid and wake up. She was off limits from the beginning with funding for a whole year riding on his behavior, and then there was her debonair lover in the big city. Just do your job and stop thinking about her.

The lush green of pine and birch forests passed under their moving shadow, and soon the great icy blue stretch of Lake Superior's shoreline loomed on the horizon. Checking his location, he said quietly to her, "Welcome to Paradise." He banked the plane into the sun and pushed the wheel forward to begin their descent. With ruthless purpose he relegated the mating eagles, Erin McIntee, and grants to the background as he nosed the plane into its landing pattern. Ignoring her startled gasp as the Piper dipped below the treetops, he guided the skittering plane along the grassy landing strip, gouged out of the trees, and taxied to the hangar. He cut the engine as he slanted one quick glance at Erin's pale face. She flashed him a diamond-bright smile, and he was suddenly grateful for the physical work that occupied him as he parked and spiked down the plane, unloaded her ample supply of baggage, and began the long drive home.

Paradise was the last sign of human habitation Erin saw as the scattered buildings of the hamlet were swallowed by the trees. She still felt a little jittery, and the washboard effect of the gravel roads added to her discomfort as the jeep bounced along. Their means of transport was an ancient green Bronco, jacked precariously high on four-wheel drive stilts. It was dusty with round blots of sand dotting its dull, short green hood and pockmarked from stones ricocheting off its rusty body.

She checked her watch; nearly an hour had passed since they left the plane, and they were still bobbing over the dusty roads of the Upper Peninsula. It seemed they were driving down a long narrow chute walled by tall pines and birch. The crisp blue sky was visible overhead and filled with small white clouds tinting in the afternoon sun. Erin tried to reconstruct the terrain as she remembered it from her bird's-eye view. From the sky it had seemed an enchanted land of mottled green forests interspersed with shimmering blue lakes and filigreed with the skeletons of once stately elms.

Taking advantage of Mitch's preoccupation with jockeying the Bronco over the worsening gravel road, she studied him carefully. He looked comfortable and relaxed, retaining an unsettling air of confidence even in a pair of worn cords and a chambray shirt. In her grandmother's home he had been intimidating in formal black, and now he was equally imposing in casual dress. Yet, somehow she couldn't picture him in the Savile Row suits and silk ties that were Warren's trademark. The fabric of his shirt strained across broad shoulders emphasized his muscular physique while the blue material brought a watercolor shade into his hazel eyes. Erin never knew when he would glance up and a trick of sun or shadow would show them blue or gold. She suspected he watched her also from time to time, but his gaze was always fleeting and casual.

She couldn't help but recall their encounter of the night before, and she was angry with herself for even thinking about it, although she had done little else. Even when she dozed in the plane she dreamed about it. She resented her wayward thoughts and was angry with him because it was obvious to her he had forgotten it altogether.

The road was steadily contracting with occasional shrubs and branches reaching out to brush the jeep's side, but now it expanded and swelled into a clearing. The trees had been removed years before and a cabin built of white pine. She formed a hasty impression of a steep-roofed, two-story building with a broad porch facing a stretch of blue lake. A chimney of native stone covered most of one wall, and the long cabin was dark with the accumulation of years of oil stain. Dark green shutters framed the windows, catching the rays of the westering sun. A long narrow cabin was also part of the homestead, but it was of more recent construction, and a variety of small outbuildings were scattered about the clearing.

A door flew open in the long cabin, and a dark-haired man of stocky build bounded toward them across the shaded yard. He appeared to be a few years older than Mitchell Cade, possibly in his early forties, and several inches shorter. He was wearing blue jeans and a khaki shirt, sporting a paunchy spare tire around his middle and a ten-gallon hat on his head. The man was smiling happily as he strode toward the jeep, but when Erin slid down from the Bronco's torn seat, he pulled up short with a dumbfounded expression on his face.

"Whoa, there! Chief, when I told you to bring me a souvenir from D.C., I thought maybe you might get me an ashtray or something, not a delicious-looking little dish like this," he drawled.

"Down, cowboy!" Mitch cautioned as he extricated the luggage from the back window of the jeep and set it on the ground. "Erin McIntee, this is Reuben Preston. Ms. McIntee is my new assistant. And Reuben is the best birdman this side of the Rockies." Smiling again, Reuben quickly crossed the distance between them and pumped her hand enthusiastically.

"Howdy, Miss McIntee. You can call me Tex." He smiled. "And you're about the prettiest little filly I ever did see." Erin caught a quick glint of shrewd amusement in his eyes as he glanced at his friend.

"Rein in on the charm, partner." Mitch mimicked the thick accent, and Reuben laughed good-naturedly. "How are things going? Everything okay?" Cade questioned, rushing his friend's admiring appraisal of his new assistant.

"Sure. Doc came while you were gone just like you wanted, and he's settled in. He's moving in slow and steady. But Cindy is missing you something fierce." Erin had been listening to their banter through a haze of fatigue, but the last exchange brought all her attention back to their conversation. Reuben went on oblivious of her interest. "I can see you had a real good time in the big city." He was beaming at Erin.

"She came with the grant," Mitch said with no intonation at all.

"That's some grant," the Texan replied, offering his arm to the woman glaring at his boss's broad back.

"I'll help you get settled in," Tex went on, guiding her toward the large cabin. From behind them she heard Cade's warning to his friend, and the words stiffened her spine. "Better be careful, cowboy; she's a liberated lady of the eighties." Erin stopped in her tracks, biting her tongue and whirling to face her tormentor. "She's also got a mean right hook," he added with a devilish grin that showed even white teeth.

Her mouth opened and closed, but no sound emerged. Giving Mitchell Cade an acid glance, she turned to smile capriciously at Tex. "Believe me, Mr. Preston, I'd never strike a gentleman."

"Ohhwee! Boss, what have you been up to?" He laughed at his friend's answering scowl. Then he added more seriously to Erin, "I tell ya, ma'am, I've got to watch this boy like a hawk. I let him out of my sight a few days, and he starts turning over a new leaf on me. Ya got to forgive him for doubling up on the ladies, though; it can get mighty lonely up here," he apologized pointedly. So he had noticed her reaction to the mention of Cindy. Her first impression was correct; beneath the down-home, good-ol'-boy exterior lurked a first-rate brain.

"Evidently not that lonely," she replied archly, watching the biologist stride away without another word. She felt a sudden stab of abandonment, but she smiled at Reuben who was scooping up her bags and heading toward the main cabin. She followed him into a large sitting room while she scanned the dim interior. Huge pine beams supported the cathedral ceiling and emphasized the massive gray stone fireplace. The furniture was hand-hewn pine, and a heavy corded rug covered the wooden floor. She could glimpse a modern kitchen and a bath at right angles to each other in the far corner of the room. To her right a stair climbed into the gloom, and the railing of a loft could be seen above them. Directly ahead Tex halted in the doorway of a small bedroom that held only a dresser and a large pine bed. Its one window was curtained in faded chintz and looked out into the trees that began at the edge of an overgrown patch of lawn.

"We don't have guests often, miss. But this is the guest room." The accent was much less noticeable than before. He set the bags on the floor and started back out the door. The house was very quiet. Voices in the yard floated clearly on the cool, crisp air, but none of them belonged to Mitchell Cade. An unbidden visualization of Cindy jumped into her mind. A petite blond beauty with dimples and a bow mouth. She'd keep her virile boss occupied for some time, or Erin missed her guess. That thought produced a decided lowering of her spirits. Why hadn't he mentioned there would be another woman present? Why indeed, she answered her own question, he was making love to you. What kind of man was he to have made love to her on the train when he knew he was coming home to another woman? Her hands clamped shut on the locks of her luggage, flipping the fastenings with unnecessary force and flinging the lid back on the cotton chenille spread that covered the bed. Because he was a man, a man like all the rest. Perhaps Cindy stayed in this very house? Perhaps she was even his wife? Erin felt a cold chill despite her anger, but a small part of her brain rejected this calumny even as it formed. There was something basic and honest in his nature that wouldn't allow that hideous a deceit.

"Mitch will be with you in a bit. I told him everything's all right, but he still wants to get the feel of the place himself." Reuben's brown eyes watched her steadily, gauging her reaction to his words.

"Yes, of course I understand," Erin said stiffly. "Is Cindy a close friend of Dr. Cade's?" The question slipped from her lips and fell heavily to the floor. She regretted asking it immediately and hated his reply even more.

"About as close as she's likely to get." He chuckled whimsically.

"Oh, I see. There is a Mrs. Cade then? He didn't mention being married." Erin hoped her voice was nonchalant, but she hated the bitterness she felt deep inside.

"No. No," Tex assured with a shake of his shaggy head. "I think Cindy has designs along those lines. You might even say she'd like to get her claws into him. . . ." he trailed off, and Erin failed to see the impish sparkle in his eyes.

"I see," she replied, snatching up a suitcase and starting to drag clothes from it.

Unsure of her reaction, Reuben spoke again. "I think I'll be on my way. Mitch is in the room next to yours. I'll fetch his stuff in and . . ."

"What did you say?" Erin demanded, the tiny wisps of smoky anger now kindling into an orangey light.

"I'll be staying in the room next to yours," Mitchell Cade answered, standing in the doorway of her room, daring her to object. Taking the words as his cue to leave, Reuben vanished into the main room and out the screen door that closed behind him with a bang.

"I'm not going to stay in the same house alone with you," she hurled at him. "I thought we settled that last night."

"Stubborn . . ." He let the word hang. "I suppose you can bunk with the boys in the long cabin," he said tightly, weariness etching new lines in his face. "You are just one of the boys, remember?" He was watching her closely for her reaction.

"I do not intend to sleep with any of you." Her color flamed at her choice of words, but she went on. "There is surely some-place I can stay—alone."

"I'm too tired and too busy to argue with you. You're staying right here. This is the safest place for you, and that's my final word on the subject." Mitch's tone grated on her ear. "I'm responsible for you, and you'll stay where I tell you to stay."

"I will not stay with you," she hissed as she began to toss her clothes helter-skelter into her bags. "And that's final!" she declared, banging the lid closed on the expensive piece of luggage. "I'm not staying with any of you."

"You'll do as I say," he repeated the statement as he filled the doorway threateningly. "You'll have all the privacy you want."

"I doubt that since I'm only one of the women you have stashed away out here."

"What the hell are you talking about?" Anger and disbelief shone in his eyes as he took a step toward her.

She backed away. "I'll stay there," she said impulsively, spying a small log shed visible outside her window.

"Absolutely not. It's nothing but a storage shed."

She grabbed up her luggage, her heart jerking in thudding beats, and stared with pure insubordination at the large man in the doorway. "Let me out of here," she echoed last night's demand. He stepped aside as she rushed out of the room afraid the confrontation would end as their last one had.

A few seconds later she stood hesitantly staring into the cool darkness of the storage shed as the door creaked open. Building character and fiber; wasn't that what Lydia wanted? She felt as if she were taking a step into a solitary cell as she lifted her chin and stepped into the dank darkness. She shuddered as her shoulders and face knocked down cobwebs from inside the door. It was very dark with only the palest gray light coming from the small dusty window and tiny licks of brightness lapping through chinks in the walls. She took a few steps forward, a startled cry escaping her lips as her head brushed against something that returned to strike her curls. She dropped her bags to swat at the creature circling her head trying to bat it away from her hair. Suddenly a bony hand above her pulled the string of the swinging light bulb suspended in the center of the musty room. Erin whirled around as the light flashed on to illuminate a ghostly wrinkled face frowning severely at her. A small scream mingled with his muffled shout.

"For Gawd sakes, girl. Are you trying to scare me to death?" the old man said, clutching his thin chest. "What in Peter Corey's hell are you doing out here in the shed anyways?"

"I . . . I . . ."

"The door was standin' open so I goes to close it and you scar't me out of a year's growth. I aint' got none to spare at my age. Who are you anyways?" the old man asked, eyeing her suspiciously. "Another bird person, I suppose. This whole damn place is full of 'em, ya know. This whole damn place is for the birds; now they add another mouth to feed. A woman who's like to scare folks to death."

"You must be George?" she whispered.

"It doesn't matter what they told ya; everyone eats what I cook and they like it. No matter what they sez."

Erin could only nod as she looked around the room gulping air and struggling to collect her wits. The bulb was still swaying, casting strange shadows that would grow and shrink on the craggy log walls and on the studs holding the tin corrugated roof. "This whole place is filled with crazy people anyways." George was shaking his head and muttering thoughtfully as he walked from the shed. "Scare a fella to death."

"I see you met George." Tex smiled as he poked his head around the edge of the door. "He's harmless, except for his cooking," he added irreverently. "The chief wants me to help you get settled in. I brought a cot, okay?" Erin smiled and nodded. "I really wish I could talk you out of staying in here, Miss McIntee." She shook her head. "That's what I was afraid of." He handed her a broom as he began to set up the cot. "This is usually where we keep the boats and motors in storage, so it's not too fancy."

"Please call me Erin, if I may call you Tex."

"Sure." He beamed at her. "You know you really don't have to stay out here, Erin. One thing I know for sure—you can count on Mitchell Cade getting you through whatever bad times you've got. I know that for a fact. Faults, yes. The chief has some god-awful faults, like he's as stubborn as a lop-eared mule, proud as an eagle, and ornery as a cross-eyed badger when he wants something and he knows he's right. He's got faults, all right, but lechery sure ain't one of them. *Comprende?*"

"Why do you call him chief?" she asked thoughtfully, intentionally avoiding a direct answer to the earnest speech.

"Ole Mitch?" Tex looked up from his assemblage of wooden legs and canvas. "I've called him that for years."

"How long have you known him?"

"I've been kicking around here with him for five years since he left Cornell the last time. But before that we spent a lifetime together in Nam one year. That's when I first got aquainted with him." He looked up at Erin, carefully questioning. "He was the chief and we were the Indians. That's how that worked. He was only a sergeant, but the rest of us knew that he would look out for us and get us home alive, no matter how many second looeys tried to get us blown away. That's all. That's how I know he can be counted on." She was silent for a while, considering his words and watching his persistent work as the cot began to take shape.

"You both like working with birds of prey?"

"Yeah, some people think that's strange. To like a predator— a killer, but we both have great respect and admiration for them. And sometimes the killers come up empty-handed, so someone has to look after them. Mitch, he's made them his life's work. I just like them." He set the cot against one wall and tested it with a blunt, strong hand. "That should do it, Erin. Now," he said, taking her hand. "I'll show you the rest of the compound."

"That won't be necessary, Tex. I'll show Erin around." Mitchell Cade spoke from the door. "You finish up your work." Erin wanted to object but didn't. He looked more relaxed, as though

72

his inspection of his domain had been a pleasing one, and she was strangely reluctant to renew hostilities.

"Sure thing, chief," the Texan acknowledged, dropping her hand. Touching his finger to his hat he left the building, relinquishing Erin to her employer. The early evening sunlight danced on the small lake as they walked through the dappled shadows to the long cabin.

Opening a door, Cade ushered her into a laboratory complete with a high lab table holding microscopes and other instruments, while several desks and tall filing cabinets stood along the wall. Colorful posters of various eagles decorated the white painted walls along with a large detailed map of the region showing, Erin assumed, the positions of known nesting sites and their status by the use of various colored pins.

"We do most of our lab work here," Mitch explained stiffly, and Erin knew he had not forgiven her for her earlier outburst. They passed into a narrow hall with several doors opening on each side. There was a small surgery, an office, and rooms she guessed belonged to the three men of the staff. "We are licensed to keep injured birds, and when Doc's here we even perform an occasional surgery." Erin listened carefully, only now beginning to realize the full extent of his work.

They stepped out the back door into a large penned area with several cages holding perches and a wire ceiling overhead, just below the tree boughs. Doc was walking toward them, a small man with curious light blue eyes darting behind wire rimmed glasses and not missing a detail. Mounted on his leather-gloved arm was a full grown bald eagle. Falconer's leather jesses circled each yellow talon and attached to a leash with a metal swivel. Its startling white head pivoted as it perched head and shoulders above its holder's tousled sandy hair. The eagle eyed Erin with its staring yellow orbs, turning its head regally to the side, affording its admirer a profile view, ruffling its proud white tail feathers. The eagle's only apparent flaw was a bandaged wing held at a dainty angle away from the shining dark brown feathers of its body.

"Erin, this is Dr. Joe Jackson and Cindy." He gestured to the bird. So this splendid raptor was the other woman. Erin was too enthralled by the impressive creature to be embarrassed by her mistake.

"She's magnificent," Erin breathed. "What happened to her?" The bird was preening coyly, cocking her head and creeing happily at the sound of Mitch's low voice.

"Besides being homesick for Mitch, she's doing pretty well with her broken wing. She was shot by some crackpot." The young veterinarian's studious eyes were watching her closely, but Tex must have clued him into her identity because he asked no further questions. "You did a great job with her wing, Mitch. She's doing just fine. Let's get her back in the cage before the sedative I gave her wears off and she decides to take a bite out of me," Doc only half joked.

Mitch smiled, erasing the tension lines from around his mouth, and picked up a leather glove similar to Doc's from a nearby table, pulling it on. He slid his hand behind the yellow taloned legs, and the bird stepped cautiously onto his hand as he took the leash Doc offered. "Thanks, Mitch. She goes about sixteen pounds," he informed Erin, flexing his tired shoulder as Mitch moved off to return the bird to her cage. "Let me show you the lab," he cajoled, the enthusiasm for his work sounding plainly in his voice. Erin accepted happily, already feeling she could come to like being in this exciting and interesting place if only she didn't have to worry about the disturbing proximity of Mitchell Cade.

She began her campaign to avoid the biologist that very evening, but it was even more difficult than she had imagined. They ate George's meal seated around a large table while he grumbled over the steaming pots in the kitchen. She listened to the tales of Texas that Reuben continued in a steady stream, and she consciously evaded Mitch's hazel eyes while the conversation moved on to shoptalk and the three men nodded through an unintelligible morass of bird jargon. After trying to keep the various birds and experiments straight in her tired brain, Erin gave up and excused herself for a long, leisurely bath.

She slid gratefully into the deep claw-footed tub in the starkly masculine room. The walls were paneled like the rest of the house, the fixtures white and old-fashioned. Mitch's razor and comb rested on a shelf below the mirror, and a bright red towel was thrown over the rack where he had left it. Erin soaked a long time in the warm brackish water stained by the tannic acid in the Tamarack swamps that drained into the lake. She lathered her hair, rinsing it thoroughly, and toweled off, using her blow dryer to feather a soft halo of dusky curves around her head. After she was dressed she studied her reflection in the steamy mirror, feeling more like herself than she had since stepping onto the train yesterday. She returned to the main room in time to accept a cup of coffee from George as she passed the kitchen. Erin settled comfortably into the worn overstuffed sofa before the crackling fire, good food, fatigue, and the soaking bath producing a drowsy euphoria.

Mitch was standing by the hearth, toe of one shoe idly kicking at a smoldering log. A tanned arm rested along the mantel, his shirt sleeve folded back to reveal the curling gold hair that covered the muscled flesh. One strong sensitive hand was curled around the steaming mug, the other hooked in the belt loop of his pants. He could be counted on, isn't that what Tex had said, he could be counted on. It was purely a matter of trust. As the reflected light turned his hazel eyes to liquid gold, she could understand why Cindy was homesick for him. She already felt she had something in common with the regal bird. Yet she was secretly very pleased that Cindy was not a two-legged beauty but a fierce confident predator. She had misjudged him again. But watching his natural leadership with the others, she felt a small shiver of apprehension course down her spine.

She could trust him, perhaps, but could she trust herself? Could she see her way clearly enough to avoid becoming lost in the overwhelming power of his personality? He smiled down at her curled sleepily into the corner, and she returned the fleeting visual caress for a brief moment. No, she couldn't trust herself, she admitted as the blood quickened in her veins. One smile from this golden man and her heart was fluttering. He was her guide, her boss, and she was the vulnerable woman who could lose her heart to him—to an eagleman.

She knew if she allowed his power to overcome her, she would lose not only her heart but her identity as well, the identity that she was sent here to seek and needed so badly to find. She took

75

one last long feasting look at his fire-shadowed face and strong, virile body and quickly excused herself from the group, stopping to compliment the mumbling chef before she left the warmth of the cabin for the blackness of the night. As she closed the door, she heard Tex say, "Chief, you can't make her stay out there . . ." But she didn't hear Mitchell Cade's reply as she hurried into the sobering chill of the May night.

CHAPTER FIVE

She hadn't been so cold since last December; it was a cold lonely chill that crept through her, but the feeling was not foreign. It seemed that every time she asserted herself in a man's world she ended up alone in the cold. She pulled her long nightgown down and hooked its ruffled bottom over her toes, enveloping her tightly curled body, and pinched the sleeping bag up to her chin. She was attempting to read the sizzling best seller that she had packed, trying to absorb a little of its heat in her bone-chilling corner of the world. Reuben had bestowed her with a few creature comforts: the sleeping bag, a straight-backed chair, and the extra bright light that was plugged with extensions to the fixture suspended in the middle of the room. He had even presented her sheepishly with a china bowl and pitcher that now sat incongruously on the greasy workbench. The dismal room reminded her of Pore Jud's house in the revival of the stage play *Oklahoma!* that she had seen so many years ago with her parents.

The last time she had shivered so much was on her wedding day just prior to the Christmas holidays. What would she be doing now if she hadn't run away leaving a mortified Warren standing on the church steps? She recalled how he had demanded her return, as if the worst thing she had done was upset his schedule. Warren had it all planned so carefully; the wedding would take place before the holiday recess, and then there would be a few days for a honeymoon. Warren wasn't new to presidential campaigns. He had worked on several of them, and he knew what he was doing. "Christmas weddings are beautiful," he assured her, and that was the only time in the next two years he would have adequate time to squeeze in their wedding and honeymoon. The names of the famous and near famous on the guest list were already accepting in gratifying numbers. Warren was pleased but not surprised. He was building his foundation of power and prestige with careful, confident hands.

Looking back he had seemed so very much what she wanted when they first met. Sophisticated, successful, he was everything a young woman could hope for. But almost immediately he began to try his subtle, polished, manipulative techniques on her. For those first months she was too blindly in love to resent his attempts to mold her into the perfect partner; then later when the doubts became stronger, she felt too committed to back out. Warren's smooth counseling voice was always there with soothing tones to ease the small, nagging fears she did find the courage to speak about.

He would tell her patiently of the future they were building together. "We'll be partners, Erin," he would say, kissing her with cool expertise, smiling his satisfaction at her quiet response to his practiced lovemaking. "You'll be the most influential, elegant hostess in the city." She would snuggle against him wanting to be reassured, wanting to believe that the things he asked and expected of her was what she really wanted also. But when he left her and withdrew the velvet-covered force of his will, she was left to think again—doubt again.

When she finally did come to her senses, came out of the deep pit he'd dropped her into that late fall night, and realized something must be done, the holidays were upon them. Eating little and sleeping less, she moved through the prenuptial celebrations like a zombie. Twice the exclusively designed raw silk wedding gown had to be taken in. Warren thought she had never looked better, and Lydia asked her frankly what was wrong with her. But she couldn't tell her grandmother whatever love she felt for Warren had dissipated in the cold gray fog of night, that she was too weak to make the effort to break free of the bonds that held her to him.

Her wedding day found her staring in her bedroom mirror, a vision of grace in the high-necked, heavily beaded gown Warren had chosen for her. His diamond weighed heavily on her finger, and soon his body would lie beside hers. Tonight and every night for the rest of her life. At least when he could squeeze her in between the computer polls, dinners, and campaign tours. She couldn't go through with it. She needed to get away from Warren or she would be eaten alive by his ambition.

"Erin, it's time to go." Lydia's voice spoke quietly from the door behind her. Their blue eyes met briefly in the mirror before Erin's gaze slid away. The declaration caused a javelin thrust of panic to slice through her. She felt doomed with no chance of reprieve; no one knew of her plight. She could only count on herself.

Regardless of her rising panic the limousine moved steadily through the holiday traffic, pulling smoothly to a halt at the foot of the church steps. Lydia was squeezing her cold hand, and Berrie fussed with the yards of illusion veil floating around Erin in the fitful wind as it began to spit icy rain again. She stood on the pavement, her eyes riveted to the party of satisfied, proud men at the top of the steps. The gray gothic spires of the First Episcopal Church loomed over her like the doom gripping her heart. The steps passed relentlessly under feet while Warren's face came closer as he left the groomsmen to assist her climb. The touch of his hand in hers detonated the charge of horror and disgust she had been keeping at bay for weeks. She knew in that instant she could not trust this man, not with her life or the lives of her future children, not today, not tomorrow—not ever.

"I won't," the words were torn from her throat. "I can't. I'm sorry, Grandmother. I'm sorry Warren." She shook from head to foot like a sapling in the wind. "I don't love you, I don't even know you . . . I thought I did . . . but I won't marry you . . ." With a muffled sob she tore away from his slackened grip and flew down the steps as though she were being chased.

"Erin! Come back! I demand you come back." Warren's harsh command floated after her on the keening wind.

She kept running, her veil streaming, the hem of her gown dragging in the muddy water at the curb's edge. On she went, heedless of the glances of startled passersby. She ran on into the rain and cold wanting only to escape, to rest, to heal herself. She was so bone-rackingly cold, wandering the nearly deserted streets of the city in a soaking, dirty wedding gown. She had dropped her beautiful bouquet of snowy orchids and sweetheart roses into the wet streets as she ran, beads flying from the delicate gown. She was cold and alone and running away from a man that wanted to conform her to his will, to control her completely.

But now she was cold and alone again running from another man. She had only met Mitchell Cade a short forty-eight hours ago, yet her instincts warned her of her heart's jeopardy. His golden, blue-flecked eyes and the memory of his touch reminded her that he was a dangerous threat to her quest for her identity.

Everything was excruciatingly quiet here in the woods. Even the creaking of Jud's cabin had ceased. She heard the men leaving the main house talking quietly while George continued rattling pans, getting ready for the next day's meals. But now everything was still. Not a sound. She could almost hear the cold creeping through the little holes in the walls and under the door. The silence was so loud it seemed to drown out the narrative of her book. What fictional plot could possibly rival the idiotic drama of her own life? Not even the television soaps would have a bright young woman in a wedding gown catching a bus to get back home from her defaulted wedding. Or have her huddled into a sleeping bag in the middle of a forest for God knows what reason, trying to conserve the little heat left in her body. Why was it she was always on the outside looking in? Warren had never tried to contact her again. He was much too insulted and much too busy with his candidate to worry about her. And she could hardly see Dr. Cade losing any sleep over the plight that she had created for herself.

It was deafeningly silent. She must remember to tell Lydia that they really didn't live on a quiet residential street. This was a silent street—a dead-end road a million miles from the rest of the world. She heard footfalls, then a stirring outside the door and a sharp rap of knuckles against wood that shredded the silence.

"Who is it?" She sat up quickly, leaning on one hand.

"It's Cade." She heard his low voice, and her pulses leaped expectantly.

"Come in." She tried to make her voice confident.

"I brought some . . ." He swung the door open and stared down at her. She knew the soft pink nightgown with its Victorian ruffle and lace yoke crossing over her breasts was not revealing, but it couldn't be proven by his expression. ". . . some blankets and a heater," Mitch finished after a leisurely inspection that left

80

her breathless once more. He dropped the blankets on the chair and carefully closed the door. He seemed to fill the whole room, casting a huge shadow that covered most of the wall and door. For an instant she felt childlike, gazing up from the low cot, but the intensity of his regard dispelled that notion. He carried a camping heater close to her bed, moving with animal grace, and set it on the floor.

"I see you're reading." He gestured to the book opened flat on the cot. His eyes traveled from the scantily clad beauty on the cover to her own breasts as they lifted the lace of her gown with each breath she took.

"I like to read." She hurried into speech, embarrassed by his study, but unwilling to have him leave. "I'm glad Reuben could find this extra light." She didn't want him to go; she wanted this radiant source of heat and life to stay with her.

"This will warm you up a little," he said, squatting on his heels to fiddle with the levers protruding from the heater.

"Oh, yes, the heater," she stammered, fearing he had read her thoughts. "Thank you for bringing it." The bold light made his beard a shadow over his chin and jaw, and she wanted to feel its roughness against her skin. He nodded and stood, walking to the door. She tapped impatiently on the paperback with a long nail causing the ruffles at her wrist to bounce. It drew his attention.

"Harold Robbins writes quite a bedtime story," he teased, holding her confused gaze and gesturing toward the book in her hands. His eyes were dark and alluring in the bright light, and his shadow duplicated his every masculine move.

"I read anything, classics and best sellers." She shrugged gracefully, but she couldn't meet his continued scrutiny so she rattled on. "Some books are like puzzles that need to be pieced together, one detail at a time; others are more like modern art, complicated collages of texture and purpose. They're all unique. Like your birds."

He stood with his back against the door, his long denim-covered legs propping him up casually and his arms folded across his broad chest. "It sounds as though you know a lot about writing, more than the average reader, anyway." She scrambled out of the sleeping bag, curling her toes under to escape the floor's chill as she laid the book carefully on the cot and walked to the door. He straightened from his careless position as she drew closer to him, and the light outlined the curves of her body within the translucent gown. He stiffened, looking about the room trying to avoid her, then gave up the delusion and watched her unabashedly.

"In college I studied literature," she said earnestly, looking up openly into his rugged face as though that explained her behavior and all of her now chaotic emotions. Shivering from the cold and his nearness and feeling small next to his large frame, she realized it was a mistake to leave the marginal comfort and safety of her sleeping bag. Butterflies chased each other in her stomach. Either from excitement or the chill of the night, she could feel her nipples rise and tense, peaked mauve-shaded impressions pushing into the thin fabric of her gown. The sensual detail didn't go unnoted or unappreciated by Mitchell Cade, who muttered an oath under his breath. He picked up a blanket from the chair, unfolding and gently draping it over her, smoothing it on her shoulders. A muscle worked along his jaw as his hands reluctantly left her and firmly lowered to his sides.

"I have some books in the house; you're welcome to read them anytime," he said at last.

"Thank you." She pushed the words past the lump in her throat. She couldn't think of anything else to say; the only thing that she could focus on was the thought of his arms around her. She didn't want him to leave. You silly fool, you are out here because you didn't want him to hold you. You didn't want to be near him. Admit it, you're afraid to be near him. But she still didn't want him to leave, and he was reaching for the latch on the door. "Cade?"

"Yes?"

His eyes were piercing her, not angry with her yet, very intense. His frank inquiring expression was making it difficult to hide the fact that she didn't know what to say. All she knew was the thought of being in Pore Jud's cabin alone was nearly unbearable. She wanted him to stay if only a few minutes longer. She wanted him to ask her to come in with him, but she knew he wouldn't. She had made him look foolish before Tex. If she wanted out of this place, she would have to swallow her pride and say so. "Thank you for the heater," she stammered.

82

"We couldn't have Mrs. Wentworth's only granddaughter catching pneumonia the first night, now could we?" A devil's smile in his eyes crinkled the lines at their corners. She could watch the play of emotions in their depths and never tire of it.

"That wouldn't look at all good in the grant report." The retort fell flat, and she clasped chilled hands tighter. He saw the gesture and the smile disappeared. Swinging open the door, he stepped down onto the gravel path from the floor of the shed, bringing her own puzzled gaze level with his.

"If it gets too cold, don't be stubborn. The door of the house will be unlocked," he said sternly.

"I'll be all right," she maintained, automatically pulling the heavy cover closer with a shaky hand. An unreadable expression crossed his face as he leaned against the doorframe. What good did it do her to observe the moods of his features when she didn't hold the key to understanding them?

"Sure you will. Good night." He moved away.

"I'll be fine." She nodded, determined to remain and prove her independence. "Really," she said to his vanishing back. "Good night," she added, unsteadily. Her last words made him stop short just beyond the rectangle of light from the door, and he turned watching her a moment silhouetted in the doorway. He hesitated, then returned.

"If you hear anything outside the cabin during the night, don't go out to investigate." His tone was casual, but he watched her carefully.

"If I hear anything?"

"Things that go bump in the night. And I don't mean mice." He grinned at her shudder and quick glance at the floor beneath her bare feet. "Just stay inside. Don't let that stubborn streak send you out to investigate on your own. It will probably be a bear."

"Bears!"

"This isn't Washington," he spoke patiently, but amusement danced in his eyes.

"Bears?" Her tumbling thoughts stuck on the last coherent utterance she had voiced.

"It's only food they're after. They think people food is great."

"Do they think people make great food?" He grinned at her

question and then answered by crooking his finger and beckoning her with it. She stepped closer to him where he stood outside the door and scanned the grounds to detect any stray bruin.

"You'll be all right as long as you don't keep food in here. And don't get carried away with sweet perfumes; they think that smells good enough to eat." He reached out suddenly twisting one dusky strand of hair around his finger, bending nearer. "Yours is just right," he complimented, watching her for a long moment; then with a cautious hand he moved her dark glistening hair and laid back the soft lace at her throat.

"I'm not wearing perfume." She could feel his warm breath on her skin, his fingers heavy on her neck, and the words came out breathlessly, lacking the sarcastic sting she meant to give them.

"I know," he murmured. "You smell very nice, flowery." His voice was husky, his eyes shadowed, searching hers. "See that window right there?" He indicated pointing to the warm yellow light coming from the window very close to the shed. "That's my bedroom. I'll only be a few feet away."

She nodded seriously, listening more to the tone of his voice than the words he spoke. "I'll be right there in a warm, comfortable, and safe bed. You can come in tonight. Your room is ready and waiting. You don't have to prove anything to me." The observation was too close to the truth, and she inched back. It was to herself the proof was needed.

"You can trust me, Erin. If you need any help you only need to call and I'll hear you."

"Just call?" She was watching the inviting glow of light, and he was watching the conflicting emotions chase across her face.

"Absolutely." She saw the calm assurance and sincerity in his eyes, and she stepped back leaning against the doorjamb with a small involuntary sigh of relief. Perhaps he did understand her gnawing need to be independent, to find for herself the elusive quality of serenity that gave him such strength.

"What should I call you?" Her voice held a hint of panic. "I mean, everyone here calls you something different. So many names. I could call you Doctor, Mitch, chief, boss, Cade. By the time I decide what to call you, it would be too late." He suppressed his amusement, tugging the blanket up around her trembling shoulders close to her neck, lightly brushing the feminine ruffle there, and lifted her chin with his thumb.

"Just whistle. I'll be here—you can count on it." He braced one hand on the log wall beside her and one hand on the doorjamb above her head. He was very close to her now, leaning into the opening with flexed muscular arms. "Can you whistle, Erin?" His eyes held hers, preventing her retreat into the dubious safety of her solitary abode. The golden light from the house cast the shadowed planes and angles of his face into coppery relief. She couldn't think about whistling or anything except him, feeling the heat pour from his body and smelling his clean spicy skin. "Just pucker your lips and blow. Go ahead and try it," he urged provocatively. She pursed her lips and blew out an airy sound, but it was cut short by his warm mouth covering hers. The sweet erotic contact made her body remember his intoxicating touch, and she craved it again as she opened her blanket and arched toward him, brushing her breasts against his heavy chambray shirt. She longed to be pulled into his strong arms, but he deprived her of that pleasure. She leaned her heat-starved body into his while her arms reached up to wind around his neck and her breasts nestled naturally against the broad wall of his powerful torso, the blanket slipping to the floor. She kissed him back, enticing first the corner of his mouth, then his mobile lips, still aching to be enfolded and molded to his length. But she couldn't summon the courage, the daring, to make such a wanton advance. She could hear the doorframe creak and groan from the increasing pressure of his stubbornly denying hands, and she felt the quivering bands of muscle across his shoulders and arms as her hands unwittingly implored him. He tasted her lips longingly and then stepped away, expelling a long ragged breath. "If you need me I'll be here. Trust me," he urged, his own voice ragged. "Good night, Erin."

"Good night," she whispered as she watched his large frame vanish around the corner of the house.

She stood at the door only a moment, then returned to her ungiving bed. Her heart was pounding, and she could still feel the impression of his kiss on her lips. She slithered deeper into the sleeping bag, snuggling down into its depths before she zipped herself in, safe from bears and cold, but not immune from her milling thoughts. He wasn't satisfied with throwing her emotions into upheaval, or being able to elicit a sexual response with a word, a smile, or a simple kiss; he wanted her trust, too. Is that why he didn't crush her in his strong arms, so she would trust him? His response to her was much more controlled than last night on the train. Was he vying for her confidence? It was a novel way of asking for trust—proving it first. She wasn't used to that tactic from men; Warren had certainly never used it.

But hadn't she known from the first moment that she met Mitchell Cade that he was unique, encompassing the qualities of men that lived in other times, in other centuries? Honor, pride, inner strength, and now concern and kindness could be added to her mental list. He had brought her blankets and a heater, and he didn't make an advance that wasn't totally welcome. But he had never really done that, she admitted honestly. Then why was he so frightening? She knew it was because he was capable of making her forget the hard lessons she had already learned.

Trust me; Mitchell Cade's words haunted her spirit. Isn't that what Warren had wanted her to do? Was there any such thing? Wasn't faith supposed to come with love? If she learned that she couldn't believe in Warren Markham, had she ever really loved him at all? Or had he really loved her? Questions were the only thing that came to mind. No answers, just questions along with painful memories crowding her head. Could she rely on any man again? "Trust me, Erin. I know about these things" is what he had asked of her that gray rainy evening in early November only a few weeks before their wedding, just an evening after election day.

"Warren," she had ventured nervously, twirling a glass of sherry between her fingers. They were sitting before the ceramic logs of the gas fireplace in her apartment. "How do you feel about children?" She had avoided the subject until after the election, but she felt she couldn't put it off much longer. Soon he would be busy planning his new campaign, and she would be blooming with his child.

He raised one brow in the gesture that never failed to make Erin feel gauche and very young. He was standing stiffly with one hand on the mantel watching the leaping blue flames in the small grate, weighing his answers as he always did. Erin bit her lip to stifle the scream of vexation that was growing in her throat. Why couldn't he just answer her? In six weeks she would be his wife. Couldn't he tell her openly what he felt, without hesitation, with no inner dialogue of discretion?

"I suppose we will start a family when the time is right." He moved to sit on the couch against which she was leaning. Warren would never sit on the floor. His hand reached out and draped itself around her chilled shoulder. Erin leaned her head on his knee, turning her face back to the fire, running her fingers through the plush pile of the cream-colored carpet.

"I mean now, Warren. How do you feel about a child now?"

His glass clattered onto the end table, and Erin flinched as his hand bit into her shoulder. He lifted her to her knees and turned her to face him. She felt like a supplicant begging for understanding from a stern mentor.

"What are you trying to say, Erin? You haven't been so foolish as to become pregnant, have you?" His voice was cold as she stared into flat gray eyes, as cool and limitless as a rainy sky.

"I don't know yet; it's possible," she confessed, wanting with all her heart to see his face reflect the joy she needed to see.

"The wedding is six weeks away," he calculated. "Have you been to see a doctor?"

"No." Ice from the gray eyes was transmitting itself to her heart.

"Good." He expelled a quick breath. "There are some very good doctors in Maryland—"

She laughed, but it was strained. "Warren, darling. There are fine obstetricians right here and pediatricians as well. I don't need to go out of the city."

"Trust me on this, Erin. I know about these things." His mind was reeling far ahead, his emotions far from her. "Now is not the right time for a child. We'll be so busy with the campaign . . ."

"Warren, the election is two years away. What are you suggesting?" she whispered as the measuring look she dreaded suffused his features. She rocked back on her heels, holding her breath.

Watching her closely, Warren made his decision. "It was foolish of you not to take precautions, love." His tone was patronizingly gentle. "I was afraid your lack of experience in these matters would do you harm, but you assured me . . . after all, you aren't a child."

"Warren, please. . . . What are you saying?" She knew really what he intended, but she couldn't bear this uncaring, dispassionate discussion of life and death another moment.

"I'm saying this is not the right time for us to start a family. You'll see that, too. I'm just thinking of you, my love," he lied smoothly. "We're gearing up for a presidential campaign . . . the wedding . . ." he trailed off, patting her absently while his calculating mind turned over alternatives. "A child would upset all our plans, our whole future." He tried again. "After all, a pregnant bride . . ."

He would never come right out and say it, she realized. Not with his training in the law and his political instincts. "Are you saying you don't want our child?" she questioned bluntly.

"I'm saying we could always have another child." He halted again, noting the bleak hardness settling into the cobalt of her darkened eyes.

"Are you suggesting an abortion, Warren?" she asked tonelessly.

"I'd never presume to ask, my dear," he said, donning the mask of sidestepping objectivity he used when he talked to the press. "I know as my wife you'd want to do what's best for both of us . . ."

"It would be our baby," she said softly, tears spilling down her cheeks, misery knotting inside her. She resented his playacting, and for a few fleeting moments she saw the truth and hated it even more. Perhaps he had been acting from the beginning. Maybe she had made love with and promised to marry a man who could only pretend to love her.

He soothed and calmed, speaking to her as though she were an hysterical child. He had almost convinced her she had misunderstood his words. Tomorrow she would see Dr. Lee, she agreed, and they would talk again. It was just the shock, the bad timing, and her carelessness that had taken him by surprise.

Dutifully, the next day she had seen the doctor, received his verdict of stress, frayed nerves, and vitamin deficiencies, and reported obediently to her fiancé. He looked relieved but didn't mention that night again. He also didn't make love to her in the weeks until the wedding. She didn't mind; it was a relief. Warren had attempted to make her fit the mold, even as far as their lovemaking. Everything must please him and him alone. Warren was trying to manipulate and control even her body and the life that might grow inside. How had she allowed herself to fall for his lines so long—trust me. But it had taken several more long miserable weeks to make the final break.

He violated her trust, her love. Wouldn't any other man do the same? She had learned her lesson well—trust was going for a very high premium these days. Although Mitchell Cade gave her the feeling of being the stable rock on which to build a foundation of trust, she knew better. She had learned her lesson well.

Erin was nearly asleep, exhausted from shivering and emotion, when the vision of his amused blue-flecked eyes somehow worked its way past remembered misery into the forefront of her mind. She pictured him tall and lean, golden brown and smelling like clean herbs and spice. Lazily she speculated what he would smell like coming directly from the shower, and that deliciously sensual thought brought her fully awake again. It wasn't until the early hours of the morning that she finally drifted off into a restless sleep.

CHAPTER SIX

The revving of the jeep's motor woke Erin from a sound, dreamless sleep. She stretched languidly, shifting the blankets that covered her, starting a chain reaction of bed linen sliding off the cot. She sighed and came fully awake at the sounds of footsteps on the gravel outside. It seemed only a few minutes ago that she'd fallen asleep. It had been that way for the past several nights; cold, yes, but no headaches, no sleeping pills. She was even getting used to the Stygian blackness and less jumpy of every sound in the darkness.

She knew that Mitch was close by, which was a source of comfort and turmoil. His handsome features were difficult to ignore. He was always around, yet he seemed so preoccupied when she was near that he barely had time to nod in greeting before he rushed off to complete another task. She was truly looking forward to this morning when she would go out on her first banding mission. Not only would she be working, but she would also have a chance to talk to Mitch again. Excitement was already starting to build in her heart, but she convinced herself that it was because she needed to be busy, have action and work that would fill her days. That would settle the restlessness she felt. Wrinkling her nose at the boxlike room, she stretched again, pushing her arms up over her head, sending her pillow skidding onto the plank floor.

Erin glanced at the travel clock on the upturned box beside the cot as she reached out to retrieve her pillow. With a start her sleep-lulled mind clicked into gear; the voices outside, the running jeep, the sounds of Doc's Ford pickup truck departing for town with George grumbling his adios to Tex—her first banding and she was late.

It was still early, barely seven o'clock, and the sun wasn't even peeking through the thick curtain of cedar forest behind the boathouse. Erin flew into her clothes, choosing what she considered her best bet for rough country. Her hurried departure from Washington had been so unexpected there had been no time to shop, so she did the best she could.

She emerged from the musty boathouse into the cool, misty morning, wiped the last cobwebs of sleep from her head, and shivered in her lightweight jacket. She stood quietly a moment watching the mist rise from the dark blue-brown water of the hazy lake.

The air was brisk, almost cold, and tangy with the scent of cedar and jack pine. She stepped onto the gravel, rounding the corner of the boathouse, coming to a halt before the frowning bulk of her employer. Erin began an automatic apology for her tardiness, but he ignored her, studying her with disgruntling scrutiny.

He was standing by the idling jeep, hands at his waist hooked into the belt loops of worn, faded blue jeans that fit his long muscular thighs too snugly for Erin's peace of mind. A dull-gold wool shirt stretched across his broad chest, revealing a triangle of tanned skin with its wiry mat of golden hair. He wore heavy leather boots, and the legs of his jeans were tucked into high-topped wool socks. His eyes traveled over her, the frown deepening as he took in the designer jeans, the open-necked white shirt, and high-collared jacket of bright poppy-red.

"You can't go out in the field like that," he said shortly.

"Is he always this grumpy in the morning?" she inquired lightly of the grinning Tex as he hefted climbing equipment into the back of the jeep. She thought she looked pretty good in what she had to work with and was disappointed by his attitude.

The few days since her arrival had passed pleasantly, and Erin saw no reason for Mitch's obvious bad humor. She was looking forward to her first chance to see them at work, and Mitch's scowl was dampening her enthusiasm more quickly than the dewy grass was wetting her nylon running shoes.

"I said you can't go out wearing that outfit," he repeated as seriously as before.

"It's all I have," she shot back, her pleasure in the new day and the experiences it would hold evaporating as quickly as the spring mist. "Your schedule gave me very little time to ready myself for the wilderness." He wasn't the only one who could be stubborn. She'd show him she refused to be bullied. Tex was watching from the far side of the jeep, his blunt face carefully noncommittal.

"You'll scare every living thing within a hundred miles in that coat," Mitch exaggerated. "Get those things off!"

Tex had sidled away from the jeep, walking back toward the long cabin at her first outburst, apparently deciding to let his friend fight his own battles. Erin was growing angrier by the second. How dare this man speak to her in that condescending tone.

"This is the best I can do," she said mutinously, hands on her hips. "Take it or leave it." Tex returned as she uttered the last defiant statement, carrying a khaki turtleneck sweater and a plaid flannel shirt that once had been green but was now various shades of mottled gray.

"I washed these in hot water," he drawled into the charged silence, ignoring the smoldering glares of the combatants. "They shrank up real good. You're welcome to them."

"No, thank you, Tex," Erin said politely, favoring him with her most winning smile. "I'll wear what I have on." This day was not going like she had planned, not at all, and she resented it.

With speed that caught her unprepared, Mitchell Cade erupted into motion, grabbing the clothes from his startled cohort and clamping his hand on Erin's wrist before she could escape. "I told you to get out of that jacket," he grated, annoyed.

"No!" She wasn't going to give in now. She couldn't and retain her self-respect. It was a test of wills, and she must make a stand for herself.

"Take them off or I'll do it for you," he threatened, and his eyes were hard, not a flicker of amusement in their steely depths. "Erin, I've given you a long tether. If you insist on being stubborn, staying out in the cold at night, that's your choice. But I'm not going to let you sabotage a banding trip just for a fashion parade. That red jacket will scare any eaglet out of the nest, and it's not warm enough."

"I'll stay here then," she countered, too angry to care what she said.

"Oh, no you don't. You're going, and you're wearing what I tell you to wear." His words were sharp, and she stared rebelliously up at him, not daring to break the contact, knowing she was unreasonable but also hating his overreaction to what she was wearing. He needn't be so angry about her attire.

"You're wasting my time, Erin. If I have to undress you myself, I will." Her mind raced, and her heart accompanied it. Surely he wouldn't carry out that threat, but his steady, icy gaze left her little assurance. She remained silent, and the grip on her wrist tightened. With a twist of his lips he shifted his weight, tossing her over his shoulder with ease.

"Put me down," she screeched. "Put me down!" She was already breathless, and her stomach jounced painfully against the hardness of his shoulder with each step he took. "Cade!"

"You want to be stubborn. You want to act like a child, I'll treat you like a child," he said, striding toward the shed, carrying her like a sack of potatoes. "Hold still!" he ordered as she pummeled his back with her fists. "Hold still, damn you!" He grunted as one punch landed on the unprotected area above his kidneys. Following up her advantage, she continued raining blows until the sharp crack of his large open palm on the seat of her pants terminated her attack with an outraged squeal. The boathouse door banged open on its rickety hinges, and Erin was deposited unceremoniously on her cot and her smarting backside.

"Get these on!" he repeated, his breathing heavy. His hand streaked out and opened her jacket with one harsh zip.

"Don't you dare touch me again," she snarled, a red mist forming before her eyes as she estimated the damage to her dignity and her person. She rolled over searching for a weapon, anything to throw at his arrogant face. She made a grab for her alarm clock to hurl at him, but he pounced on her, pinning her hand to the cot and leaning over her threateningly, unmoving as she pushed against his shoulder. He was still holding the disputed articles of clothing, and a return of prudence stilled the harsh oaths Erin was sifting in her mind. "Let go of me!" She shook her curls from her flushed face and bore into her oppressor with fiery eyes.

"I've been trying my damnedest to keep my hands off of you," he snarled. "And now you pull this stunt. Get these on now." Each word was snapped off so distinctly Erin could hear the sound of his straight white teeth coming together. "I'm not going to let you hold up my work."

"I . . . I don't want you to touch me." She hurled the words at him. "I hate you," she lied. "You're crude . . ."

"My, my," he said mildly, pulling her up from the cot and pinning her clawing hands behind her back. "What's the matter? Can't you even admit you might be attracted to an ordinary man? No politician, no society lawyer." A muscle flexed along his jaw, and his eyes narrowed. Ordinary man! Erin's swirling brain clamped onto the words. Ordinary man; the thought was ludicrous. "I'm warning you, Erin, get these on, now. Or I'll do it for you. As you say, I'm crude." He actually wouldn't stay to watch her dress. Or would he? His stubborn determined face gave her no comfort. He was worse than Warren, worse than any man, and she was totally dependent on him for the next six weeks. Even as the thoughts bounded into her brain, a small treacherous flutter of heat began to build in the pit of her stomach. Two could play at this game, she gambled, watching a small spark lighten the darkness of his eyes, replacing their coldness with a hazel glow. He was surely bluffing, and she was going to call it.

"I said no, and I meant no," she reiterated, waiting confidently for him to back down. When he had done so, she told herself, and tendered a suitable apology, she would put on Tex's clothes, and they would proceed on a much smoother course.

"Then I'll have to do it for you," he stated, watching her thoughts chase across her face. His anger seemed to be dissipating as determined fingers unfastened the top button of her soft white blouse and started on the second. This bluffing game had gone too far, and Erin began to wrench away from his arms, but he held her firmly. She felt helpless as well as involuntarily responsive to the fleeting touch of his powerful hands. Humiliation flooded over her along with the delicious feelings aroused by his relentless fingers.

"Lydia will hear about this," she threatened. "You're certainly not the man she thinks you are," Erin hissed, trying to writhe

94

away from persistent, methodical hands that continued with their task.

"I want you to know the kind of man I am. What I say I will do—I do."

"Let me go!" She struggled against him, only managing to wriggle the shirt and jacket from her shoulders, parting the blouse that was now completely unfastened. She was bound by the soft quiana clinging and binding on her upper arms as well as by his steely grip. He let his eyes trail over her woman's curves with unadulterated admiration, causing a scarlet stain to creep up from her deep, scented cleavage. Her low-cut bra held her round, full breasts temptingly high as they thrust against him with every breath she took, their softness straining against his power. He pressed on her wrists still confined behind her, nearly lifting her from the floor, arching her heaving bosom higher still and merging their lower bodies, a cloud of stinging desire in her veins. She could no longer deny her wanton longing for him to caress and possess her body, yet she struggled against him so he wouldn't see her quivering need. She tried to writhe from his grasp, which only caused another wave of desire as her nipples, protected only by a wisp of lace, brushed against the titillating roughness of his wool shirt.

"Let me go!" she begged. "Don't—"

His mouth clamped on hers quickly and completely, stopping her plea and eliciting an immediate response to his harsh demanding control, stealing her breath and sapping her will to resist. But her mutinous mouth refused to fall prey to his ravaging tongue seeking entrance past her quivering lips. She held firm trying to escape him until he tightened his grip and pulled on her wrist, wrenching a small angry cry from her. He plundered her parted lips, invading the moist softness within, demanding at first and then tender as she surrendered to the sweet victory of his kiss.

"There's no use to fight me, Erin," he breathed against the delicate velvet of her cheek. He tempted her with another firm kiss, and this time she weakened, accepting the probing insistence of his tongue, as a large knowing hand trailed down her throat, sweeping over the flushed voluptuous mounds, initiating a trembling ripple in its wake. She knew there was no use to fight him. He was all too aware of the sweet chaos he was causing in her. She didn't want to respond to his touch, didn't want him to see her desire. Yet she pressed her breasts into the hard expanse of his chest needing the coarseness of the contact as he slid her shirt off her arms and down to her manacled wrists. A faint smile lightened his eyes but disappeared before it reached his lips as he tugged on the sleeves of her jacket and blouse. They fell away like a shell sending a chill of cool air over her bare back and shoulders. "I never bluff, Erin. I always finish what I start. Always." He bent his head and caressed her mouth tenderly as he released her hands, only to surround her in a warming embrace.

The hands that were so menacing moments ago flowed over her flesh in a fountain of pleasure. Her anger was gone now, spiraling away as another wave of weakening desire burned through her, and she melted closer to him, willingly accepting his exploring kiss. Her hands, freed of their bondage, wound around his neck, caressing the corded muscles of his shoulders under the harsh wool. His hands moved possessively, fondling her breast as though touching an exquisite treasure. His eyes explored the translucent porcelain of her skin usually hidden from the sun but now exposed to his burning gaze. Bold fingers slipped inside the lacy cup of her bra, stroking and exciting the mauve nipple. His kisses trailed fire from her trembling lips to her throat as his hands continued their tactile discovery of her breasts, knowingly teasing and caressing the tip until it peaked and tightened into a firm, perfect bud. She was beyond thinking, enjoying his mastery of her body, leaning into the pleasure that he gave her.

Her hands grew bolder as they wandered down over his ribs to fasten around the firmness of his waist, her fingertips slipping inside the waistband of the taut denim to caress the smooth flesh of his stomach. Breaking the contact of their mingling tongues, he chuckled softly against her mouth, and she opened passion-bright eyes to share in his amusement. His lips hovered over hers, planting tiny, nibbling caresses on their parted moistness. One hand rested lightly on her hip, and the other held her wrist, his thumb tracing patterns over the sensitive skin of the inner surface.

96

"You can spit fire at me as much as you want," he smiled against her searching lips, his hold increasing as he felt her stiffen. "You can tell me you hate me, but your beautiful body says something else, and that's the message that comes through loud and clear." He looked down at her, and the smile was gone; there was resentment in his eyes and something else. Her world of pleasure was crumbling about her. "I never bluff." His voice was cold and hard. "I keep my word; you can count on it. Don't expect the sophisticated gambits you're used to from the other men in your life." He released her completely, still regarding her startled face and her jutting breasts as they strained against the lacy fabric. "Don't push me too far," he warned, his voice ragged with an emotion Erin was too distraught to decipher. He scooped up the forgotten garments and put them in her limp hands. "You'd better get these on. We've got to get going. It's an hour's drive to the first nest. Hurry up!"

She glared at him, hating his insufferable calm and self-righteousness. She resented his manipulation of her desire. He was worse than all the other men she had known. He could elicit a riot of emotions clambering through her veins with just a touch of his hand or a cutting word. He spun on his heel, leaving her standing, the shame and horror at her own behavior mingling with anger and a grudging respect for the ease with which he had beaten her at her own game.

Erin pushed her chair away from the desk, pulling the cover over the portable typewriter and stretching cramped muscles, raising her arms to reach high above her head. It was so quiet. Erin was surprised at how quickly she'd grown fond of Reuben's corny jokes, Doc's earnest concerns, and even George's grumbling. The noisy confusion of their everyday comings and goings was preferable to the silence that now reigned over the compound. They had left early this morning, setting out for a series of nests that would keep them on the road for the next several days. George was accompanying them, complaining about the inconvenience and his rheumatism but, Erin suspected, secretly pleased they preferred his cooking to their own.

She had been right; being busy had settled her into the routine of this male society. After taking data in the field and gathering

Mitch's notes from the lab, she typed them all and filed the information on each active eagle nest they visited. Each aerie had its own file of recorded history for the last five years. It was identified by code, correlated with the numbers of all the eagles banded in that nest, and a chemical history compiled after Mitch had studied eggshell fragments, castings, and scraps of food retrieved from the fishy-smelling aeries.

It was her duty as his assistant to coordinate the information and organize the material in a concise, readable form before filing it. She was very efficient in her work, if not in the ways of her heart. And of course there was her other duty. She had already sent a report to her grandmother for the Wentworth Fund on the status of the work being done. It was a very formal report, clinically rendered and closed only with her initials. Yet she couldn't help wondering how Lydia was doing, wishing their parting hadn't been so hostile. She wanted to prove her worth to her grandmother, and she wanted their relationship back on its old easy footing. She was still angry with Lydia for her compromising blackmail, but she recognized the underlying motives. Still, the older woman's scheming had catapulted her into the stubborn hands of an unknown eagleman. Erin was aware she had projected her anger onto the young biologist, yet in the past week her anger was dissipating, replaced by a growing respect for his work and for the man. In her obstinacy she had been continually mistaken about Mitchell Cade. Now she couldn't help but feel a grudging respect for the man, even after their fiery encounters. Unbidden, that respect was beginning to accelerate into a guarded admiration. She had drastically misjudged the steel strength of his determination, disguised by his amiable smile and quiet reserve. It was a strength that could overpower her, along with sexual prowess that reduced her to quivering jelly in his arms. After his humiliating rejection the morning of their first banding, she vowed never to allow him that advantage again. He was a dangerous man. She knew she dared not underestimate his magnetism and the growing extent of his power over her senses. He drew her eyes, her mind, and her heart like a powerful invisible force. She enjoyed watching him climb, enjoyed his quiet assurance as he worked with complete concentration in the lab. He was dedicated, involved in work he enjoyed and believed in regardless of its isolation and lack of reward and personal gain. She hadn't known a man like that in many years. In some ways he reminded her of her father. Both men had shared a true love and commitment to their work and their integrity. Both men had the special quality of being totally devoted to the things they loved.

One of Lydia's favorite family tales was relating her daughter's stormy courtship with Duncan McIntee. "At the time Duncan was a hardworking, hard-nosed foreman on our ranch," Lydia would faithfully begin, and Erin would settle back, eager to hear the familiar story once again. "He was handsome, wily, strong, just like the land itself. And Claudia!" She would laugh, which was Erin's cue to giggle. "She was fresh from finishing school, so sure she knew everything there was to know. She was also convinced she was in love with a boy-from Baltimore, until her father introduced her to Duncan." Lydia would smile dreamily, possibly remembering her own romance with Erin's grandfather. "In the process of reacquainting Claudia with the ranch, Duncan fell in love with her and convinced her that he was a man to be reckoned with." At this point in the story her mother would lean over and kiss Duncan McIntee on his lean, tan cheek and smile.

"Your father was the most stubborn and honest man I'd ever met. He refused to take no for an answer." Her parents were strong individuals, and their tempers clashed with frequency, but the storms were always brief, all sound and fury. In all her short life with them Erin never doubted her father's love for her or for her mother.

Claudia's smile faded from her mind as she moved idly into the hallway from the small windowless office, drawn by the sounds of activity in the cages behind the long cabin. Had Lydia discerned the same qualities in Mitchell Cade that had been so strong in the men she cared for most? Erin couldn't be sure, but she was having more and more difficulty convincing herself that her growing attraction for this stubborn man was only physical. She laid open the embroidered collar of her short-sleeved white blouse, then shoved her hands deep into the pockets of her gray flannel slacks as she reflectively watched the birds and the eagle-man.

Noisy, creeing calls were issuing from the eagle swaying on the branched perch in the flight cage while Mitchell Cade sprayed her with a light mist from a length of green garden hose. He was talking soothingly, and the shameless hussy was clearly delighted with his undivided attention. The feathers curling from her strong legs gave Erin the impression the eagle was wearing a fashionable pair of dark brown knickers cuffed coquettishly just above the strong bright yellow talons where her aluminum band still was held in place. She turned on her perch, provocatively fanning her tail feathers and waggling them invitingly as the light mist drifted over her. She preened coyly, watching him, as the spray made rainbows in the brilliant morning sunshine filtering through the new leaves overhead.

Erin smiled, laughing at herself for projecting human qualities and emotions onto the creature. And she could hardly blame her, she decided. Mitchell Cade made an impressive sight, his bronzed torso bare above the low-riding cutoffs with long muscular thighs and arms stretching and flexing. His tousled hair as well as the tightly curled golden hair on his body sparkled with drops of moisture from the fine spray, glinting in the sun while smooth muscles worked across his back and broad shoulders. Erin watched, quietly enjoying the visual feast of man and nature. Cindy preened and postured, twisting her snowy white head to avidly follow the man's movements with an inquisitive yellow eye. And Erin imagined that the bird enjoyed the sight of his masculine body also. As Erin walked toward the cage, she watched the eagle clamp her talons in a mating dance. Erin's appearance caught the raptor's quick attention, and she stretched her wings, striking a pose that reminded Erin of the top of a flagpole. She gave a harsh cry of warning to the man outside her cage, obviously unhappy at Erin's disturbance of their tête-à-tête.

"I've finished the filing and typed up the reports you wanted. Is there anything else you'd like me to do?" She didn't want to fall to the lure of his smiling blue-flecked eyes and spoke sharply, concentrating on the antics of the great bird. His eyes were blue again today. She would never grow used to his changeable hazel spheres.

"You can help me finish up here," he suggested, shutting off the spray and stepping into the work area where she was standing. "When we finish there's a nest about an hour's drive from here. I think we can manage it by ourselves if you're game." It was a challenge, and she accepted with alacrity, eager to prove her worth.

"I can be ready in fifteen minutes." Her smile was genuine and totally captivating. Mitch reached out, catching her hand. Suddenly the smile died from her lips, replaced by an anxious, wary frown, and she pulled her hand away from his. She turned away, unwilling to let him take her heart on another tumbling roller coaster ride. When she felt composed enough, she glanced at him. He had moved to a table where his muscles worked in quick harsh movements as he cut a thawed rabbit carcass into suitable pieces for his charge. Erin felt as helpless as the rabbit in his hands, all the inner strength and life gone, only the weak flesh remaining.

"You're becoming very efficient," he offered tonelessly after his flurry of motion.

"That's exactly what I said about you in my report to my grandmother," she replied; extremely efficient at manipulating my emotions, she continued unspoken.

"You're taking your work seriously; I didn't expect you to become so quickly involved," he said, ignoring her and putting a haunch of rabbit meat into the cage for the eagle.

"I assumed you would be pleased . . . that the report is favorable," she said, arching a dark brow. He was silent as he placed another piece of meat near the water pan. He left Erin hanging in a limbo of confusion as he turned his full attention to the giant bird again.

"I know I do my work well," he said flatly with simple pride. The eagle pounced on his offering, tearing greedily at the meat, no longer interested in the humans around her. Mitch had carefully mapped out the eagle's rehabilitation, wanting to make her return to the wild as successful and as soon as possible. When he considered the injured bird strong enough, she would be allowed to make her own kill; the dead meat would be replaced with live fish and trapped prey. It would be as successful as his manipulation of her life, eliciting just the desired response he wanted from both of them at will.

Erin said no more, watching as he moved with cool confidence to put food out for the red-shouldered hawk that also occupied the flight cage, the victim of a collision with a power line.

"How soon do you plan to return to the city now that you've finished your report?" The question caught her by surprise, and she stammered a reply.

"I don't know . . . whenever my grandmother sends for me. I'm not sure," she said hesitantly. She glanced over at him. Was he finished toying with her schoolgirl emotions and wanting her to leave now? She couldn't explain her real reason for being here. He would think her even more foolish. How could she say her grandmother didn't feel she was mature enough to handle her own finances? But she didn't need to explain anything to him. Her transformation would be complete by the time she left Paradise; she would be a whole fulfilled woman with a purpose, independently wealthy and unencumbered by any man—free. A lump rose in her throat.

Sliding into a change of subject, she addressed the sated and curious bird. "No one can keep us down, can they, Cindy? You look as though you may be leaving soon, too. If you can tear yourself away from Mitch, that is." She gave him a brief smile, hoping to show she could easily tear herself away from his magnetism. But his steady, penetrating gaze stifled her confidence and caused her pain.

"She won't be strong enough to release before fall," he said quietly. "So I'll be able to hold her awhile longer." He still studied her, and his brows clamped together in a quick frown. "After that she'll fly." He moved with catlike grace to stand behind her. The vibrations in her body told her he was close even though they didn't touch.

"So you'll be losing her," she said, pushing the words through her constricted throat.

"No. I'll be freeing her. I would find no pleasure in holding a creature so wild and beautiful against her will." She stiffened, rubbing her wrists, remembering the evocative bondage of his viselike grip, flushing when she admitted that even his rough hold on her wasn't truly against her will. "It won't take long for a beauty like her to find a mate. She's a mature female, but I

102

doubt she's mated yet." His voice was low, very near, and her wayward heart skipped several beats. "Bald eagles are one of those rare species that mate for life."

"Unlike people." She was giving a curt imitation of weary sophistication.

"Unlike some people," he corrected her, stepping imposingly closer. "And next spring Cindy will return to give me a brood of eaglets to band and study, won't you, girl?" Cindy bobbed her head as if answering his request, and they both laughed at her antics. The sound of their laughter seemed to please the bird, and Erin couldn't take her eyes from her feathered cloak for fear she would see Mitch and he would guess her weakening resolve, or see the response of a dewy-eyed fool. Turning her to face him, and lifting her chin gently with his fingers, he asked, "Where will you be next spring, Erin?" His intensity caught her off guard, initiating a tightening twist deep in her center.

"I don't know." Her words were too sincere, not etched with the cavalier tone she wanted, but they slipped out in a tumbling stream. "But wherever I am, I'll be missing Paradise." Her blue eyes were shadowed as she crossed her arms and curled her hands around herself, shivering from his encompassing look. He watched her questioning features carefully as though he were trying to peel back the layers of protective shell and memorize the Erin that lay beneath.

"I know another group that will miss you," he said slowly, infusing the words with deeper meaning, but Erin refused to dwell on the connotations. "Your adopted family over there," he went on, pointing to the three downy, orphaned, barred owl chicks nesting in a protected wooden brooder.

She laughed shakily. "They think I'm their mother. Who knows, if I play the role long enough maybe I'll become wise like an owl." The light words caused her a tiny, sharp pang. Perhaps she would stop losing her heart to men who wouldn't return her love without trying to change her.

"You'll have to keep feeding them to know for sure. You wouldn't want to neglect your family now, would you?"

"Of course not!" She laughed musically, snatching up some food and preparing to feed the gawky, noisy youngsters. Relieved at the opportunity to break away from the emotionally charged atmosphere near him, she began to drop bits of raw meat into their open, clamoring beaks. Suddenly Mitch was behind her again, pulling her back into his arms.

"Easy little mother," he cautioned. "Your babies are getting bigger every day. Those beaks could snap off the end of your finger." His words barely registered in her thoughts; she was only aware that she was leaning back against his powerful naked chest and he was surrounding her with his arms. She tried to keep from melting into his rugged frame, attempting to concentrate on the deeper purpose of her wilderness venture. She meant to come out of this a totally free woman. Yet in his arms she could feel herself being swallowed up by his strength and the inexplicable sphere of force that was building up around her. It should be a warning, she thought, distracted by the feel of his hair-roughened skin through the thin gauze of her shirt. Both large tanned hands were gliding over her shoulders, caressing down the length of her smooth arms. It should be a warning; she couldn't delude herself in this fantasy world. There was no guarantee that she could share her life with a man and retain her own integrity. It wasn't preordained that in love you would find a world in which two separate personalities could live together and remain whole and equal. She had wanted that with Warren, and he had betrayed her dreams. But Mitch had started her wanting again. It should be a warning—a warning. She stepped abruptly away from his caressing hands, whirling to face him.

"I'll be more careful in the future," she said firmly, promising herself also. Damn the man; she had to remember the attraction was only physical. She had felt it immediately even at their first meeting in her grandmother's house. But so did that damn eagle! You're jealous of a bird! She could almost laugh at the lunacy of her untenable position with romantic fantasy and reality colliding in an emotional mass of confusion. "I'll go get changed now," she said quietly, backing away from his stony features. "I'll meet you at the jeep." He didn't answer as she rushed from the cage back into the long cabin. A narrow escape. She slumped weakly against the wall, quaking in the dark hallway, trying to collect her splintered emotions and her last shreds of dignity. She couldn't allow the humiliation of another rejection. She had to get away. During her flight she didn't look back to see Mitchell Cade smash one bunched fist into the wall of the long cabin as she rushed blindly away.

CHAPTER SEVEN

Erin pulled the blanket back over her shoulder, gooseflesh rising on her arm as the shed took on all the warmth and charm of an icebox. She glanced again at the empty camp heater and debated whether it was worth getting dressed to go back to the main house and ask Mitch for more fuel. She shivered again, lowering her book and glancing at the clock; nearly midnight and she wasn't sleep, even though it had been a long, busy day. Now it was going to be a long, cold night.

She tried to concentrate on the book in her hands. She hadn't done this much reading since college, she thought wryly. At least that was a plus for this wilderness sojourn. She felt, however, she was receiving a degree in survival instead of a B.A. in Literature. Erin pushed at the pillow behind her back, trying to find a comfortable position on the unyielding cot. She wriggled around, and the blanket dropped lower. "I'll end up with pneumonia," she gasped aloud as the cold night air washed over her breasts, only partially concealed by the low-cut neckline of her voile nightgown. The lace bodice and capped peasant sleeves of the filmy fabric gave her little protection from the cold. Erin looked around the solitude of the storage shed, tired of the smell of motor oil, dust, and mildew. It was a dirty cell of a building, and leaving the warmth and comfort of the main house and Mitch's company was growing harder with each passing day.

She toyed with the idea of moving her things into the main house tomorrow, before Reuben and Doc's return. Independence was one thing, but freezing to death was something else entirely. What good was it to have pride and independence if she were found frozen to death on this infernal army cot? Certainly even her Wentworth pride and temper could afford a little compromise and horse trading. Couldn't she be self-reliant and warm at the same time? But along with her trade for a warm bed, she would have to graciously suffer Mitch's complacent smile and Reuben's impertinent questions, and decided against it.

Doggedly she returned to the Hemingway novel with deliberate interest. She hadn't read Hemingway since her days at the university and wouldn't be now if Mitch hadn't loaned her the book and mentioned the author's love of this part of the world. Hemingway had spent his childhood summers in Michigan, and many of his early stories used the area for their settings. In many ways the man who had given her the book of short stories resembled a Hemingway hero. Mitch was at peace with himself and his environment, understanding nature as well as being a part of it. He grew with the wilderness, becoming like the land while caring for the fragile existence of a bold endangered species. He knew about life and death, about mating and . . .

And I'm thinking much too much about Mitchell Cade, she charged with chagrin. The image of his body, his smile, his eyes, invaded her thoughts. The things he said, his kisses and caresses, were branded on her memory. Now she was projecting him into the characters of a book—into her life. The man and his work were creeping into her plans for the future. His personality was permeating her wilderness life. She was falling in love with him.

No! No! No! Compromise was one thing, but how could she be an independent woman and allow a man to dominate her life as before? Hadn't she learned that lesson already? Her time in the woods had cleansed her spirit and healed her wounds. She was thinking much less about Warren Markham and Washington and the cynical tangled web of expediency that fueled that city of political razzle-dazzle. But should she forget the cruel lessons she learned there? She couldn't be falling in love with Mitchell Cade. She wouldn't allow it. Absolutely not.

Too restless to continue with the young soldier Nick Adams in "Big Two-Hearted River," she closed the leather-bound volume, placing it on the box beside her bed. Pulling the blanket around her shoulders, she moved to the one window and stared out at the still landscape. A full moon hung above the treetops, reaching her even in the dismal shed. Every leaf and branch was outlined with its pearly luminescence, and the night breeze carried a sharp earth scent of fern, moss, and pine. Growing more chilled with the passing minutes, she snatched the cord of the bright overhead light and curled into her sleeping bag, courting sleep. But her mind refused to rest, conjuring images of the day's climb, replaying the scenes behind closed lids.

After Erin's shaky parting from her employer earlier in the day, they were both determinedly lighthearted, perhaps both intent on making this climb and the time they had left together happy. They had left the jeep at the trail's end, walking the last five hundred yards to the nest through the forest, lugging the climbing equipment in framed backpacks. They picked and threaded their way through the forest as quietly as possible, and their stealth was rewarded. As they approached the clearing near the base of the nesting tree, Mitch nudged her.

"There she is," he whispered, pointing to the huge nest perched on the dead pine as a mature female bald eagle zeroed in on their movement from the edge of the aerie. She seemed to have delayed her departure just for them, because as they watched she unfurled her seven-foot wings and lifted off with mighty strokes into the blue sky. In the quiet of the forest they could hear the pulsing even beats of the raptor winging into flight.

"She's beautiful!" Erin breathed.

"Yes, she is," he agreed, watching her fascinated features.

Soon the eagle was gliding on the wind, banking to circle her home and offspring, her white head and tail feathers gleaming in the sun, her dark body and wings framed by scudding white clouds. To Erin's delight the large female was soon joined by her smaller mate, and the two soared together over the nest, keeping vigil, riding the wind currents with matchless grace.

"Will it be safe for you to go up while the parents are so close?" she asked, concerned, visualizing Cindy's savage talons.

"It'll be all right," he said, readjusting the weight of his pack as he watched the birds. "Eagles don't attack to protect their nest."

"They must know you're only trying to help and wouldn't hurt them or the eaglets," she said ingenuously, still watching the soaring pair, thinking that Dr. Mitchell Cade wouldn't hurt any living creature, but especially not a new life.

"Absolutely." His quiet word brought her eyes from the perfect sky back to his handsome face. He was studying her carefully, and she blushed. He was too good at reading her thoughts. "Just ask any eagle in the area," he added facetiously. "I'm a very trustworthy fellow." A smile accented the leathered creases around his eyes but only tugged at a corner of his mouth as he stepped past her, and they moved on to the base of the tall pine that held the aerie.

The long trek down dusty rutted roads and even rougher logging trails to find the forbidding dead pine topped with its crown of thorns was worth the effort. The avian architects had worked on this nest over thirty breeding seasons, accumulating more than a ton of sticks in the room-sized platform, Mitch informed her as he shrugged off his pack. Erin narrowed her eyes against the bright sun as she dropped her heavy backpack beside his while watching the unmistakable dark head of a curious eaglet pop over the side of the nest.

Mitch, muscles working in smooth precision and sharp irons biting solidly into the dark wood, leaned back into his climbing belt as he ascended through the verdant lower branches to the gray dead skeleton jutting into the blue sky. The wind ruffled his burnished gold hair and glinted off the hooked stick dangling from his belt as he climbed. Erin held her breath as she watched him begin the dangerous ascent. Her heart skipped several beats, and she called his name as the irons of one boot hit a soft spot on the trunk with an ominous hollow ring and he slipped, was caught by his safety rope and held as a shower of bark and debris rained down. Erin swallowed a shriek, biting her lip and returning Mitch's reassuring wave with a good imitation of savoir faire as he continued his climb, gingerly testing each branch and each step he took.

At the top the nest protruded far out from the trunk, and he rested a moment before hanging suspended, then traversing almost parallel to the ground across the bottom of the aerie before hoisting his head and shoulders over the lip. Securing himself with his rope, his hands were free to work with his reaching stick and riveter. Erin relaxed after he was secure, amazed the slender trunk could support his added weight. He smiled and waved down to her, teasing her about the eaglet's lack of charm. "A face only a mother could love," he chuckled. He seemed determined to make the afternoon a pleasant one as he called the information down to her, and Erin laughed in return.

The banding evidently caught the large gawky eaglet by surprise, as its cries filled the air, and its five-foot wingspan carried it in frantic leaps above the nest. With deceptive ease Mitch corraled the eaglet, turning it on its back and snapping the riveted band into place while calling down details that Erin quickly jotted onto her notebook: sex, age, one unhatched egg in the nest, basic facts that would be expanded in a more convenient setting. She was busy using her own hastily concocted shorthand, intent on correctly interpreting Mitch's hurried impressions and directions when he gave a frustrated shout and Erin looked up to see the frightened eaglet break from his grasp. The frenzied bird teetered and flopped on the edge of the large aerie, launching itself into space with a noisy squawk. Erin shaded her eyes, watching the half-falling, half-flying youngster as it vanished into the trees with the distressed parent birds circling above calling for their progeny with harried cries.

Gauging the eaglet's flight path as best she could, Erin moved into the dense undergrowth ignoring Mitch's commands for her to wait. How many times had she heard the men speak about the importance of getting to a "jumper" as quickly as possible. This was her first experience with a frightened eaglet leaving the security of the nest, but she knew there was no way the large wings of the parent birds could maneuver in the dense understory of the forest. It was up to her to find and return the baby to the nest.

The going was rough; low-hanging branches snaked out to snag her clothes and scratch and bruise her delicate skin, fallen trees blocked her path, and brambles tangled in her hair as she rushed in the direction of the flapping flight pattern. After a breathless scramble up the side of a low hill, she stopped, trying to orient herself in the green-on-green silence. The quiet was intense, yet filled with life, and she took a cautious step forward as though emerging from a soft, giant green womb into the new world of a sun-spangled clearing. Her eyes traveled over the fern-covered ground where trillium bloomed below the fronds. Before her there was a small space where all the fern had been carefully matted down in a compact circle. She took one step, two, then sank to her knees, oblivious to a faraway echo of her name as she peered down into the quiet nest.

Its occupant was a tiny fawn curled into a ball, completely protected on a bed of fern, hidden from view by the waving fronds in the sunlit clearing. Large liquid eyes moved, following the movements of the fascinated intruder. Instinctive fear claimed the little creature, as every muscle under the soft brown spotted hide quaked, yet the baby didn't try to escape. For a moment Erin was completely overwhelmed by the tender new life, beautiful and still, and awed by the revelation of this regeneration of nature quivering at her feet. Erin looked around in puzzlement, searching for signs of the doe, but only a blue jay in a nearby tree disturbed the peace of the setting. She was conscious only of the pounding of two heartbeats.

"Poor baby," she soothed. "I scared your mother away, didn't I?" The delicate ears twitched at the alien sound of her speech, while moist mahogany eyes continued to stare up at her. Erin rubbed her palms along denim-covered legs, itching to touch the soft speckled fawn, but declining, knowing that human scent on the baby would mean abandonment and certain death for the little one. The echo of her name was closer. Mitch was searching for her now as well as for the eaglet. She didn't answer, unwilling to frighten the shivering bit of new life further. Yet she couldn't think of anyone that she would rather share this moment with than the man who called her name. She wanted to find him, show him the beauty that certainly he would understand; then perhaps the absent doe would return to her fawn. But she couldn't tear herself away. The fawn lifted its head curiously; the sensitive nostrils quivered with the scent of this strange trespasser. The large eyes brimmed as though at any second crystal tears would drop like dew on the carpet of old leaves that covered the forest floor.

"Okay, I'm leaving," Erin whispered again. "Your mom can return, and you can tell her all about me." The strident call of the jay and the rustle of a rising wind covered the sounds of Mitch's approach. Almost without warning he emerged into the clearing, covering the distance separating them in two long strides, pulling her into his arms with demanding urgency.

"My God, are you all right? Why didn't you answer me?" he asked roughly. "Don't ever take off like that again!" He gave her a shake to emphasize his words.

"I won't . . ." He was chastizing her again, yet she ignored his exasperated tone, placing a slender finger on his lips.

"Shhhh, he's frightened enough already." Eyes shining with emotion, she looked openly into his determined features, pointing to the young deer and watching anxiety melt from his hazel eyes. She stole another look at Mitch, trying to imagine his reaction to holding a tiny bundle of baby and blanket. She put her hand on his strong forearm, wondering what this powerful man would do with a feather-light infant.

"Mitch?" He smiled at her and wrapped an arm around her waist. "Will the mother return?"

"Sure. She's watching and waiting for us to leave, I imagine," he said, relaxing, but not loosening his hold around her. She leaned into him just for a moment remembering a child she thought she was going to have, dreaming of children she might have. And the eagleman who held her not saying a word, he, too, was part of the dream, part of the fantasy, she realized with a start.

She knew that since the disappointment of her suspected pregnancy she wanted a child very much, although this was the first time since Warren's betrayal that she imagined a father for her children. Shying away from the depth of feeling she was stirring, she recalled her purpose with a guilty start. ". . . the eaglet . . ."

"Can't be far from here; the parents are circling about a hundred yards away. I'm afraid you're going to have to give up your charge to his rightful mother and come with me."

His careless words pricked the magic bubble of peace she had found in his arms, and tears welled into the sapphire pools before she could hide them. Was it possible that he was another man with a cavalier, uncaring attitude toward children?

"The fawn will be better off," he assured, misunderstanding her distress. "What's wrong, Erin?" Mitch asked, tenderly drawing her into his embrace with a ragged sigh. His palms captured and cradled her upturned face as he vowed, "Someday you'll trust me, tell me what makes you sad." Had she only imagined

112

the callousness of his words? She watched his face for the sincerity she'd heard in his voice.

Her eyes traveled over the rugged contours studying the sensitive, sensual line of his mouth, and her fingers ached to trace the curve of his cheek. Her lips parted as her perusal recalled his caresses and the taste of his mouth. With a ragged groan he covered her trembling lips with his. Satisfied with what she had read in gold-flecked eyes, Erin accepted the domination of his mouth. The conviction was growing within her, strengthening like the bonds he was weaving around her heart. He would understand and know the damage Warren's callous complacency had done to her soul, how cruelly his easy rejection of their possible child had eaten at the fabric of her femininity. But now even these thoughts faded as his tongue mingled with hers, coaxing desire from the depths of her being, warming and healing the cold aching places of her heart.

That had been hours ago, and the memory of the afternoon warmed her now in this lonely cold shed with the heater not working and her mind worrying about the same question over and over. Was she falling in love with Dr. Mitchell Cade? Her heart held only one answer—absolutely. She smiled guiding her thoughts back to the wooded glen; he had ended the kiss reluctantly, pulling her with him back into the sheltering trees, standing motionless but achingly aware of the length of his body pressed to hers. From beyond a lacy screen of cedar boughs, together they had watched the delicate beauty of the white-tailed doe return and gently nose her infant.

"Come on, Erin. Now we can find our large, squawking eaglet and return it to its mother." His words were so low she had to strain to catch them as his breath sent an evocative signal along the sensitive skin of her hairline where his lips rested for an instant. She smiled and placed her hand in his powerful grasp, content to have him lead her into this exciting and living land.

CHAPTER EIGHT

The persistent chill numbed her brain, but strange sounds were penetrating the frozen edges of her consciousness. Erin was still hovering between thought and sleep when another crash startled her into full awareness. She could hear heavy footsteps outside, aimlessly grinding the sod and twigs. Why would anyone be out this time of night? Then with a prickling along her scalp she remembered. The others were gone, Mitch would be asleep by now, and there must be intruders in the compound.

"Bears," she breathed. Now she could hear an occasional grunt and the banging of a burglarized garbage can lid. Someone must have failed to close the heavy wooden door of the box that covered the receptacles. She reached for the flashlight Tex had provided for her the first night and stole out of her bed. She tiptoed across the shed floor, avoiding the stone-cold camp heater and various other obstacles in her path. How often would she have the opportunity to see a bear completely free and untamed? Certainly not in Washington. She moved with conviction and curiosity to the door and eased it open, trying to minimize the creaks of its rusty hinges.

She stepped cautiously into the darkness, noting the moon was high, lighting the far corner of the house. The dewy grass chilled her bare feet and dampened the bottom edge of her gown as she glided stealthily toward her quarry. Two bear cubs stood out clearly in the moonlight. They were half frolic and half hunter as they probed dark shaggy heads into the box, tipping light brown noses into the air and smiling with low chuckling growls as they crashed the lids with sturdy paws. Erin wanted to laugh at their obvious interest in the discoveries of their nocturnal raillery. Dark shadowed faces nuzzled one another, playfully

114

growling and tugging on rounded furry ears. Erin was thoroughly entertained by the comedic twins as they delved deeper into the can. One was balancing on the edge of the box and lip of the can, and the other clung to the side with strong pigeon-toed paws, craning his short neck to see over the edge.

But in the blink of an eye, play turned to danger as a cub bumped the lid of the box and it came crashing down. One twin escaped, but the other's head and front paws were caught by the barrier. Unthinking, Erin took several steps closer, trying to decide whether to help the squalling infant when she was stopped in her tracks by a low, powerful growl behind her. The surly threatening rumble caused her spine to lock and the hair to rise on the back of her neck. In her preoccupation with the cub's plight, she had forgotten about the sow, and her hasty steps had propelled her into the no-man's-land between mother and son.

Erin turned slowly to face the threat while the trapped cub tumbled to the ground with an outraged bleat as the lid pinched its tender nose and forefeet. The large she-bear was a vague sinister shadow at the corner of the shed, shifting her weight indecisively between her front paws. Erin knew she had to get away, move from between the sow and her cub, but she had never felt so small and alone in her entire life. If only she could get to the corner of the house, she could break and run for the sanctuary of her shed.

She swung the beam of her flashlight at the animal as though the rays would hold the wildly reflecting eyes at bay. Abruptly, the sow reared on her back legs, swaying aggressively as she growled through yellowed teeth. Erin was paralyzed for a moment. She knew she should run, but her feet would not obey her commands. The cub's whining continued behind her, and the bear began to snarl in answer to her baby's distress. Erin froze, a pale statue with fear draining her faculties. Why was she so very much alone? There was no one to help her; she would have to fend for herself. She felt deserted, trapped between an angered parent and her cub. How had she gotten herself into this predicament? The bruin gave her little time to ponder the answer as she dropped to all fours and started a whooshing, snorting charge.

Erin's feet moved of their own will as she scrambled around the corner and dashed for her shed. She couldn't stop the scream

115

that tore from her throat as the silence rebounded with the explosion of a gunshot. Her pounding heart drowned out a second blast and the frightened snarls of the bears as they broke and ran into the dark cover of the trees. Adrenaline coursed through her, lending wings to her bare feet as she bounded into the shed, slamming the door and huddling on the cot, hiding her face and sobbing.

The door blasted open, splintering into flying shrapnel, and gulping sobs tore through her as Erin buried her face in the covers, pleading. The light came on, blinding her as she was pulled up from the bed by human hands, but she fought and screamed until she recognized the strong arms and flung herself gratefully into the man's safe embrace.

"It's okay, honey. I'm here. You're all right, baby." A low voice crooned. He held her in the cradle of his arms and smoothed her hair as terror shuddered from her body in waves. It was so wonderful to feel the comforting human contact, not to be alone, even if she had to remember the strong arms holding her could never be her haven forever. But she was still trembling, sorting ponderously through her disordered thoughts, so she clung to the muscled fortress that protected her, shedding her fear of desolate solitude in the healing tears that rolled down her cheeks. The male voice still soothed and comforted her. "You're mine, Erin. I'll take care of you always," it promised over and over. "I won't let anything hurt you, ever."

She nestled thankfully in his arms as he stroked her with soothing hands and held her silently for long heavenly moments. A hand tipped her face up, gently wiping away her tears, kissing her cheeks and closed eyelids, then moving to her mouth with lingering tenderness. She responded to the firm lips on hers, wrapping one arm around his powerful trunk and exploring the curling coarse hair on his chest with the other seeking hand. His kiss deepened along with her desire, dazzling her frayed nerves with a new excitement as she melted into his embrace.

He lifted his head, and Erin opened tear-laden lashes to find herself staring into the dark, alluring eyes and rugged features of Mitchell Cade. She was elated at first, clinging to the warmth and security of his body, but then a fire of indignant humiliation stung her. She was in his arms again—he was smiling—he had

116

heard her whimpering like a little girl lost in the forest. Her eyes hardened into icy gems, and even though her voice trembled, she forced the words out as she tried to wriggle from him. "Let me go," she hissed. She wouldn't allow him to watch her make a fool of herself any longer. She wrenched away from his supporting strength.

She glared at his stunned features, transformed to a carved mask by the latent rage that bubbled below the surface of his calm exterior. "Get out of my cabin," she insisted hysterically, unable to meet his eyes. She kept her gaze lowered, watching his hands ball into fists.

He apparently didn't trust his voice or his temper as he backed away a few steps. Erin swallowed and choked on a sob but refused to release it. No more tears! Her rubbery legs collapsed her back onto the cot, and she raised a shaking hand to her temple trying to order her thoughts. She flinched instinctively when Mitchell Cade did speak. "That does it, Erin," he said intimidatingly.

His dominance filled the shed, determination etched in every line of his tensed athletic body. For the first time she noticed he wore only a pair of faded jeans that rode low on his narrow hips. Her breath caught in her throat as he started toward her, biceps flexing and his breath coming in harsh, angry spurts. He covered the distance between them in a step, bumping the hanging light with his shoulder and sending the whole room reeling. She was painfully aware of her vulnerability and wondered if the bear might not have been an easier foe to face than the rage that loomed over her now.

"You're moving into the house," he growled, snatching up her nerveless hand and pulling her up to her feet.

"I will not!"

"I don't intend to lose any more sleep over you," he snarled, swinging her toward the door. She tried to flail away from him, but he held her in a vicelike grip, dragging her along while he strode forward. "I've let you get away with too much already."

"Don't touch me," she commanded, but her voice was thin and quavering and he paid no attention.

"I think you need your wings clipped just a little," he announced pulling her menacingly close to him. "You've turned

117

my whole life upside down." He was nearly shouting, and Erin had never seen him so angry before. She struggled against him, alarmed by the depth of his emotion. Her unexpected attack gained her release, and she backed skittishly away from him. His fierce advance continued to dictate her retreat out of the door and around the corner of the building. Erin couldn't take her eyes from the apparition he had become; his chest was heaving while long blue veins stood out on his forearms.

"Turned your life upside down," she spluttered, pouncing on his last utterance as she rubbed her aching arms. "What about my life?" she hurled back. "One day I'm at a perfectly civilized cocktail party in Washington and the next I'm in the middle of nowhere—shanghaied by a . . . a . . . birdman."

"I knew it was a mistake to bring you here," he breathed, brushing distractedly at the thatch of unruly golden hair that fell forward onto his forehead. "You defy me at every turn, make a shambles of my authority with my men." Then he rounded on her unexpectedly, glaring at her arrogant, upturned face. "What are you doing here? Why did your grandmother send you light-years from the life you were leading if everything was so wonderful there? What in hell are you really doing here?" She backed around the corner of the house as he stalked after her, pressing for answers that she couldn't articulate even for herself.

"You have no right to ask me that," she stalled. "You act like my schoolteacher. Well school days are over, professor." She sliced the title past him with disdain, turning her back and walking boldly away. With dizzying speed he grabbed her arm and twirled her around to face him once again.

"If that's the case, you've failed the course," he thundered. "I told you explicitly to stay inside if there were bears in the compound."

"I wanted to see one."

"Damnit, Erin!" he shouted, quickly flicking a pained frown from his forehead with a hurried hand.

"You said you would always be there to help me if the bears came. All I needed to do was whistle, you said," she aimed sarcastically. "Where were you?" she screamed, remembering her total isolation as she faced the animal alone. "Where were you?"

118

"Didn't you hear the shots?" he asked, astonishment showing through the anger on his face. "What do you think scared them away? I didn't want to shoot for fear you would do something stupid like run or fight—and you did." He caught his breath and her wrist as she spun away from the stinging barbs of his words. "Don't you know when a bear charges you're supposed to play dead?" He sounded exasperated, and it grated the lacerated edges of her feelings. His hand shifted to her upper arms, and he shook her until her teeth chattered in her head.

"Play dead?" A laugh bubbled up in her, and she forced it down. If she started laughing now, she would never be able to stop. Play dead—she was sure she had been facing death as the bear rushed toward her. She was shaking with renewed rage and the nearly hysterical urgency to get away from the man that had protected her.

"I think if I have to learn one more survival skill, it will kill me!" she shouted. "I can't help it if I'm not the cool, brave war hero you are. Reuben says . . ."

"Reuben talks too damn much," he grated, slowly releasing her.

Erin was too wound up to back down now. "Everyone thinks you're so wonderful," she sniped. "Reuben admires you. Thurston thinks you're a bona fide hero. Lydia is positive you're a paragon of virtue. . . ."

His gleaming hazel eyes narrowed. "What do you think of me, Erin?" he quizzed, holding her gaze with his magnetic power.

"I think . . . I . . ." His handsome features mellowed under her searching appraisal as she peered up into his moonlit face. She thought he was wonderful too, no matter how aggravating he was. He was honest and proud and she had never met a man who stirred her as he did. He could be angry with her; he could reject and chastise her; but he couldn't make her stop loving him. And that was the simple truth of the matter; she loved him. She was trying to convince herself that she didn't, but she was failing miserably. He could fill her lonely void; he could comfort and protect her. But he could also sap away what little independence she was able to muster. Could she allow a man to become so important in her life again? Could she make a commitment and remain complete and whole? He frightened her—scared her to

119

death. Would he try to remake her in the image he desired, as Warren had done? "I refuse to be treated like a child any longer. I will not allow you to bully me." She realized he was backing her toward the rear door of the main house, and she sidestepped quickly toward the long cabin. He lunged after her with catlike grace, and she whirled, standing her ground as he continued his advance. "Stay away from me . . . you . . ."

"A man! That's what I am, Erin. A man!" he yelled. "And you'd damn well better not forget it." His voice held an urgent threat and an echo of a promise as he moved nearer. She could hardly forget his gender with his imposing body so close to hers extracting an uncontrolled feminine response to his vigorous charge. His male domination stung her, heightening her splintered senses as his savage features loomed over her, merely a breath away.

"Yes!" she shrieked in extorted admission, her exclamation piercing the quiet of the forest night. "A man—just like all the rest," she lied, "just like Warren. You're even worse." Her voice was hoarse and rasped in her throat. She backed farther away from his power, pacing before him, not allowing him to regain his physical control of her. "You manipulate and coerce, all right, and if that doesn't work you just pick me up and drag me off."

"Damnit! I'm not trying to control your life," he retorted, goaded by her continued resistance. He reached for her arm, but she batted his hand away and ran from him. "Erin, come back here, for God's sake."

"Not trying to control me. What do you call this?" she hurled over her shoulder breathless with haste and beginning to feel the cold predawn chill in every aching bone. Her feet were numb, and the hem of her gown-was drenched by the heavy dew on the long thick grass.

"I call this trying to make you see reason," he yelled his answer, pursuing her with single-minded purpose. "I want to see you in a warm, comfortable, safe place . . ." He trailed off. "I'm only trying to talk some sense into you." He quickened his pace, clutching her hand and swinging her around to collide with his rock-hard torso. One strong arm held her tightly, crushing her unprotected breasts against him, while the other hand tangled in

120

her dark hair pulling her head back to meet his kiss. He captured her mouth in a commanding caress, defying her rebellion and flirting with a sensual danger that threatened to consume them both in a torrid flame. He kissed her relentlessly, not lifting his head or softening his plundering tongue until he felt her body soften and mold to his. If she spoke aloud her words would deny her love, but her body was more honest, not withholding its answer to his seeking hands and tongue.

Mortified by his easy victory, she spat her defiance when he freed her traitorous lips. "I'm not staying with you," she vowed breathlessly, "if that's your idea of talking some sense into me." He released her in an instant, his chest working and the muscle along his jaw jumping ominously.

"You are staying in the house. You can't go back to the shed; the door is broken." His words came out in jagged spurts through his tightly clenched teeth. "You are going to stay in the house." He was appraising her with a scathing look, not missing a detail of her fetching disarray, and his eyes impaled her as they sensuously disrobed her.

"I'm warning you," she called out with brassy bravado. Stung by his heated regard, she retreated more quickly, unable to look away from his powerful virility. "I refuse to be manipulated by anyone again—ever. You have no right to treat me like a child, like an object, like . . ."

". . . Like a woman, Erin?" he asked quietly.

"Don't!" The words tumbled out, unleashed from somewhere deep inside her. "I won't be subjected to this any longer. I am a person, do you hear? I am me. Erin McIntee. Not Lydia Wentworth's granddaughter, not . . ." Her brave speech was cut short as she backed heavily into the side of the pump house. It confused her for an instant, and then she lunged for the door, knowing it connected with the long cabin and offered her an avenue of escape from this man who excited and jeopardized every atom of her being. She tugged viciously at the recalcitrant door until his voice at her ear startled a quailing shriek from her throat.

"What are you doing here in my world, Erin McIntee?" he questioned as she looked up to see his long sturdy hands holding the door shut.

121

She whirled to face him. "I'm here to become an independent person," she snapped bitterly. "So I won't need Warren. I won't need Lydia. And I most certainly won't need you." She tried to move away from him, but she was made aware of his entrapment as he snaked both hands down the door to rest on either side of her hips, blocking her way.

"Yes, Ms. McIntee, you've made it very clear you want to be a totally independent person. Just remember it's a very lonely life not having anyone to rely on but yourself," he added harshly. "And while we're at it, how is a cold, self-sufficient lady like you going to manage to have all those babies you want all by yourself?"

She was stunned by the question, gazing at him with wide inquiring eyes, star-spangled in the moonlit darkness. How did he know these things? "What are you talking about?"

"It's not hard to figure, when you mother every creature around. That's what got you into trouble tonight, wasn't it?" She wriggled to get away from him. She needed to escape his clairvoyant insight. But he used a large hand to push her back against the door, his patience wearing thin. His rough handling lowered the rounded neckline of her gown, exposing the peachy skin of one shoulder. His grip softened as his thumb trailed lightly down the column of her throat, sweeping across her partially draped breast in a light caress before returning to sensuously knead her shoulder. He intentionally brushed the unyielding wall of his chest over the rising swell of her breasts as he shifted his position. Erin held her breath, trying to quell his seductive powers.

"There may be test-tube babies, but they aren't made from scratch. You'll still need someone, Ms. McIntee," he said, his eyes shining. With callous ease his searing masculine body flirted with her hardening nipples, effecting a dramatic chord change in Erin's harmonizing form as her eyelids fluttered shut and a shuddering contraction gripped her. Unmercifully he leaned his torso lightly against her, and a hand moved to the door beside her head as his strong fingers aimlessly separated a lock from her dark tumbled curls and his eyes scanned her for every hint of a mood. Her breasts rose and pressed to him with her captured inhaled breath, and her heart thundered in her ears.

"Me—I'm still very partial to the old-fashioned way of making babies," he said evocatively. Stampeded by his intensity, she spun away, yanking on the door handle in abstracted panic, looking for an avenue of escape. "It would be easier for both of us if you'd just go into the cabin."

"I'm not going to sleep with you," she charged, spinning again, using her hip to barge past the barriers of his hands. As she ran from the pump house, a stray glimpse of reflected light from the jeep's window caught her eye. She could get away in the jeep. Even her muddled reasoning told her he was herding her in a circle, wearing her down. She angled toward the parked vehicle, but it seemed so far away and he was only a step behind her. She raced along, stopping abruptly at the picnic table in the yard to catch her breath and put a solid object between them. They circled the table like boxers in the ring, each sizing up their opponent, not able or willing to step in close for the big punch.

"Why are you chasing me?"

"Why are you running?"

"Stop doing this to me!"

"You're the one that's got me on a merry-go-round," he replied, keeping his hands lightly on the table and his weight on his toes, ready to bob and weave, ready to spring in either direction if she decided to flee. His calm sparring was wearing her nerves to a thin tight band ready to snap at any second. She was completely drained by his self-assurance and weakened by her own doubt. She was intimidated by him, yet there was nothing else she would rather do than be surrounded in his arms. Still, she fought on into the middle rounds of the bout, swinging wildly and out of control.

"You are the most conniving, horrible—"

"Don't forget crude—" he interrupted, before she continued her jabbing thrust of words.

"Crude, rude, contemptible, self-righteous—" she hurled vehemently.

"You forgot honest and proud—" he parried.

"Honest, proud," she repeated until she realized she was paying homage, so she restarted in a ragged fury. ". . . aggravating and arrogant man I've ever met." She shouted with a climactic finish that rattled her whole body.

"Why do I frighten you so, Erin?" His words penetrated like

123

a numbing blow between the eyes. He was so peacefully confident, that his dark eyes mellowed into a warm gold light. The silver glow from the moon played over the lines and angles of his body, and Erin's stomach contracted with a dull ache. The light glistened on his body, reminding her of an ancient gladiator fighting in the arena. He was doing it again, she cautioned, he's controlling your emotions again. "Why Erin?" he pressed, seeing he had the momentum of this round. "You can't control me with your sophisticated charms and wit, and that scares you." She was beginning to sputter an angry retort when he finished her off with cool confidence. "Just admit it. I can feel it in your body when I hold you. You don't want to run from me," he said with what seemed insufferable patience and serenity.

"Damn you! You can feel my silly schoolgirl sexual response to you, and you think you have to teach me lessons. You think it's your noble duty to teach this innocent little female the ways of the world." She spiked, reserves of strength coming from someplace deep within her. "Believe me, professor, there's no need. My education has not been neglected. Warren Markham taught me more than I ever wanted to know about men." She catapulted the words across the table in a roundhouse blast, and they shattered Mitchell Cade's illusion of calm. He made a dash around the table, but she stayed ahead of him. They were into the final rounds, and she was suddenly spent, feeling spent, wondering whether she would be able to go the distance in this no-holds-barred match. She pushed the words out of her trembling depths, amazed at her own cruelty. "He taught me how to dress, what to say and think, where to go." She swallowed the tears and delivered her knockout punch. "He even taught me his idea of sex. I don't need any more lessons from you." He flinched as though she'd actually struck a blow. She had finally hurt him, nailed the words into his flesh, and she instantly hated herself. He pounded both powerful fists on the table, and a vein throbbed at his temple.

"Shut up!" He bellowed at her. "That's enough!" She could read pain and resentment in his expression, and she knew she'd seen it before. She ran to the end of the table, brushing by his outstretched arms, and charged for the jeep, away from the man she loved. Certainly he would let her go now—certainly he would hate her enough—he would be glad to have her go. She could see the jeep in the shadows ahead as she ran hindered by the long gown. She was afraid to look back for fear—he wouldn't be following her. She glanced over her shoulder, relieved to see his dogged advance, but catching her racing feet in the ruffle of her skirt, she tumbled to the ground, soaking her gown in the dewy grass. The fall knocked the wind out of her, and Cade increased his speed, covering the distance between them in determined strides. She gathered herself up, pulling her gown up to her thighs and running as fast as she could to the jeep.

Wedging her body into the crack, she forced the sprung door of the jeep open, breathing so hard she thought her lungs would burst. Bouncing onto the seat, she slammed the uncooperative door, fumbling for the light switch and the key to the ignition in the shadows. She was frantic to get away from this man that so endangered her heart and goals. He seemed able to read her mind, or could he merely read her body? She knew he was right, knew that deep down she didn't want to run away. She wanted to throw herself into his arms. Her tears and the darkness trapped her as completely as a blind person searching desperately for the key she couldn't see.

"The key? Damn it!" Erin swore, hearing a tinkling, jingling sound as she saw Mitchell Cade watching her, dangling the keys from a sure hand outside the window. Her tears started again as she pounded on the wheel, but he terminated her tantrum by flinging open the door, nearly pulling the screeching iron from its hinges. She slid across the seat and scrambled out the other side, holding the door in front of her like a riddled shield while Mitch rounded the front fender of the Bronco. She kept him at bay with the rusty armor as she glanced around for another means of escape.

"There's no place else for us to go, Erin," he said quietly.

"Give me the keys to the jeep. You don't want me here; let me go," she pleaded, pretending to reason. But she was beyond reasoning and listening; all she could do was feel. And she suddenly felt cold, damp, miserable—and so alone. "I think I need to get away from you. I think if given half a chance you would take over my life, my world."

"Like you've taken over mine?"

"You're too strong, too brave. You would swallow me up. I won't let another man control my life. Warren tried that and he nearly succeeded." Her thoughts took her away for a moment, and Mitch stepped closer. Startled again, she swung the creaking door at him to keep him back. "You'll never teach me not to respond to you. You'll never teach me not to . . ." Not to love you, was what nearly came out, but she couldn't allow the humiliation of those words. "I can't be trapped again." The plea tumbled out, and she ran from the jeep; holding her gown up to her thighs and taking long deerlike strides, she ran to the main house, slipped inside the back door, and locked it. Leaning against the safety it afforded her, she began to cry. She could hear him knocking and pounding on the door, trying the lock, but she just sobbed. She was locking out the man that held the keys to her heart, and she would be imprisoned in her cell of misery for the rest of her life. She backed away from the door, withdrawing further from him, knowing that her future was a shadowed veil. Even her proposed wealth couldn't buy her light or freedom. She felt completely alone, fragmented. She couldn't have been more torn apart or mauled by the attacking bear. And she remembered how comforting and safe she had felt held in Mitch's arms and wondered why she had ever left his strength. Why did she fight and hurt him? She must be a child for blindly driving him away; she needed him and she wanted him.

"Erin?" His voice was low and steady, very close behind her. She spun around, not knowing where he came from, but he was there filling the room with his warmth, and that was all that mattered.

He moved toward her, and she did not back away, allowing him to enfold her in his embrace. She wrapped her arms around him, pressing her curves to his length, not wanting to chance being torn from him.

"You're where you belong now," he whispered. "Just remember," he cautioned warmly, lifting her chin with his thumb to look into blue fluid pools, "you locked yourself in here. I didn't trap you."

"I'll remember," she nodded.

He kissed her lightly, testing her mood, tasting her lips with a tender yearning that swept into a grass fire inferno of desire.

He folded her in his arms, kissing her with a lusty hunger as though he would never let her go. She was greedy too, arching toward him, savoring every caress, every kiss. She would let him make love to her tonight; the joy of belonging to him would be worth the heartache she was certain lay in store for her.

His feverish lips were burning away her cold, desolate fear of being alone forever. She felt nearly complete, with the complement of his hard masculine body pressed to her soft feminine form. Together they could make a whole. She surrendered her body to his roaming hands as they grazed over the curve of her back, and he surrounded her with a protective arm. He kissed her parted lips, drinking in the fountain of her sensuality, and she was on fire, alive to every nuance of his hands and lips, aching to be filled and fulfilled. What did it matter if he didn't say he loved her? She couldn't delude herself any longer; she was in love with her golden eagleman. It was love already stronger than she wanted to admit. She knew she couldn't be complete without Mitchell Cade. He was her missing half, the half that would make her whole.

His hand trailed over her ribs across her quivering abdomen to rest below her breast with his thumb stroking the base of the curve. She leaned into his warmth, shivering with anticipation, and placed a kiss on his mobile mouth. Lulled by the contact, she relaxed against him, but he suddenly jerked her off her feet and into his arms with an abrupt movement.

"Mitch? Mitch, please." Her voice echoed the confusion she felt as he carried her quickly toward the bedroom next to his own.

"I know, Erin. You're not going to sleep with me," he ground out. "I'm not trying to control your life. I'm just trying to get you safe in your bed. Safe from the cold, the bears. And this birdman," he admitted grudgingly. He flipped on the light and set her on her feet near the bed. She couldn't bear to be out of his arms, so she wound her own around his neck. He pulled her arms free of him like a gardener pruning vines. It was as though he couldn't endure her touch. "I promised myself if I ever held you in my arms again I would show you that you could trust me." His teeth clenched on his last words, and the muscles that worked his jaw ground his teeth together.

127

"Mitch." Her voice and eyes were pleading, but he didn't look at her as he brusquely turned back the blankets on the bed and patted it, silently commanding her as though she were an unruly child.

"Into bed and I promise I won't bother you anymore," he said in a cold tone. She was numbed by his withdrawal from her; she stood dazed and motionless by the bed. "Just get into bed, Erin," he said with growing frustration. Had she only imagined his tenderness? Was she only projecting her desires onto his actions?

"My gown is wet," she said woodenly, demoralized by his coldness when all she wanted was to be with him. He stared at her a moment, a flicker of indecision and doubt showing in his eyes. The material clung to her, outlining her every curve as he stepped close to her, grasping the damp filmy fabric at her thighs and pulling it over her head and upraised arms. He looked around, then tossed the lilac garment on the floor, his gaze returning to her with guarded reluctance. Her haunting blue eyes held his gaze at first, but then it lowered to the freed beauty of her proud, pouty breasts that thrust invitingly toward him climaxing in perfect tight nipples. Below the swell of her breasts her flat abdomen rose and fell with deep jagged breaths as lacy bikini panties hugged her curvacious hips. His breath came out in a rush, and he broke the contact of their eyes looking over her head at the far wall while tears welled in the sapphire pools. She was his, body and soul, and he didn't want her. The devastating reality bore in on her like a cold wind. She could see him so close, and yet he was beyond her grasp, barricaded behind a wall of iron-willed calm. All the source of heat and energy she would ever need was taking her light away from her. He took her by the shoulders and set her down on the bed, swinging her legs onto the mattress and lifting the blankets to cover her. She lay quiescent as she watched his deliberate movements. He gently covered her and frowned at the tears he could see floating in her eyes. She was trying to be strong, but she had spent her final reserves arguing with him. This man could invoke all her emotions in a matter of minutes. She kept telling herself over and over, she would be strong, she would have to accept his rejection. But her fear of being alone was crushing her resolve. He bent over her, settling the blankets around her as she caught his large strong hand, sitting up, uncovering the glory of her breasts as the blanket slipped to her waist.

"Mitch, please don't go," she pleaded, trying to sound brave.

"I'll be in the next room," he said gruffly as though he were anxious to leave her.

"Please don't leave me alone," she begged, a fraction of her emotion creeping into her voice. "Stay with me just for a little while." She reached up, clutching at his forearm, sliding a beseeching hand to the hard steel bands of his powerful upper arm. She expected him to flick her off like an annoying insect, but instead he sank to the bed. Half sitting, half lying on the soft mattress, he braced himself against the headboard. She wanted to break down the last barriers between them, but her brain still refused to obey her commands to speak of Warren's betrayal.

"I know you're scared. But I promise, Erin, I won't hurt you." She cuddled against him, longing for his warmth and understanding. "You can trust me, always," he whispered. "I know you don't want to belong to me, yet. You're beautiful and free like the soaring eagles." She heard a catch in his voice and his soft groan as she nestled against his hair-roughened chest, rolling onto a rounded hip to lean her slender, silky thigh along his denim-covered leg.

"Hold me!" she said. He cradled her in his arms, giving her a reassurring hug. She could pretend in the comfort of his embrace that he loved her, that he would never let her go, because now she knew that she loved him, and for that condition there was no remedy. The birdman who could care for and nurture his wild charges back to health couldn't cure her of her love for him. "I'm an incurable coward," Erin sniffed. "I'm so afraid to be alone." She realized now that it didn't matter how many people she would be with, or how many children she might someday have; she would always be alone if she didn't have Mitchell Cade's love.

"You felt deserted when you thought the bear was coming after you," he chuckled, the sexual tension diminishing as a drowsy euphoria crept over the exhausted combatants. She nodded. "I thought so." His simple confirmation and his tightening embrace filled her with emotion. "As long as you stay here with me, you don't need to worry about being alone." He kissed her hair so lightly she couldn't be sure he had. She should tell him how much she regretted her spiteful, caustic words, but he continued speaking and the moment was lost. "I'll be here; all you need to do is whistle." She choked on a sobbing laugh at his cheering words as she repeated the last phrase.

"Just whistle? You must think I'm still a child, and you don't need a child slowing you down, complicating your life." For the first time an image of his tanned, golden child playing on the lawn in front of the main house invaded her thoughts, and she suppressed the disturbing picture.

"I find it extremely difficult to think of you as a child," he replied. "Absolutely impossible at the moment."

"But you heard me whimpering and begging like a little girl. I was crying like a baby," she confessed, ashamed and even more self-conscious in the silence that followed her words. He seemed to be scarcely breathing. She braced herself on an arm to look questioningly at his face.

"That doesn't mean you're a child or a coward, Erin. It means you're scared. That's all." Tears came to her eyes once more as he pulled her into the circle of his arms. Now he seemed to be drawing warmth from her as he flicked a thumb over her shoulder. It was a novel sensation, and she liked the idea that he could need her comfort, too. "I've heard a lot of soldiers calling for their mothers in a firefight," he went on, dark shadows and ghosts hovering in his tone. "I know what fear sounds like. Different words, different languages, but always it sounds the same. I'd recognize it anywhere. That's how I know you're frightened of me."

Was frightened of you, she wanted to say, but not anymore. If she was frightened of anything now, it was the depth of her own feelings for him.

"You'll come to trust me."

"I've only been here a short time . . ." she began hesitantly.

"I know someone hurt you before, Erin." He interrupted her, apparently unwilling to listen to any mention of time. "I know you're not ready for anyone to make love to you, yet. I can wait," he pledged. "I can wait until you're ready to come to me." Those words seemed to end the discussion, and he was silent a long while, holding and stroking her bare back and soft hair, lulling her into a state of well-being. She relaxed in his arms, listening to his steady, even breathing and drifting toward the edges of sleep. "But not too long, my love," he whispered into the gray dawn. "Not too long."

Pale light was filtering through the closed curtains of the window as the steady drumming of his heart in her ear shifted away. "Mitch? Don't go." She was barely awake as she felt him lower her onto the bed, and she frowned at the loss of his body heat.

"I told you—you can trust me always. But I'm no saint, Erin. I can't lie beside you all night and not make love to you."

"I'm sorry," she apologized sleepily. She regretted her early angry outbursts and was sorry that he thought he couldn't make love to her. She was still so sleepy, and her heavy lids closed despite her efforts to keep them open, his words sounding blurred and far away.

"So am I, my love. So am I."

CHAPTER NINE

A loon called out on the lake, an eerie melancholy cry that raised the short hairs on the back of Mitch's neck as he remained in the shadow of the crooked pine by the lake's edge. Great streaks of purple and orange filled the horizon, stretching to vast heights and repeating their hues in the rippling water. The loon called again, and its mate answered from the far shore. And Mitch wondered idly if he would ever hear the answering call of his mate. A canoe was visible against the fiery sunset, its occupants silhouetted against the light. Water was flashing in metallic arcs from the stroking paddles, and Doc's patient instructions were muffled by Erin's silvery laugh as it carried clearly across the lake. The sound sliced through him, triggering that familiar fever of desire. His hands itched to touch her again, to feel her breasts blossom to ripe perfection beneath his gentle stroking. But he hadn't touched her since the night she had locked herself into his cabin, and he wasn't sure how much longer he could restrain himself.

Three straight days of wind and rain made it good to be outside again. This afternoon the gray persistent ground-hugging clouds had finally lifted, chased away by a clean west wind. It had been three straight days of having Erin with him, smelling her violet scent as she leaned close to him in the lab questioning him about his notes, or watching her reading before the fire, curled in the corner of the sofa like a contented kitten. It had been three long days of trying to avoid her; after all, he was still waiting for her to come to him. And he might never be that lucky. He didn't even have the luck of that loon with his echoing mating call. Damn it, Cade, you knew all along she would only be here a short time. You're a fool to think she'd stay.

132

Now that the sun was sinking behind the serrated tops of the pine trees on the western shore, the wind had settled also. Only a faint breeze remained to ruffle the surface of the darkly reflecting lake. Tex was sitting out on the dock on an old boat cushion leaning back against a weathered post. A cigarette was dangling loosely in one hand while smoke curled into the air. As Cade moved out onto the dock, the wet planking vibrated under his weight, alerting his friend to his presence, but Tex didn't change position. Keen, blue-flecked eyes followed the direction of Tex's gaze as Mitch lowered himself onto the balls of his feet and rested his elbows on his thighs.

"Certainly was a nice day after all the rough weather we've been havin'," Tex drawled. "Very pretty scenery we're watchin', too. Think you two can handle those nests on the Big Two-Hearted?" he questioned casually.

"She'll be all right," Mitch answered shortly, intent on the canoeing lesson. But he didn't know yet how he was going to get through a night alone with her in an isolated cabin. He couldn't tell Tex he was afraid he couldn't keep his hands off Erin if they were alone together.

"I ain't worried about her," Tex shot back, taking a long drag on the cigarette. "She ain't the one keeping me up half the night banging around in the office."

"Oh, hell!" Mitch swore emphatically, hoping to dispel his suspicions and change the subject. "Then you shouldn't have been so determined to see me start that damn book. I have to work on it somewhere." He was unwilling to discuss Erin McIntee with anyone, not even Tex. He hadn't sorted out the enigma of soft woman and angry fighter in his own mind yet. Erin laughed again, and he lifted his eyes from the splintered wood following the sound with hungry longing. He couldn't help watching her and listening to her laughter, regretting that he couldn't be the one to make her smile, wondering if he would ever see her truly content before he must set her free to soar in the wind.

". . . It's like that eagle today," Tex began pontifically. "Latchin' onto that fish that was too much for him to handle alone and ending up in the drink. He sure did look funny paddling ashore using his wings like a pair of oars. Just goes to show even

133

the great hunters come up empty now and again. Bite off more than they can chew, so to speak. Just because you want something doesn't mean it's going to happen automatically." Mitch felt the distinct brewing of a homegrown lecture in the Texan's shaggy head. When Reuben got wound up he could harangue with all the fire and brimstone zeal of a Baptist preacher. But Mitch wasn't sure he was in the mood for any homilies today.

"I'm not fishing or hunting for anything," he said firmly.

"Ummm." Tex didn't sound convinced. Mitch refused to look at his friend's concerned face, and Tex shook his head, closing his eyes against the spiraling smoke. They both knew Mitch was evading the real issue.

"Cowboy, if you've got something on your mind, you'd better spit it out," he capitulated after a lengthy pause.

"I'm just wonderin' what's on your mind." The Texan studied Mitchell Cade with a persistent stare. "I know it's that girl." He gestured with his cigarette. "You don't need to deny it. You ain't been this jumpy since Nam. The question I'm wantin' answered is what's going on between you two?"

"Nothing!" He gave his quick honest reply. "Absolutely nothing."

"And that's what's botherin' you." Tex chuckled. Cade ignored his friend, watching the arc and splutter of Tex's cigarette stub as it hit the water. He was always amazed at Reuben's perception and was irritated at how easily he could read his mind. He'd had that uncanny ability for years, even in Nam. Maybe that's what had made him such a good point man.

Knowing he only had himself to blame for the mess didn't make it any easier. He'd wanted her to trust him, and now she did. But he couldn't trust himself anymore. Thoughts of her were taking over most of his waking hours and all of his nights. Her smile, a word, a gesture, would insinuate itself into his thoughts, interfering with his work and his sleep. Erin's laughter floated to him, and his gaze homed in on her; it was second nature to him now. He could find her anywhere, and if she wasn't around, he could conjure a perfect image of her. He couldn't even picture the compound, his lab, or the cabin without Erin in it. He swallowed hard, scowling at his hands that were balled into bronzed fists, the knuckles showing white under the skin.

"Yes, sir," Tex chortled, "you're proud just like those eagles up there. You do a lot of flappin' and squawkin'. And spread your wings and strut, but it's really the little lady who calls the shots in the mating dance."

Mitch didn't answer the chuckling comment. The words were much too close to the truth for them to be funny. He stood restlessly as the canoe headed their way. No woman had ever put him through an emotional wringer the way Erin McIntee was doing. Since she'd moved into the house, he'd been on a sexual tightrope; before that it was bad enough, not having slept a whole night since she came. At least the night she needed him he was awake and ready to scare the bears away. God, she'd felt so good and natural in his arms, and then she'd become so frightened of him. . . .

"I think we better start giving Cindy live food now. She's getting stronger. She'll be leaving soon. What do you think?" He nudged Tex with his leather boot, coming back to reality.

"I think that's about right," Tex answered, watching Mitch with concern, seeing his big fists open and close, but never quite relaxing, while he watched the canoe glide steadily closer. Erin smiled and waved, the sleeves of his red plaid wool jacket rolled above her wrists. It didn't fit her, but the color suited her, highlighting the delicate tint in her cheeks and repeating in her moist red lips. She looked happy, at peace with herself, and her smile reflected a new found contentment. The boat glided alongside the dock, and Tex reached down to grab Doc's paddle and steady the craft. Mitch leaned over extending his hand, and Erin took it without hesitation. He pulled her up and set her lightly on the dock, his hands resting proprietarily on the feminine curve of her waist. Her eyes watched his steadily, the anxiety gone from their clear depths, but they remained shuttered.

"She'll do fine on the river, Mitch." Doc complimented his pupil. "She's a fast learner."

"I've got a good teacher." She smiled capriciously at the younger man, and he colored to the roots of his ginger hair as he noted Mitch's narrowed eyes.

"How about a Coke?" Doc asked, trying to change the subject and evaporate the confusion of her heady smile.

"I'd love it. Do you suppose George is done in the kitchen, or

135

will we have to use the lab beakers like last night?" She stepped past Mitch to follow Doc's retreat, still recalling the late evening raid on the kitchen that had sent the two culprits lightheartedly out into the rain to pop corn over a Bunsen burner and get drunk on beer.

Mitch stayed where he was, almost unaware of the frown that pulled dark gold brows together and deepened the lines around his eyes. Was she toying with him? Seeing how far she could push him before he cracked and begged her to let him make love to her? Did she realize what the sight of her returning from the lab last night had done to him, all rain-swept and laughing as she swayed uncertainly in the doorway? Did she know how hard it was to listen to the myriad enticing sounds she made splashing in the deep old tub in his bathroom? She had tortured him with her every move while she dried her hair before the fire, every line and curve of her graceful form limned by the fire's glow.

"Wonder how long it'll be before she gets to missing her friends in Washington?" Tex persisted from where he was securing the canoe for the night.

"I'm not going to wait to find out!" Mitch stated harshly. "I'm sending her back as soon as possible. I canceled the grant and mailed the congresswoman's check back a few days ago. I should have never let her talk me into bringing Erin here at all. She doesn't belong out here." He knew he couldn't keep his agreement with Lydia. He wanted Erin more than he needed the grant. It was the only honest thing to do, return the money, but he couldn't bear the thought of returning Erin. Lydia would send for her soon enough as it was.

"What the hell did you do that for?" Tex demanded.

"You know me, a proud and honorable S.O.B., just like the eagles," Cade said gratingly.

"Now I got the feelin' you're a sonovabitch in love; that's the only reason I can think of to explain such goshawful foolishness. A fool in love. That's the worst kind, and it's no time to be noble, chief."

"Love's got nothing to do with it," he lied. He knew he wasn't noble enough to keep his hands off Erin, that was for sure. He gave a low, cynical laugh. Not nearly noble enough. "She doesn't belong here; it's too rough, the work's too dangerous."

"She looks right at home to me," Tex snorted, wiping his fists on stained jeans and scrutinizing Mitch's shadowed face. The sun was completely gone, and the high-pitched whine of mosquitoes filled the air.

"Haven't you asked yourself what she's doing here? How many grants have we had, and none were set up like this one? Why is she really here?" Mitch's voice was bitter as he turned to watch the last of the daylight fade from the sky. "I've tried to get her to tell me, but she won't." There were too many things he didn't know about her. He couldn't really reconcile himself to having her here. She was as rare and unexpected as an orchid among the jack-in-the-pulpits and sweet william on the forest floor.

"You won't ask her a simple question because you're afraid of what she might tell you," Tex prodded, looking up at the red-streaked cirrus clouds as if calling for divine inspiration. "Chief, I'm gonna give you a piece of advice whether you want it or not. A woman like that don't come along more than once in a lifetime. Any fool can see you're falling in love with her. Tell her." He paused for a moment, continuing after the implied admission of the truth in Mitch's silence. "You're not sure how she feels, and you're afraid she'll go back on her own, so you're gonna send her back. That would be real mule-headed and noble and the biggest mistake of your ornery life." Tex was still observing him with a measuring look, waiting for his reply.

"It's a different world here than in Washington. She's completely dependent on us out here. I can't force her into some kind of commitment she'll regret as soon as she gets away from me. I can't take advantage of her like that." He kept his eyes on the far shore, following the noisy flight of a pair of mallards as they winged out of sight.

"I got the feelin' she won't go just 'cause you tell her to. Not if she's got her own reasons for staying like you think," Tex replied cryptically, lighting another cigarette as he talked, narrowing his eyes against the spiraling, acrid smoke. "I've done all I can for ya, just like a good point man should. Now tell the gal you love her before it's too late." He slapped at a mosquito buzzing around his head and sighed. "It's too early to tell how much of an indentation I made on that thick skull of yours, pardner, so let's get inside before these critters eat us alive."

They walked back to the house in silence; treadmill thoughts blinded Mitch to the beauty of a waning moon as it rode low above the treetops. Tex was right about a lot of things, but not about love. He wasn't in love with Erin McIntee no matter what foolish words he'd whispered. He couldn't afford to be. When she left, he'd get over her in no time. He had his work, his book . . . It was just physical, just one of those things. But having her so near and still beyond his reach was tearing him apart. The sooner she was gone the better. He'd forget her quickly enough when she was out of his life and he could get off this merry-go-round. But until then he was faced with the bittersweet torture of another sleepless night and more self-deception like he was practicing now. Hearing the final lonely call of the loon, Cade hesitated a moment, waiting for the female's answering cry; but it never came, and the night's chill crept through him.

The sound of the Bronco's wheezing engine faded into the distance taking Tex and Doc on to their next assignment leaving Erin standing on the concrete bridge above the river. Mitch was on the bank below her already loading the canoe, and the silence was broken only by the rush of wind and the sound of swiftly moving water. She looked down at the clear red-brown river uncertainly. It looked fast and narrow, more difficult to maneuver in the lightweight aluminum canoe than the placid waters of the small lake. But Doc and Tex said it would be easy, the current would do a lot of the work, and she hoped so.

"Hey, throw those sleeping bags down here," Mitch called, squinting up at her from the water's edge.

"Sorry," she called back, dropping the down-filled, plastic-covered bundles over the metal railing. "I was daydreaming."

"About what?" he asked conversationally as he swung the bundles into the canoe, tying them securely in the bottom of the craft.

"That Hemingway story," she confessed a little sheepishly. "I can't orient myself. There's no railroad, no town named Seney; isn't this the Big Two-Hearted River in the short story?" She leaned over the metal railing, the movement accenting the graceful curves of her lithe body. A quick frown furrowed his wide forehead, but it disappeared as he grinned up at her.

"That's because the story was written about the Fox River; it's around fifty miles west of here."

"Oh." It didn't really explain anything, but she grabbed the remaining waterproofed pack and scrambled down the steep bank to Mitch's side.

"Hemingway made that fishing trip himself after the First World War. It was autobiographical like a lot of his Nick Adams stories."

"Was he trying to protect his favorite fishing spot?" she asked lightly, watching as he stowed and lashed the last of the gear in the craft. She was trying to recall details of the short story, but it all blended together in her mind; only bits and pieces of the young soldier's struggle to heal his mind and body in the solitary trek returned to her. Mitch steadied the canoe while she took her place in the front seat, not answering right away.

"Some people do think he was protecting his favorite trout stream, but that's not the real reason he changed the name of the river." Erin was watching the rust and gray rocks beneath the clear water and looked up at the quiet emotion in his voice. He was very close, bending forward, getting ready to push the boat out into the current. His eyes were dark, reflecting the movement of the trees and water. "When people asked him why he had done it, Hemingway just smiled and said, 'Big Two-Hearted River is poetry.' " The words caught her by surprise as he pushed them out into the middle of the stream and seated himself lightly behind her.

"It is poetry in a wild and untamed way." She voiced her thoughts aloud. "I've never been so close to anything so beautiful and free."

He agreed quietly as the craft skimmed gracefully over the smooth surface of the river. His paddle dipped into the brown water, barely making a sound and rippling the water, with eddies scurrying from his strong, efficient J-stroke. "It's a rough life up here," he added after several moments. "The winters are long and cold, but you take the good with the bad." The canoe glided into the sunshine, and the water took on a sparkling red color as the bright light penetrated, arcing into its depths. "It gets in your blood, stays with you wherever you go. Maybe it's being close to the beginning and ending of life, rebirth and renewal in the spring and then the killing winters. You don't have the time or energy to worry about things that aren't important."

They paddled steadily for some time, and Erin concentrated on keeping the canoe in the middle of the current, avoiding snags and rocks whose only clue to their potential danger was a mere rippling of the smooth surface. Mitch's powerful, even strokes moved them quickly and quietly forward, while his words and the wild beauty of the river kept Erin silent as well. He pointed out birds nesting along the banks, calling her attention to a kingfisher posing jauntily on a branch tipping his gray topknot at them. A red-headed woodpecker could be heard tapping his wooden beat, the sound echoing through the treetops that arched above them. Occasionally a tree that had fallen across the river slowed their pace but speeded up the partially dammed current as it pressed on to Lake Superior.

Mitch was a steady bulwark behind her, at ease with his surroundings, but withdrawn and uncommunicative as he had been since the night she moved into the room next to him. They spent many hours together, but they were like prisoners in two separate cells, unable to reach out and touch each other. For Erin it was a time of waiting—she was going to make love with this aggravating, captivating man. The only question was when. When would he take her into his arms again and kiss her like there was no tomorrow?

He was teaching her to trust again, renewing her faith, and for no other reason than that she could love him. She was beginning to believe she could give herself to him and still retain that important feeling of self-worth that was growing within her. She could feel his warm regard on her back, as satisfying and comforting as the leaf-spangled sun on her shoulders.

If it weren't for the nagging doubts that came to haunt the dark hours of the night, she'd be content. Someday she would have to tell him about her trust fund. What would he say when he found out Lydia was using him, too? He was proud and straightforward in his dealings. Erin couldn't be sure of his reaction to her deception and omissions, and it was one of the reasons she hadn't sought an opportunity to bring the matter up.

Not with Tex and Doc continually underfoot and George's constant mumblings from the small kitchen. She was gambling that she would know the right moment when it presented itself. This overnight trip on a wilderness river would be the perfect opportunity, and a ripple of apprehension skittered over her nerves. Nothing must go wrong with her explanation; the possibility of her future happiness depended on it.

She'd done a lot of hard thinking in the past few days. But most often her thoughts strayed back to the night she left the shed. If she had possessed the courage to tell him the real reasons for her being here, and the reasons for her reluctance when he asked, by now she would be completely and irrevocably his. Somewhere in the recollections of her sleep-drugged intellect she could hear the words he spoke that night. He had called her his love, and for a man like Mitch that would carry the full meaning of the word. It wasn't the casual endearment, the everyday greeting of her Washington acquaintances. She hugged the memory of the words to her, sending a glow of radiant heat through her. Why was it so much more complicated to love a man who was proud and sure and filled with scruples? The angry, bitter young woman she had been those few short weeks ago was not capable of sharing any love. She was certainly not that same person anymore. He'd given her trust and contentment and a measure of peace, even though their relationship was far from placid. She knew she could believe him, his words, and his work. She knew she could rely on him; she could count on his honesty and his strength. Now she was sure of what she really wanted, to be completely his, to be the missing half of his whole, and to be totally independent and separate from loneliness. She needed him and hoped that someday he would need her also. She would tell him everything, be as open and honest as he was—as soon as the time was right.

CHAPTER TEN

"Mitch, wake up, we don't have time for you to catnap," Erin admonished as she repacked the remains of their lunch in the Styrofoam-lined cooler.

"Just resting my eyes," the recumbent form answered, and she stopped her self-appointed task to feast her eyes on his long virile body and rugged profile as he lay on the sandbar, his head pillowed on his crossed arms and his tight-muscled legs stretched negligently toward the water. Dark gold lashes fanned out over high cheekbones, and his mouth was a sensual curve above the strong stubborn line of his chin. The warmth of the noonday sun had tempted him to unbutton his cotton shirt, and her eyes strayed farther, lingering on the broad expanse of his bold naked chest. She followed the line of curling hair as it tapered over his flat stomach and disappeared below the unnatural barrier of his cutoffs.

What would he do if she stretched out beside him on the sun-bleached sand? She longed to run her hand through the mat of tightly curled hair on his chest as she snuggled against him to nibble at his earlobe. Would he forget the restraint he'd placed on himself these past few days, gather her to him and make love to her? It was another beguiling erotic fantasy, and they seemed to be invading her thoughts with increasing frequency. She smiled to herself, a satisfied, catlike smile; who would have thought that Erin McIntee would be sitting on a sandbar in the middle of the North Woods calmly, lovingly planning to seduce the man she loved? She felt like laughing. No one in her faraway Washington world would recognize her at all.

She could hardly recognize herself. She had never wanted to behave so wantonly before in her life. It was exhilarating and a

142

little frightening. She tried another approach, thinking conversation would be preferable to her rambling fancies.

"A penny for your thoughts." Erin curled tanned legs under her, leaning back against the cooler, still watching Mitch, who was soaking up the rays of welcome sunlight.

"I was thinking about the book."

"Well, prestigious authors must muse now and then." She smiled at him, but he couldn't see the respect she held for him in her gaze. "It's going to be a very good book," she praised frankly. Erin didn't pretend to understand the complexities of the technical experiments and lab work on which Mitch was basing his writing. But she knew his style was clear and concise, and from the outline he had given her he was building a complete profile of the bald eagle and its vanishing environment. There were very few books written on the subject and none so comprehensive and solely dedicated to the North American predator. "You are a man outstanding in your field, Dr. Cade!" She added with enthusiasm. She wanted to kiss his smiling lips as he lay in confident male splendor on the sand.

"The second chapter is ready for your critique," he teased, opening a careless eye to squint at her in the sunlight, "if you think you can work up to the standards of a famous author. There's probably only a couple dozen people in the United States who have a genuine interest in the damn thing." He chuckled. "Along with hundreds of aspiring ornithology, conservation, or nature science students. Thank God for captured audiences."

"Ah, dedicated birdmen, one and all," she sighed theatrically, studying her own eagleman stretched golden and still in the sun like the sacrifice of a pagan ritual.

"You've been a big help to me, Erin," he said seriously. "I've had it all in my head for a long time." He rolled over, his fingers tracing meaningless patterns in the sand. Erin shivered with remembered sensations as she relived the erotic movements of those same hands on her skin, reviving again the excitement of his stroking caresses on her breasts and hair. His touch could bring her alive. Even that first night on the train he had taught her heart to beat with a new rhythm and her body to sing a new song.

"I may have never started this book without you." He was watching her steadily, his dark eyes waiting for her reply.

"I've enjoyed—working with the book very much," she side-stepped. "I'll be glad to help you for as long as I can stay here." It was the wrong answer. His brows snapped together, and he rolled onto his back again. She tried to keep him talking, not understanding the sudden change in his attitude. "When the banding's finished, you can go back to Cornell to write," she said stiffly. "I'm sure you'll be able to find a willing young coed to take your notes and correct your spelling." And warm your bed, she thought jealously. She wanted to do everything, help with his work, warm his bed—have his child. If he would only ask her to stay, she could tell him everything, bring it out in the open and begin a new life with him here and now. Tell him she would give up everything in her old world, but Lydia and Thurston, to stay here with him forever in Paradise. Erin blinked back tears of frustration when he remained silent staring at the cloudless sky above them. She tried to concentrate on the tranquility of their surroundings, watching the sway of grasses on the bank across the narrow channel through a blur of unshed tears.

"We'd better be going," Mitch advised, sitting up and rising to his feet in one swift move. He reached down with a powerful brown hand to help her to her feet. The touch of his fingers, so soon on the heels of her thoughts, was a shock that sent a bolt of longing jolting through her. She marveled at his strength as he propelled her up. She wanted to fly into his arms, but he turned and bent to lift the cooler, the frown returning to his face as she climbed into the canoe.

It didn't do any good to dwell on situations that she couldn't remedy, so Erin tried to keep her mind on staying in the middle of the river as they swung out into the swift current. Its width had been steadily narrowing since they left the site of the nest where Mitch had banded two large, gawky chocolate-colored eaglets. Now a patch of foaming water appeared in front of them, and Erin's hands tightened on her paddle as they shot through, spray flying with Mitch's sure control carrying them safely past hidden snags and water-smoothed boulders. The brown water rolled over the obstacles foaming like root beer soda, but at other times the sun would shine into the translucent river, turning the

144

water to a brooding red. Hemingway would choose a bloody river to write about, she mused. The blood of this artery was pumping vigorously through the narrow banks at an alarming rate.

The sun was high overhead, and she was glad she had stripped down to the short-sleeved royal blue shirt and khaki shorts, shedding her heavier clothes. Unexpectedly the river widened again as they rounded a high banked curve, and Erin leaned over to let her hands dangle in the clear blue-brown water. It was icy cold, and she gasped at the shock as Mitch chuckled wryly behind her.

"Not exactly bath temperature, is it?"

"It certainly isn't." She laughed, shaking the crystal drops from her fingers before returning her paddle to the water. He sounded more relaxed, and she didn't want to do anything to rock the boat, literally or figuratively. "How much farther to the old cabin that you told me about?"

"Close to half an hour's paddling. I'll check out the nest near there before dark; then we can get an early start in the morning."

"Will Tex meet us somewhere?" She hurried on, not wanting to let him hear the excitement that was growing in her at the thought of spending the night alone with him in a deserted logger's cabin. The mechanics of a canoe trip were new to Erin, but she knew they couldn't paddle back upstream against this current.

"He's leaving the jeep at the mouth of the river. There's a campground at the point where it empties into Lake Superior."

"I'm looking forward to seeing the lake," she said dreamily, her eyes on the overhanging branches trailing their leaves in the water as they floated by. The current was pushing them along quickly when the river twisted around on itself once more. The bow of the canoe shot toward the far bank, running them onto the submerged branches of a fallen tree that was partially blocking the channel.

"Erin, sit still; I'll try to back off and push us out around the trunk," Mitch called, his voice calm and confident, but the light, loaded canoe was pitching violently. Erin stretched over the side trying to gain a hold with her paddle on a branch, but the blade slipped off the mossy surface, pitching her weight forward and tipping the canoe. She clutched frantically at the side of the boat as the dark swirling water came racing closer and she was flung headfirst into the icy river.

One frightened scream pushed its way out of her paralyzed throat before the freezing water closed over her head, sucking her down and dragging her tumbling body along until she was slammed into the reaching, clutching branches of the submerged tree. The current pressed her back into the tangled branches, trapping her in the cold darkness. She didn't feel the pain of scrapes and bruises as she struggled in horrified solitude against the never-ending blast of water that was holding her body captive. Her eyes were wide open, but she could see little in the murky swirl. Gaining a semblance of control, she applied all her strength and concentration to freeing her hands. One arm was pinned against her body, and the other draped over a branch as the current worked to tear it from her body. She couldn't move them against the savage pull of the water, and she was exhausted from the struggle. She was drowning, she realized, still imprisoned after her frenzied effort, her lungs aching, and the fear of death pounding in her head.

"Erin!" She could hear Mitch calling, but that was impossible above the rush of blood and water. "Erin, my God!" Still she watched for him, staring into the light that shimmered above her. The oxygen in her body was nearly gone, and a sense of peace was settling over her as panic passed away. She didn't know why Mitch was delayed, but she knew he would come. She wanted to call out to him, tell him where she was, and one last despairing cry was building in her heart. Yet remnants of coherent thought told her that when it burst from her throat rising to the surface, the water would rush into her lungs, snuffing out her life before it had really begun, before she had really loved. She struggled silently on, holding her last breath—knowing she wasn't alone.

Her movements were slowing down, the frantic fear that goaded her to escape washed away with the river, and she drifted into pondering. Perhaps it wasn't so hard to die after all. She felt lighter than air now, and the branches were loosening their hold. Hands reached out to her. Was it Mitch? She couldn't tell, but the red darkness was growing brighter, the sun was shining in

146

rippling splendor just above her face, and suddenly the suffocating weight of water was gone and she burst into air and light.

She spluttered and coughed as her head popped above the surface, dragging great gulps of air into her tortured lungs, clinging to Mitch's strength as he dragged her from the waters of the Big Two-Hearted—both tasted love and poetry as he held her in his arms.

His breath was as ragged as her own, and his face was white and drawn. "Erin, are you all right?"

"I'm okay, really. Don't squeeze me so hard," she gasped, but she refused to release her own hold on the steel band of his arm.

"I couldn't find you, my God. I dove again and again," he rasped against her streaming hair as he lay holding her on the warm sand. "The current carried you into the branches. My God, I thought I'd lost you." They were quiet for a few minutes while Mitch caught his breath, and Erin marveled at her return to life and light from the cold depths of despair.

"Will you be all right for a minute," Mitch inquired, searching her pale face intently but not releasing her completely. "I've got to get the canoe upright before it works loose and we're stranded. Do you understand?" The arms that held her still shook, and she mustered her resources to belay her lingering terror. She nodded, struggling to a sitting position. "Go ahead." It was all she could manage, and not very convincing, but he kissed her once again, quick and hard, before letting her go and wading back out into the river. The canoe was wedged into a fork of the tree, and Mitch worked doggedly to free the craft and right it before the relentless river sucked it under the tree and crushed it beyond repair.

He secured the canoe to the bank, rested a little, gasping for breath as he held to its side, and swam off again with bold sure strokes to retrieve Erin's paddle and the one waterproof bundle that had worked its way loose, and washed ashore. It seemed miraculous to Erin's befuddled faculties that the rest of their cargo was still tied securely between the thwarts of the beleaguered canoe. She waited passively, still numb with cold and terror, until he waded ashore and gathered her into his arms. She rested against him, listening to the soothing rumble of his voice

147

while the warm sun overhead stole a little of the chill from her bones and her brain began to function once more.

"We have to keep going, Erin. The cabin isn't much, but it beats staying out here all night." She would gladly stay here in his arms forever rather than face that cold water again.

"I'll be fine. Let's get going." She tried to sound confident, but she felt like a mass of quivering jelly. For Erin the next minutes passed in a surreal blur, and she could remember very little of the trip when she tried to retrace it later. She could only recall how thankful she was to see the tilted chimney of the rough-sided cabin in its tiny clearing. Mitch tied the craft securely to a stump, steadying it and studying her white, tired face with a frown between his eyes.

He loosened the ties and grabbed several bundles as he led her toward the lopsided porch on the building. She waited behind him while he fished under the eaves for a rusty key, manhandling the padlock until the warped door opened to reveal an empty dusty room and blackened fireplace. Erin stood shivering uncertainly in her soggy shoes and damp clothes while he unpacked a soft down-filled sleeping bag from its nylon pouch and spread it on the floor before the hearth

"Get those wet things off," he said as he walked out the door. She could hear his footsteps on the porch again and realized he was going to retrieve more bundles from the canoe. She dropped down onto the soft flannel lining of the sleeping bag, wrapping her arms around her knees in an effort to stop the deep shudders running through her. Now she wasn't sure anymore whether she was trembling from the numbing chill or from the thought of the deadly water covering her face, but she was exhausted from the wasted energy of trying to vibrate life back into her limbs.

"Get your clothes off and wrap up in the bag," Mitch told her when he returned a second time, bringing the rest of the packs. "We'll get them drying in the sun." He crossed the room and helped her work at the stiff laces of her shoes, pulling them from her icy feet. She stared at him. He looked down at her, meeting her nearly black eyes, brushing a damp curl from her forehead and running his hands over the chilled flesh of her arms.

"I'll get you something warm," he said roughly, reaching with a long arm to drag a pack toward him. "You need something to warm you inside and out." He was already digging into the knapsack, pulling a glass bottle of amber liquid from one pocket and extracting a long-sleeved shirt from the plastic-wrapped depths of another. "Drink this," he commanded, pushing the bottle into her trembling hands. "And put this on," he added, dropping a dry flannel garment beside her.

"What is it?" she questioned, eyeing the liquid dubiously.

"Some of George's applejack." A smile sounded in his tone. "Drink some, it'll warm you up." He was talking as he removed the lid and tipped the bottle up, assisting her slow, shaky movements. She took a long burning swallow and coughed. "Drink some more," he urged, holding the bottle to her lips once more. The liquor was warming her and so was his steadying strong arm around her shoulders. She could feel his body heat flowing from him, and it revived her much more quickly than the applejack scorching her throat.

"Erin, you need to get out of your wet clothes," he said with the authority of experience. Then his voice softened. "You can change while I scrounge up some wood for the fire." She wanted to beg him to hold her in his arms, she needed his warmth, she needed him; her lips parted but the words never formed as he rose quickly and walked to the door.

She didn't really notice his exit as the fiery liquor exploded in her head. The smooth cidery taste warmed her throat all the way down, and she took one more long swallow before relinquishing it, setting it at the edge of the bag as she stood on shaky legs. She was cold and clammy, and she struggled out of her damp shorts and shirt staring at the gaping, empty fireplace. Even the lacy fabric of her bra felt cold and constricting. Her hands and fingers worked slowly like blocks of wood that needed to be manipulated one at a time. The hook of her bra was stubborn, finally coming loose, and she peeled her clinging panties from her wet skin. Naked, she knelt on the soft down sleeping bag to pick up the heathery flannel shirt from beside the pile of her damp clothes. Her mind was still sluggish, requiring a specific command to move on to each new task.

It wouldn't do to remember the cold furious grip of the river's current; it caused the flesh to rise on her arms, making it even harder to move her marionette hands and fingers. She would remember Mitch's touch, his caresses, heated and vital, making every inch of her body warm and alive. She was holding the shirt to her, lost in her dreams, when the door opened behind her and his powerful outline filled the rectangle of light. She watched him over her shoulder, his strong body frozen in a defensive stance. His arms were filled with wood, and he strode past her, barely glancing down at her dazed face or her naked body as he dropped to his heels before the hearth.

"I told you to put that shirt on," he drawled. He was concentrating fully on placing the wood carefully in the fireplace.

"I will." Her voice was very small, and she sat motionless, mesmerized by the play of muscles across his back. He had removed his own shirt and wet shoes, and his damp cutoffs clung to muscular thighs like a second skin. His back was stiff and erect as he worked with the kindling and handful of dead leaves to start the fire. He continued to watch it long after the sparks grew into a hungry flame that licked at the larger pieces of wood. Finally he turned and looked down at her, fists clenched at his sides, and the muscle flicked along his stubborn jaw. What was she doing, she questioned wildly as the leaping flame in his hazel eyes recalled her near nudity. She hadn't moved to put on the shirt, still sitting on her heels holding it to her breasts with hands that shook. She could feel her desire for him growing and filling her every cell.

"Erin, get dressed and get under the covers," he said, his voice gruff.

"My back hurts," she complained timidly as though that expressed her feelings. He moved toward her, a still brown giant as Erin turned a slender shoulder to show him the angry red welts across her creamy flesh. She heard his quick intake of breath as he reached out to inspect the abrasion. She could sense the concern in his gentleness, and the need to be held by him washed over her in a tidal wave.

"It must have happened under water. I don't remember . . ." Her voice came out in a delicate whisper, quavering in spite of her attempt to steady it.

"I'll get something for it." He stood abruptly, forgetting his anger, and she clutched the shirt to her bosom, listening as he searched through the supplies for the first-aid kit. He returned, carrying the medication and a blanket to kneel behind her. "Now, let's get this fixed up." His voice was husky, and Erin swiveled her head to watch him smooth the cool cream on the injury. His hand trembled, and a tightening curl of desire coiled in Erin as his gentle fingers applied the ointment to her velvet flesh.

"I think that will do," he stated, starting to rise from the floor. As she turned to face him, she knew it wasn't nearly enough, she must feel his caress even if he did reject her again. She held the shirt to her with one hand and pointed with a pink-tipped nail to a small scratch just above the curve of her collarbone. She studied his face, watching the telltale muscle flex along his lean jaw, noting the emotions racing across his chiseled features, her attention drawn to the deep hollow of his throat where a pulse beat steadily. He moved his hand over her skin, and the pulse raced. A new dawning settled into her befuddled brain—she had power also. He, too, was susceptible to a word, a touch; she could elicit his response as easily as he did hers. She gave him a brief pleased smile, anxious to further test her exciting new theory. He was a biologist, wasn't he? Certainly he would understand her scientific curiosity. She moved her hand to point to a cut on the back of the opposite wrist. She studied the leaping artery in his throat as his thudding heart pushed the response through while the shirt dipped farther down her breast, stopping with tantalizing precision just above the swelling point of her excited nipples. He took a breath, quick and hard, but massaged the cream into the injury.

What would a kiss do to his tightly leashed control? she wondered, her mind floating in a rainbow-hued limbo of tactile sensations. Just a simple kiss? Would it sweep away the constraint he had treated her with these last days? She pointed expressively to her curving cherry lips as she rose to her knees, watching his dark eyes, feeling his warm breath as she moved closer. She wasn't Erin McIntee any longer, afraid and uncertain. She was a siren, a wanton loving creature seeking the ecstatic fulfillment of joining herself to the man she loved.

She leaned toward him; her fingers sensitized the outline of his full lower lip, entreating his kiss. She wound her arms languidly around his neck as the shirt fell unheeded to the floor, her breasts molding to his hardness, and he moaned against her lips claiming them in a possessive, demanding kiss as he surrounded her in his embrace, his hands exploring her back. She arched against him, but he held her hips away with the heels of his hands, denying the contact of her yearning pelvis.

"My God, Erin—don't," he rasped against her cheek. "I'm only human."

Erin laid her hand against his beard-roughened cheek, imploring the touch of his lips once again, darting a pointed tongue across their fullness to taste his lightly salty skin. She was rapidly succumbing to her own uncontrolled experiment.

"I want you to make love to me, Mitchell Cade," she whispered, watching the darkening hazel eyes intently. "I've wanted it for a long time."

"I don't want you to ever regret making love to me, Erin. You're too vulnerable. I can't take advantage of you like this." His voice was hoarse against her throat, and he repeated the phrase as though trying to convince himself of its veracity. "I know I can't keep you." His words speared through her as he pulled her to him, pressing her hips harshly into his prodding desire as the fabric of his clothes scratched her thighs. Every detail of his body was imprinted on her flesh. The surge of wanton desire that bit through her as he crushed her to him was so intense she nearly cried out. It didn't matter what he did or didn't say. Nothing mattered now except the hair-roughened texture of his skin along her silkiness and the swell of his passion against her conforming softness. Radiating swirls of desire quivered through her, unlike anything she had ever felt before. She shivered with the overwhelming wonder of her feelings.

He took her lips again, besieging their moist darkness with a marauding tongue as he played her body with a master's hand. His lips returned to nuzzle her now defenseless lips, his tongue drinking their nectar, giving her a tantalizing promise of the experience yet in store. With the luminous eyes and shining smile of a woman being loved, she slid her hands along the ridge of sinewy ribs to the waistband of his still-damp cutoffs. Boldly she pulled at the resistant snap, tugging the tight fabric down over his slender hips. With a muttered, impatient oath he stood and pulled them off, supremely unconscious of the glory of his nakedness as he knelt again and pushed her down onto the sleeping bag's softness.

"Kissing you isn't enough, loving you won't be enough if you leave me when it's over," he whispered against her hair.

"I'm not going anywhere." She cuddled along his bronzed length, pressing closer and savoring the feel of his corded thighs against her legs. Running blind hands over the angled contours of his torso, she let them move shamelessly lower to trace the flat hard surface of his stomach. She caught her lips between her teeth and let her questing fingers slip lower to trace the thrusting power of his manhood with butterfly delicacy.

"Mitch, love me now," she whispered.

His breath caught with a groan as her caress grew bolder, and he rolled onto her, chasing the last of her coherent thoughts into the background. His mouth covered hers, establishing his territory as his plundering tongue claimed the spoils. His lips left hers an eternity later to trail over her cheeks, kissing her eyelids, nibbling the tender lobes of her ears while his hands teased and excited her already taut nipples. Erin sighed, giving herself up to the joy of a woman totally desired. Her hands tangled in his soft, dull-gold hair as his lips descended in a fiery comet's tail of kisses to fasten onto her aching breast, in a soothing, nipping bite that vibrated along the invisible connection to her womb. She arched against him, inviting more intimate caresses as his fingers lightly roamed over her, exploring the velvet of inner thighs, seeking and finding hidden treasure as he massaged the petal-soft moistness within, preparing her for his entry. Her wings gracefully unfurled, fluttering in a swirl of pleasure, her body poised and ready for a flight of ecstasy.

Her legs parted invitingly, and she basked in the warming glow of his body, as he shifted his weight, resting his bulk above her. She explored his length with heady abandon, seeking his sensuous mouth and closing her eyes against the exquisite sensations of their joining. Erin was soaring above the trees, wings spread, spiraling higher above the earth, meeting and coupling to her eagleman. She pulled him closer as his slow gentle thrusts increased, sending through her a smoldering excitement that was stealing her breath away. She trailed her fingers over his spine and the flare of tightly muscled buttocks, painlessly cutting a path with her fingertips over his back to the ridged muscles of shoulders and arms. His lips returned to claim hers again, and the controlled movements of his body in hers became more urgent, invoking an instinctive answer from deep within her. Together they ascended and soared to dizzying heights in perfect unison, shattering into a myriad of fiery fragments as passion exploded within them, shuddering and lifting them to the zenith of delight.

"Erin, I love you," he breathed hoarsely. "I love you." His voice was distant, but the words sang through her heart. His love flowed into her as he kissed her parted lips, their tongues entwined in a unison so complete, so true, that tears came to Erin's eyes. They started their plunging descent from soaring heights, but she didn't care, as she clung to him gasping. She had heard the words—he loved her! His erratic rhythms inside her were answered by her own repeating choir. Diving, gaining speed, joining together in free-fall, she bowed his head down—her proud eagleman—and kissed him fervently, sharing her love in complete trust and ecstatic passion. His strong wings lifted her, guiding her, taking away the fast approaching spinning earth. She rested safely in his cradling arms, and they clung together, spent and replete.

Erin turned her head, looking at her lover, marveling at the intensity of their shared passion. Mitch's weight on her was heavy and satisfying, and she hugged him tightly, their bodies still merged and intertwined. The sound of his breath in her ear and the steady thud of his heart against her breast filled her with contentment. He gazed down at her seriously.

"You aren't shivering anymore; you must be warmer now."

She smiled with the confidence of a woman completely desired and loved. "I'm toasty warm. And very much alive, thanks to you," she said, moving gentle fingers over his cheek to flick his earlobe.

"All you need to do is whistle; rescuing damsels in distress is becoming my speciality," he teased.

She hadn't thanked him for saving her, and the ingratitude stung her. "Mitch. Thank you for everything." She kissed his mouth, and for a moment he was frowning down at her.

"Erin, I don't ever want you to regret this," he stated seriously.

"I don't regret anything. I love you, Mitch. And I love making love with you."

The frown dissolved, and he was exciting her with gold-flecked hazel eyes. His words were low and intense. "I was soaring with the eagles; we were wing to wing."

"I know." She spoke with perfect sincerity. They were together even in the fantasy of sensual flight. She lifted up to wrap welcome arms around his neck, hoping to share feelings beyond mere words. She nuzzled the strong column of his throat until he captured her tender lips with his, tasting and seeking entry with his tongue as she slowly lowered to the fleecy lining. He lifted his head, resting his weight on his forearms and tangling his fingers in her dusky curls.

"I'm tempted to never set foot outside this cabin again."

"Ummm," she murmured her agreement, bracing her hands on his chest and smiling up into his eyes. "That sounds like a marvelous idea. But, won't you be bored?" she asked playfully, outlining the flat smoothness of his nipples with her fingertips.

"I don't think I'll have any trouble thinking of something to keep me occupied," he whispered, bending to plant a row of kisses along her hairline. "Are you ready for another flying lesson?" he breathed against her cheek.

"Anytime you are, professor." She smiled mischievously up into his masculine features. "Mitch!" She could feel him harden within her once more, and her eyes widened in surprise.

"I warned you before, Erin, I never bluff," he returned with a devilish chuckle, as his teasing lips moved on to linger over the pulse beating unsteadily at the base of her throat. "Just remember who started this."

"I'll never forget," she promised, recalling her wanton seduction with a blush. His knowing hand fondled her breast, fingers flicking over the pouting nipple, squeezing lightly. A moan escaped her parting lips as he began the slow enchanting movements within her that sent singing vibrations racing through her once again.

"Unless you're too tired and need your rest," he taunted,

suspending the addictive pleasure, but her hands flew to clutch him to her.

"I need you!" came her breathless reply, as he captured her lips in an endless whirlpool kiss that set her free to soar again, releasing the sensuous loving creature inside her as they started their dizzying ascent. Wave after wave of delight raced through her as she met each thrust of his body with her own. Their passionate flight was shared, reaching fruition in perfect unison, and she gloried in it, strong arms guiding and holding her as they spiraled down into the soft clouds of sleep.

Erin returned from a soft, comfortable other world, slowly, by degrees, as the sounds of movement registered on her drowsy consciousness. A blanket kept her warm, but she missed the strong living heat of the man she loved. She opened heavy-lidded eyes to see Mitch coaxing life into the reluctant fire. She lay quietly watching as the flame rose from the coals at last, taking an interest in its work and racing upward to catch the dry wood he had added, but her real interest was in the man before her. The fire played over the lines and angles of his physique, and Erin's stomach contracted with pleasurable excitement. The light glistened in his hair, gilding his body, reminding her of an ancient golden statue of a warrior king. Her breathing was uneven; her pulses racing as she feasted her eyes on the granite perfection of his naked body. She watched the flexing and stretching of sinew and tendon as he picked up another piece of wood and added it to the greedy feeding fire.

She looked away quickly, feeling her desire for him rising again. Her bemused gaze strayed to the one small window, and she was surprised to see it was fully dark outside. She had slept the afternoon away. Mitch straightened and turned to look down where she lay on the sleeping bag covered only by the light blanket they carried with them, her head pillowed on the second rolled bag. He must have covered her as she slept, she decided. "How long have you been awake?" she asked curiously.

"Awhile. Are you hungry?" She shook her head wondering what he would say next. She lifted the blanket in silent invitation, and he turned to throw another log on the fire before sliding in beside her and pulling her close to his rugged frame. She cuddled into his strength beginning to realize that she would never be

156

content to sleep alone again. She could admit now that she needed Mitchell Cade's love to become the complete strong human being she longed to be. It was ironic but true; the bonds that one man sought to hold her with diminished her, but the gentle unbreakable bands Mitch was weaving around her strengthened and complemented the innate abilities she already possessed.

"We have to talk, Erin," Mitch said firmly. She liked the sound of his voice rumbling in his chest, fitting firmly against her back, even if the words sent a pang through her. "I'm not in the habit of being seduced by blue-eyed hellcats."

"I'm not in the habit of seducing birdmen," she retorted. "You're the very first." His silence frightened her.

"Erin, I know you'll be going back to Washington soon." He held her tighter when he felt her body stiffen next to him. "I know I can't keep you here."

She rolled to face him, cut to the quick that he was willing to send her away after what they had shared. She stared unbelieving at his fire-shadowed face. "I love you," she said amazed.

"You love me now—in this cabin. After the frightening experience you had today, you're grateful to me. But, what about tomorrow?"

"I love you," she stated, her temper matching the orange light of the fire. "Isn't that enough?"

"No. Not nearly enough when you're fifteen hundred miles away from me," he answered bitterly. "But you may take part of me back to Washington with you. You may have my baby growing in you already."

"A baby!" Her eyes flew open at the word, and she stared into the bottomless liquid gold of his fire-reflecting orbs, her brain spinning frantically. Oh dear God, don't let him say anything I can't bear to hear, she prayed, her thoughts fragmenting, hurling her back in time, edging her with heartbreak.

"Didn't it occur to you, this delightful activity was designed for that purpose? You could be pregnant now." His fingers were kneading her arm with a harsh pressure, and she shrugged his hand away.

"Aren't you taking a lot for granted," she temporized, thrown into cold confusion by his words. "There are always solutions to that problem. I will be responsible for any child I might conceive," she said stiffly, her mind flooded with pain.

He rolled her onto her back, pinning her shoulders with two strong hands. "What are you talking about?" he ground out, the lover gone, replaced by an angry stranger. She shut her eyes fighting tears as stinging barbs of memory replayed in her mind. How could the wonder of the afternoon be replaced so quickly by misery?

"Unwanted babies don't have to be born." She couldn't look at him. "Is that what you want to hear? If I should be so silly as to become pregnant with your child, you won't have to worry about the consequences." Tears trickled into her hair followed by small tight sobs that choked their way past her clamped lips. Mitch was deathly still for long moments, then he swore quietly, gathering her back against him, rocking her slowly until the strangled sobs ceased and she lay peacefully beside him.

"Erin, if you are pregnant, I'd welcome it. I wouldn't let you or anyone else harm our child." His tone was determined and strong. "I can't think of any better way to create a link between us than for you to have my baby. You'd never be able to be rid of me, no matter how hard you tried or how far you went." He held her close, searching her frightened eyes and trembling lips. "I know you could never abort a new life. Why try to make me think you could?" She opened her mouth, but no sound emerged. Perhaps he read the answer in the suffering revealed in the inky blue pools of her eyes. "Is that why you broke off your engagement to your society lawyer?" he asked, with the uncanny insight she had faced so often before.

"I thought I was pregnant," she began in a tight emotionless voice released into the painful silence. "Warren didn't want a child—my child—any child, I suppose." It was harder than she had thought to tell him, but she went on. "I was so confused, so manipulated, I might have gone through with an abortion, but it was a false alarm." Her hands clenched together. "I couldn't marry him then. I could never trust him again, and I couldn't give up control of my life to him." Her words were bitter, and she couldn't see the pain for her that suffused his rugged features.

It was a relief to speak of it at last, to tell Mitch how much she had been hurt. "Now I know I never loved him. At least I learned that much about myself."

"You're going to love me," Mitch said fiercely. "I'll do everything in my power to keep you tied to me, Erin." His lips covered whatever protests she was going to make, and her breath caught in her throat, the clamoring fears and doubts suffocated by the emotion his questing hands and lips aroused. She watched him closely, the silence of the night broken only by their breathing and the fire as it danced behind her in the grate. Mitch held her closely, and she rested against him, relishing the fiery heat of his body, trying to formulate a way to tell him all the rest of the things that bothered her. She could tell him everything later when the marvel of this moment was less intense. When she could bear the commonplace to intrude on their silent world. She wasn't ready to soil this fantasy—with the reality of money. She was falling prey to his plundering hands as they began a welcome assault on her defenses. With butterfly lightness she began her own erotic exploration of his frame, her hands gliding over the curly mat of his chest to toy with the smoothness of his nipples, tracing audaciously to the narrowing taper of his waist.

His hands matched hers, wandering over the curves and valleys while his lips traced evocative patterns on her throat and shoulder, circling nearer to the sensitive peaks of her breasts. His teeth fastened on a tender bud filling her with renewed longing. Her hands flew upwards to press the dark gold head even closer. His leg slipped between hers, nudging her thighs apart while his hands roamed at will over her silken skin.

"I can teach you to fly free, Erin. I'll only keep you as long as you want to stay, but it will kill me to let you go," he whispered.

The sensations he evoked, the longings he stirred in her were far beyond her experience. She felt complete and whole, willing to share her life with Mitchell Cade now and forever. She knew she could never learn the survival skill of living without him if he ever let her go. Erin's hands tangled in his hair, and she nibbled at his lip, seeking the warm moistness of his mouth, inviting with cherry lips the entry of his seeking tongue. Greedy for further pleasure, she moved with sensuous grace as she guided him to her, experiencing once again the soaring endless delight of their union and the dreamy satisfaction of sleeping in his arms.

CHAPTER ELEVEN

A light kiss brought Erin awake, brightening her limpid, sleep-shaded eyes and tinting her cheeks a dusky red. "Good morning," she sighed sleepily. The fairy-tale quality of the night was fading away, deepening her flush of color as she realized the fantasy of firelit lovemaking was real and not a lovely dream.

"Good morning, Erin." The second kiss was deeper, more stirring, and the sleepy lethargy deserted her as Mitch's caress renewed her desire like warm breath stirring the red embers of the fire. "As much as I'd like to spend this morning making love to you," he murmured, tightening his hold on her, his beard rough against her cheek, "we have work to do." Contenting himself with one last kiss, he stood up and moved away. "Up and at 'em, gaboon; duty calls. The facilities and ladies' room are that way." He gestured to the door. "I'll get breakfast while you're washing up. We have a nest to catalogue this morning, and Tex will be wondering what became of us." Mitch was already dressed in the heavy shirt and jeans he wore for climbing, she noticed as her surroundings settled into focus again. He turned back to his packing as she sat up pulling at the light blanket to cover her breasts. She was suddenly a little shy of him, reluctant to face reality after their night of shared bliss, and she grabbed up her clothes in haste. Wrapping the light blanket firmly around her, she fastened it under her arms and hurried out into the summer morning.

The red-brown water was icy, and Erin made a face at the prospect of washing in the stream, but after the initial shock of contact it was surprisingly invigorating. All at once she was ravenously hungry, so she dressed quickly in the privacy of a cedar copse. Mitch was waiting for her on the rickety porch of the cabin, looking rakish and a little disreputable with a two days growth of beard. The food was spread out beside him, and Erin accepted her fruit and plastic-wrapped roll with alacrity. "I'm so glad we didn't lose our supplies on the river," she mumbled around a bite of sweet, juicy cherries. "I'm suddenly starved."

"The first thing you learn in this business is to tie down your packs and waterproof them in the bargain." He laughed, handing her a small container of fruit juice. "My grandfather would have snorted at these citified conveniences," he added, indicating the rolls and juice. "He always believed you should have a real breakfast, flapjacks, eggs, bacon . . . but I think he would have forgiven me if he'd known what a warm bed I had to drag myself away from this morning." Mitch chuckled, perusing her scrubbed, dewy freshness with unabashed pleasure.

"Is your grandfather still living?" she quizzed, trying to hide her blush. In the bright morning light she realized there were so many things she didn't know about him. She knew she loved him, but little else. Mitch knew everything about her—almost everything—she amended with a fleeting frown, and she wanted to enjoy the same knowledge of his life.

"No." Sadness crept into his blue-flecked eyes and intensified the hazel irises. "He's gone now—but I still miss him." Erin nodded, understanding his grief without the need of spoken words, appreciating that this was the first time he had spoken of his family to her. "He left me the land up here. And he gave me a never-ending appreciation of birds and the wilderness. He loved this country and the things that belong to it. Leaving me the house and land was the base I needed to start my work. I had enough money saved to build the long cabin, and I borrowed enough for the equipment. So I didn't need to work as an assistant prof at Cornell anymore." He reminisced. "The first couple seasons Tex worked for his meals, and I still pay Doc a pittance, but he wants the chance to study raptors, so he puts up with it."

What would he say if she told him she had more than enough money for both of them? That he wouldn't have to worry about funds ever again? Instead she continued her tender inquisition as they finished the food and sat quietly while the last of the haze lifted from the water in ragged tatters. "Tell me some more about your family," she demanded, threading her arm through his, snuggling close in the lingering chill.

"What brings on this sudden curiosity about my antecedents?" he chided, the pensive mood that the mention of his grandfather created passing away as quickly as the sun was evaporating the mist. His eyes were laughing down at her, bringing to the forefront of her memory their conversation in the darkness before the fire. She could feel her color rise again at his continued scrutiny, but she smiled. "I know something about your work, your friends, but not your family," she pressed.

"I see." He nodded and began reciting the salient points, looking pleased at her interest. "My parents just celebrated their fortieth wedding anniversary and live in Chicago. My dad's an architect, retired now, and my mother's a professional volunteer. She heads more fund drives and chairs more committees than anyone else I know. She has more energy than OPEC, and my dad stays young keeping up with her."

"She sounds like my grandmother. Lydia's the most organized woman I know." Erin chuckled, wondering how the two dynamic women would react to each other. Mitch nodded agreement at the comparison and continued.

"I have one older brother who is an airline pilot. And then there is Mindy, the baby of the family; she's about your age, married, living in California and expecting her third child around Thanksgiving. That will make"—he paused a moment as though tallying a score and then went on—"six nieces and nephews of assorted sizes and ages. Any more information you require?"

"No," she remarked dreamily, "but I'd like to meet them all someday." She was projecting herself into the midst of a large noisy family gathering, and the happy echo of those thoughts transmitted itself to the man beside her.

"I'd like that too, Erin, very much." They continued to sit in companionable silence for several minutes, watching the day begin. Again she couldn't find the words to speak of crass money matters or the childish behavior that had led her on such a convoluted path to present happiness. The enchantment of their night together was still fresh in her thoughts, sending a glow of satisfaction through her entire being as they loaded the canoe and closed up the cabin. There were problems to be faced, and she would have the courage to bring them out into the open soon and bury their remains forever. Mitch checked the nest a short distance down the now quiet and slowly widening river only to find it abandoned.

"What happened to them?" Erin asked, surveying the deserted aerie as though it might give her an answer. She shaded her eyes with her hand, hoping to find something to justify another dangerous climb for Mitch.

"It's hard to tell." His voice was low and disappointed as he unstrapped the climbing irons and jotted down additional notes on the pad Erin handed him. "This particular pair was very prolific, a successful fledgling every season. We'll probably never know what happened to them unless somebody turns in a tag." He sounded discouraged suddenly, and it was the first time she had glimpsed the frustration his work produced. "Someday I'm going to get transmitters to put on fledglings so I can keep track of them. The chances of anyone finding the eagles that used to inhabit this nest are next to nonexistent." Erin couldn't help wondering what had happened to them also, and the nagging mystery preoccupied her thoughts on the long ride home.

Home—it had come very close to being that in the last few weeks, and now that she knew how much it meant to the man beside her, it seemed even more important to her.

The sunlight danced on the whitecaps of the choppy lake, and dark patches of shade dotted the sparse grass along the drive. As the jeep bounced into the empty compound, Erin slid over to the passenger's side, hoping the flush on her cheeks would be attributed to the genial warmth of the summer's day. She was still so dazed by her happiness that she didn't want to share it immediately, not even with Doc and Tex. The door of the long cabin swung open as they rolled to a stop, and the Texan emerged, moving with uncommon energy as Erin jumped from the Bronco's high seat and turned to walk toward the house. At that moment a warm bath and clean clothes seemed more important to her than any news Tex could have to impart.

"We've got company," Tex announced as Mitch grabbed several bundles and shoved them toward his burly friend. "The congresswoman's here lookin' for Erin."

"Lydia?" Erin halted in her tracks, spinning to face the two men, a curious prickling sensation racing over her skin. Lydia would definitely complicate things. What was she doing here? There were too many things she needed to explain to Mitch before her other life intervened. "She called last night from the Soo, and I picked her up at the airstrip," Tex explained, watching his friend closely, but Mitch didn't venture any comment as Erin moved off again leading the way into the house.

Lydia was seated before the empty fireplace in the main room, which was pleasantly cool after the bright sunshine outside. She looked elegant and relaxed in brown linen slacks and a creamy-colored blouse, her hair in soft waves around her head.

"Erin!" Lydia's face was wreathed in smiles as she rose gracefully to embrace her disheveled granddaughter. "I've been worried about you. Not a word since your first report and . . ."

"I've been so busy," Erin fabricated. She couldn't explain how all the reports she was going to send raved about the eagleman instead of his work. "I have some to mail you. Let me show them to you while Mitch and Tex unload the jeep." She tried to hurry Lydia from the room, hoping to curb her disclosure of any information about the trust fund before she explained the situation.

"Nonsense, Erin, that will wait. I've come to see you and to speak with Dr. Cade." She leveled an inquiring look at the doctor. "Tex was telling me that you two were checking on two very remote nests," she went on leadingly.

"Lydia . . ." Erin started.

"I've decided to kill two birds with one stone, so to speak." She smiled in the direction of the biologist, apologizing for her choice of clichés. "I have the trust papers with me for you to sign, Erin." She surged ahead, each word a knell to Erin's shrinking contentment. "We might as well settle that business while I'm here. And I want a full explanation from you, sir." She didn't wait for his reply, but continued. "I do apologize for using you to keep watch over my granddaughter . . ." She was aware of the growing tension between the couple and came to a halt.

"We can discuss the trust fund later, Grandmother," Erin interjected firmly. "Now just tell me how you got here." The ruse

165

didn't work. Lydia was determined to pursue her own topic, and Erin was becoming more apprehensive.

"I was wrong to ask this of you, dear," she admitted, grasping the younger woman by the hands. "I've been upset ever since you left. Forgive me for trying to make you conform to my standards. I've endorsed the trust, and everything is ready for you. All I need now is your signature, and the funds will be turned over to your control. Then we can both go home." She stopped abruptly as Mitch stepped forward and whirled Erin around to face him.

"What is she talking about?" His eyes were hard like the agates she scooped from the foam-laced edge of the Superior shoreline. "You've been staying here just to get control of your money? Is that what she's saying?"

"Mitch, please let me explain." But he wasn't listening, and the words wouldn't come. She had waited too long. "I tried to tell you . . ." Her words trailed off. She couldn't say that her faculties deserted her whenever he touched her, not in front of Lydia. How could she tell him that when he held her in his arms all she could think about was his loving her, filling her with his strength and vitality? He spun on his heel and jerked from her restraining hand, stalking from the room.

"Erin, please tell me what's happening. What have I said?" Lydia begged as Erin faced her puzzled grandparent.

"I have to go to him, Grandma. I have to explain and make him understand," Erin said in distraction. She flew out the door, but Mitch was already at the jeep, his face a mask of thunderous rage. Erin had never seen him so angry, so unheeding.

"Please, Mitch, wait," she gasped, grabbing on to the jeep's door, trying to keep him from opening it and leaving her.

"Don't bother, Erin. The charade is over. You've been lying to me all along, haven't you? The Washington society princess tested by making her stay with the backwoods birdman. I've got to hand it to you and Lydia, you've got real flare. I bet you've both enjoyed the joke. How much is it going to be worth to you, princess, a couple of million?"

"More like fifteen," she shot back, goaded into anger by his attack. She had to lash out at him or she would fold up right there and die of misery.

"And Warren? Was that all a story too, or did you hope to

replace his baby with mine?" Her hand shot out, colliding with his unshaven cheek in a stinging slap. He didn't retaliate, his eyes bleak and staring straight through her as if she no longer existed for him. "I don't expect you to be here when I get back," he ground out between clenched teeth. "It'll be better that way." He jumped into the Bronco, grinding the starter viciously as the gears clashed, and he roared out of the compound, drowning out her last attempt to make him stay.

"Mitch, please don't go. I love you." The flying gravel from under the tires and the cloud of sandy dust thrown into the air attested to the violence of his feelings, and Erin was alone again.

Tears of pain and frustration flooded her eyes as Tex appeared behind her, and she turned to face him. "He wouldn't listen to me. Tex, where's the pickup? I have to go after him, make him understand." Her eyes searched wildly for the other vehicle, but it was nowhere in sight.

"Doc's got it and Mitch is a damn fool," Tex answered succinctly. "He don't go off half-cocked like that too often, but when he does it's a doozy." He thoughtfully scratched his shaggy head. "All he knows is Representative Wentworth wants to take you away. Made a damn fool of himself, didn't he? A man tends to do that when he's in love."

"I have to find him, Tex, make it right somehow," she whispered, stunned at the sudden collapse of her fragile happiness. Tears collected on her lashes, and she dashed them away impatiently.

"He'll be back when he cools off and comes to his senses," Tex assured, unnerved by a threat of feminine tears. "You just go inside and get it all straightened out with your grandma first; then we'll worry about that ornery boss of ours." She smiled for his benefit, but the pain in her heart came close to choking her. "Things'll come out right in the end," Tex went on. "They usually do."

"Do you want to return to Washington with me, Erin?" Lydia was standing a few feet behind her, the worried confusion on her face accenting the lines around her eyes and mouth. "Tex will take us to the airport as soon as there is a vehicle available." She glanced at the Texan for confirmation of her words, and he nodded his cooperation, but his face showed disapproval of the plan.

"No." Erin's tone was decisive. Her chin came up as Tex and Lydia exchanged quick glances. "I'm not leaving here until he makes me go. I waited too long to explain. I was a coward again, but this time I have too much at stake to give up. I love him. I know that beyond a shadow of a doubt, and if he doesn't want me, he's going to have to prove it." Her eyes were shining behind her tears.

Lydia came forward to put her arms around her unhappy grandchild. "Come inside with me and we'll have a long talk. I've been a coward too, Erin. Let me help you now, as I should have done all along." It was a difficult admission for the older woman to make, and Erin hugged her fiercely while Tex kicked dust from the toes of his scuffed boots and watched the two women enter the house before turning back to the long cabin.

Once inside Lydia shooed Erin into the bathroom with instructions to take a long bath, wash her hair, order her thoughts, and then they would talk. It was so like Lydia to diffuse the drama of the situation with such practical suggestions that Erin went without a murmur of protest, smiling despite her misery. Regardless of the chaos around her, Lydia proceeded in an orderly, businesslike manner.

The bath did help, and even though she had no appetite, she ate enough of the fluffy, redolent omelet Lydia set before her a half hour later to satisfy her anxious grandparent. Lydia looked at the plate, nodded in satisfaction, and poured a second cup of coffee for them both. Replacing the coffeepot on the stove, she led the way out onto the broad enclosed porch and seated herself in a padded wooden rocker.

"Now from the beginning, tell me all about it." Her command was gentle but cognizant, as though she knew what Erin was going to say. Her grandmother smiled confidently at her, and Erin wondered if she recognized that the woman who sat beside her was an entirely different person from the immature granddaughter she had sent here. The story tumbled out, all the doubts and fear, the indecision, and the final blow that killed what little respect she still held for Warren Markham. And how Mitchell Cade had tried to corral her stampeding fears, how she had fought him every step of the way, and how he protected her, and taught her things. So many things about trust and love. . . .

"But Mitch is different than any other man, Grandma. And like a fool I thought the money wouldn't be a problem, but I was wrong."

"No, you weren't," Lydia said decisively, moving from her seat to the large picture window absorbing the beauty of sky and water beyond. "He's known you were my only heir from the beginning. We aren't the Rockefellers or the Gettys, but Wentworth is a prominent name in financial circles. And Dr. Cade may spend a great deal of time in the wilderness, but he's no stranger to the business world. He had to be aware of your possible inheritance."

"It's not just the money itself," Erin clarified, her hands circling the heavy ironstone cup. "It's a matter of trust. I couldn't bring myself to tell him why I was here, and then it made everything else I told him sound like lies." Tears threatened to overtake her again, and she concentrated her energy on keeping them at bay. "He can't love me now if he can't believe me. He thinks I won't stay with him and share his life."

"Nonsense," Lydia said briskly. "I suspect he loves you very much; any fool could see that. He returned the grant check. That indicates to me how much he does love you."

"What? He can't do that; that's what he was going to use to finish his book. . . . Why did he do such a thing?"

"That's my fault too, dear. I'm just a romantic old fool," Lydia admitted. Erin was more stunned than ever. She'd never thought of her grandmother as having a chink in her all-business armor, and certainly not romance. "Dr. Cade reminded me so much of your father and grandfather . . ." Her voice faded away but came up strong again. "Just as an afterthought I made the stipulation that he must stay away from you, no entanglements."

"Grandmother!"

"It seemed right at the time." The older woman defended her decision, slightly ruffled. "And it seemed to work magic the first time. That's what your father was told when Claudia was put in his care. Your grandfather lost a good foreman for a few weeks but gained a fine son-in-law and business partner for the next

169

twenty years," she stated with a beaming smile. This was a new revelation on the familiar story that Erin had heard so many times. And she was at once appalled and charmed by her grandmother's schemings. Lydia's back was to her, but her voice was soft. "I will help you all I can, my dear. It's my fault this all came about. I should have never forced you into this situation. Perhaps I let old memories cloud my judgment? I'll never forgive myself if he's broken your heart, Erin."

Lydia's hands were knotted together, and Erin put her cup on the floor, rising from her chair to embrace her grandmother. "You saw my life going in circles, and you knew I needed a guide. He's everything you wanted him to be. Honest, proud, giving, and I fell in love with him. But I betrayed his trust. That's not your fault. It was my own misjudgment, and I let it get beyond control."

"You sound just like your mother did thirty years ago," Lydia said, tears in her eyes, which she brushed briskly away. "Now. What do you intend to do? Have you got a plan to remedy the situation with your stubborn Dr. Cade?" she asked, instilling confidence with her words. "You'll straighten this out with Mitch, and you'll have a love that will last your entire lives. Warren Markham was too weak for you. He sensed your strength and resolve before you knew you possessed them yourself. That's why he felt he needed to control you from the very beginning. But I was wrong, too. I wanted you to learn for yourself that he wasn't the man for you. I should have spoken much sooner."

"I did almost wait too long. But I made the right choice in the end." But had she made the same mistake a second time? Had she waited too long to set things right with the man she loved? "Last winter I had no idea what I wanted from life; now I do," Erin said thoughtfully. "I want Mitch. I want to share his life, have his children, and I want to do the best job I can managing my own affairs. You've carried that burden alone for too many years."

Tears shone in Lydia's matching blue eyes, but she smiled happily. "You don't know how long I've waited to hear you speak so decisively, and so enthusiastically. You've grown into the woman I always knew you could be. I'm so proud of you."

She held her granddaughter close for a long moment before sniffing away her excess of emotion and saying in her usual brisk tone, "Now show me around this new home of yours, and we'll discuss ways and means of bringing about a happy ending."

CHAPTER TWELVE

The eagle on the perch eyed Erin suspiciously as she tossed the wriggling fish onto the floor of the flight cage. Cindy was clearly disappointed with the appearance of her keeper, but she hopped down off the dead branch and efficiently dispatched the offering as Erin turned to hose the fishy odor from her hands.

Two long nights had passed, and Mitch was still gone. She had gotten a little comfort from sleeping in his bed, yet she was still alone. She had decided to move her things into his room to allow Lydia her bed, but once there she intended to remain by any means she could. She was going to make it as difficult as possible for him to erase her from his life. She, too, possessed the Wentworth ruthlessness, she was discovering—at least when she had a reason worth fighting for.

This morning Doc and George had loaded Lydia into the pickup to begin the long drive to Sault Ste. Marie. From there Lydia would start her long flight back to Washington. "I have to make more connections than the lobbyists on the Hill," she had joked. Her grandmother's presence had helped keep Erin confident, bolstering her courage and abetting Tex in plans to circumvent the tiresome ethics of his boss and cash the grant check. He would get Mitch to sign it or else, he chuckled, tucking the paper into his shirt pocket and patting it with a large satisfied hand.

"I believe you will too, Mr. Preston, and please don't let these two wait for a big, fancy wedding," Lydia pleaded.

"Yes, ma'am. Short, sweet, and to the point. It still gets the job done."

"Marry him as fast and as legally as you can manage, Erin," she directed in her parting words. "The way you two keep

172

misunderstanding each other, it will be your only excuse to stay together!" Tex guffawed in appreciation at her sally as Lydia smiled and leaned out of the pickup window to kiss Erin good-bye. "Don't worry any more than you have to; your love is strong, and you are a Wentworth, dear. That will last you a lifetime." Erin's spirits surged upward on a renewed hope as she waved farewell to her grandmother. But that was early morning, and the day dragged on into the afternoon as doubts returned to eat away at her resolve. Where was he? So many things could happen to a man alone. What if she couldn't make him listen to her when he returned? Endless circling, nagging fears picked at her, keeping her short temper on edge.

"You'll have to wait him out if you're really set on havin' him," Tex told her with the patience of experience as she sat picking at a late lunch. And that's what she was going to do if it took years.

The barred owl chicks were clamoring to be fed, and Erin dropped the carcass of a dead mouse before each one, being more than careful to keep her fingers out of harm's way. The downy fluff that had covered them was nearly gone, and their beaks and talons were a real danger. They were almost ready to fly, and Tex would soon take them out in a hack box and teach them to hunt for themselves. Time was passing so quickly, yet the minute hand of the clock stayed still.

"He's back," Tex announced from the entrance to the long cabin. "He's sitting in the house, and he's in no mood to talk to me. I think he needs to see you," he went on. "He doesn't know you're still here . . ."

"Thanks, Tex." She smiled thinly and picked up a bar of soap to stall for time, trying to calm the panicked roiling of her stomach. Thoughts aligned, broke ranks, then regrouped. She rehearsed her words over and over as she washed her hands in the sink by the door, concentrating on making lather in the soft cold water and drying them painstakingly on the towel. That important task accomplished, she smiled once again for Tex.

"I'm going to head into town and have a beer and catch a double feature until the dust clears," Reuben answered. "The other guys won't be back till evening. You've got plenty of time to talk some sense into him." He winked at her, and she felt a blush stain her cheeks. She swallowed hard, gave his arm a squeeze, and rushed toward the house.

The screen banged behind her with a satisfying whack, but Mitch didn't stir from his chair near the fireplace. His beard was thicker, and his eyes stared at her from dark hollows. She wasn't sure what she had expected his reaction to be, but she didn't like the stoic silence that greeted her. The only thing worse would be his total rejection. Her courage was crumbling, her joy ebbing from her as he continued to stare, his eyes dull and flat.

"Mitch, I've been so worried about you," she said clearly. He flinched at the sound of her voice. His eyes narrowed as she repeated her statement, taking a step forward that moved her out of the reflected glare of sunlight from the window. "Are you all right?" The fears that she had shunted aside when she first saw him were returning. Why didn't he speak to her?

Mitch jerked to life at her movement, levering himself up out of the chair, his riveting gaze never leaving her face. The sleeves of his shirt were rolled back to reveal corded forearms, and she reached out to him, needing the reassurance of touching him.

"Erin?" He smiled briefly, lighting her darkness, but almost immediately the smile was transformed into a questioning frown. "Why are you still here?" It was a cold, impersonal inquiry, and she clamped her lips on a stammered reply as she identified the resentment in his words. This reunion was not what she wanted at all.

"I just spent two of the longest days of my life trying to convince myself that I didn't need to see you again . . ." He reached out and grabbed her shoulders. "Why didn't you leave with your grandmother? What are you still doing here?" His voice was a rough croak that purged her mind of practiced speeches, of carefully laid arguments, draining her of all her false courage. She wanted him to want her. She wanted to stay with him here, always, but he spoke as if she were a stranger.

"Are you telling me to go?" she asked in an unwavering tone, balancing on her wobbly legs.

"I don't like long good-byes," he said obliquely, a vacant expression erasing the irritated frown.

"That doesn't answer my question. Do you want me to go?" She searched his eyes for the answer she wanted to find. There

174

was pain lurking below the surface in the changeable hazel depths, but she could only take his silence as an affirmative answer. "I wanted to make sure you were all right before I go." She choked on the lie, swallowing the bitter disappointment she felt as her hand slid from his forearm. She refused to beg for his love. He nodded his silent reply, avoiding her eyes as his tortured hands released their punishing grip on her shoulders and lowered to his sides.

"I'll need someone to take me to the airport," she said solemnly, her lips feeling drained and numb, her heart breaking as she turned to step toward the blackened fireplace. He was cold-bloodedly cutting her out of his life. She felt like a tumor, a malignancy he wanted to surgically remove, neatly incise, and discard from his life like some of the specimens he examined in the lab. His detached calm was mocking her needs and tearing at her soul. She couldn't let it be this neat, this easy for him to be rid of her. It should be as painful for him as for her. Damn the man! "Why didn't you tell me about canceling the Wentworth grant?" she assailed him, her rebellious spirit rallying.

"I couldn't honor my part of the bargain," he growled a hint of animation sparking in his eyes. "Why were you so shy about explaining the strings attached to your inheritance? I gave you plenty of chances to tell me. Why did you keep it from me?" he demanded in return.

She turned away again. For the first time in her life, Erin wished she were someone else, a sophisticated, clever woman that could play this scene like a sultry character created by Tennessee Williams. She felt like an actess trapped in a nightmare play with an unhappy ending.

"Were you afraid I was after your money?" he questioned stiffly. "Is that why you didn't trust me enough to explain."

"Of course not," she breathed, an astonished expression on her pale features. How could he ask such a thing? She needed something to do with her hands, and she grabbed a large lighter from the mantel as she spun to face him once again. She was strong enough to regain her grandmother's confidence and her inheritance, but not woman enough to win the man she loved. Was she still a failure?

"I was wrong. Just as you were wrong not to tell me about

175

terminating the grant." She was beginning to recognize her best defense was to attack this aggravating, proud man as her eyes hardened into icy blue gems. He still loved her. He had to or he wouldn't lash out like this. He was hurting as badly as she. She had to break through the shell of hurt pride that he had erected around himself. She was backed against the edge of a deep crevasse and she had nothing else to lose. "Just when did you intend to give me my walking papers? After you got tired of me warming your cold, lonely bed?"

"Don't try that line on me, Erin," he ground out. He stepped toward her and then supplied his own answer. "Because you were using me to get what you wanted all along." She shook her head, but he ignored it. "Just a summer roll in the hay for the poor little rich girl while she sweet-talked Grandma into giving her the money. My assistant," he snorted bitterly. "Believe me, you put on a good show. You were very convincing. And like a jerk I fell for your act, hook, line, and sinker."

"Mitch, don't say anything else we'll both regret," she pleaded, a simmering rage growing deep in her vitals.

"You didn't even plan to tell me if you were pregnant, did you? You were just going to go back to Washington as if nothing had ever happened . . ." He stopped in midsentence, silenced by her frustrated shriek. She came toward him, spitting fire and impaling him with a burning glare.

"You can accuse me of anything you want. You can use me, spend every cent I have, I don't mind," she screamed. "But don't ever tell me I don't love you, do you hear? You've been so damn busy telling me what I feel, you obviously think I'm too confused to know my own feeble little mind. Well I'm not confused anymore. I know exactly how I feel." She hurled the lighter at him, and he caught it as she reached for another weapon, firing a wooden carving across the room.

"What did you say, Erin?" he asked, the angry hurt in his features being replaced by a subtle triumph.

"I'm not using you," she shouted, the words coming from the tips of her toes. "And don't ever tell me that I don't love you," she repeated, as her hand sliced through the air, emphasizing each word until her fist was brandishing like a sword.

"Are you sure you love me?" He began inching away from her

temperamental bursts, angling across the main room, dodging the sundry missiles she continued to hurl at him. His retreat drew her steadily forward as he sidestepped the furniture and fended off the rain of books, magazines, and ashtrays that she hurled in his general direction.

Her arsenal temporarily depleted, Erin stopped to catch her breath, her breasts straining against the soft fabric of her blouse. She brushed a curl off her forehead with an impatient hand wondering what he was going to do next. "Don't touch me," she hissed as he moved closer. "I can't stay angry at you when you hold me, and I want to be boiling mad. I'll be damned if I'll make it easy for you to send me away."

"My, my, you're beginning to swear like a trooper." He whistled as he watched the hurricane before him with a smile tugging at the corner of his mobile mouth. He reached out for her, but she darted away.

"I learned that from you too, Mitchell Cade!" she snarled. "I learned about eagles, bears, canoes, trust, love. . . ."

"Flying?"

She swallowed hard, for an instant unable to speak, remembering their soaring embraces and fantasy nights of love. "No! I may never fly again. I can't afford any more crash landings like this one," she started shakily, her breathing unpredictable. She shook her head, dispelling the lingering heady recall of his hands on her skin. "I'm a Wentworth," she told herself as well as him. "I've got Wentworth blood in these veins." She pointed to her narrow wrist as she pressed his retreat. "I finish what I start, and that includes this job." She snatched up a throw pillow from the couch and hurled it at his grinning face. "I'm going to stay until the banding is done. I'm going to finish what I started."

"You began working on my book," he baited as he continued backing away, slowing to a snail's pace if he got too far ahead of her.

"I'll . . . I'll . . ." Tears of frustration welled up in the stormy blue of her eyes. Why was he torturing her so?

"I think we might come to some arrangement about your work," he said, glancing about as he entered his bedroom, eyeing the signs of her feminine invasion, her comb and brush nestled by his on the dresser, her robe hanging on a hook by the door.

"A business arrangement," she repeated boldly. The twinkling skepticism in his eyes made her vaguely aware that he was not retreating, but leading her into his trap. She couldn't back down now, and her heart was pounding against her ribs as hope began to surge through her again. She lifted her chin defiantly. "You've been so busy informing me that I don't belong here, that you were too damned proud to ask me to stay. I want to stay. I want to be yours, no strings attached. But you blew it, professor," she said, reaching up with splayed fingers to shove on the unyielding wall of his chest. He stepped past the foot of the bed and backed away from her attack in a calculated ambush.

"And you love me." It was a statement not a question, but she answered it anyway.

"That is correct."

"I can't ask you to stay, Erin," he began seriously.

Stung by his words, she pivoted away from him, but he caught her above the elbow, swinging her back into his arms as they tumbled onto the bed.

"Let me go, Mitchell Cade! Let me off this crazy merry-go-round," she breathed as she tried to push him away.

"Not a chance. I'm never going to let you go again."

"I'm not staying where I'm not wanted," she gasped as she strained against his arms.

"You're exactly where I want you," he growled, rolling over with her and trapping her writhing body to the mattress with his length. She struck him on the shoulders with her fists, confused and dismayed by the sudden turn the confrontation had taken. He captured her dangerous right hand and pinned it to the pillow above her head, leaning his weight on her wrist. He levered himself up from her heaving breasts, but he used his legs to keep her from trying to kick free.

"I love you, but I can't ask you to stay," he grunted above her struggles, "until I ask you to marry me, you hellcat," he fumed, pressing on her. "Will you be my wife and have my children?"

She was still pounding his shoulders with her free hand when he bent down and captured her mouth with a savage kiss, nipping her tender lips with his teeth and dueling with her tongue. Her pummeling hand ceased its attack and reached to soothe the sensitive skin below his ear and angled up to curl into the soft hairs at the nape of his neck. She moaned softly as that familiar traitorous sensation flickered in her lower abdomen. But he didn't relinquish his power over her until he felt her rigid body become pliant, surrendering sweetly beneath him. Only then did he lift his head and speak in a husky tone.

"Answer me, Erin, will you marry me?"

"Did I hear you say you loved me?" she asked pensively, tugging at his earlobe with her free hand.

"Absolutely." He smiled down at her, starting a whole new song winging through her heart.

"Yes, I'll marry you, birdman." She returned his admiring look, guessing that those three little words were going to come on rare occasions from this proud eagleman. But it didn't matter as long as his feelings were true and lasted forever. Their lips met in a promising kiss, exchanging their love in a tender, breathless vow.

"I just want you to remember who forced me into this bedroom," he said, his eyes glittering and his mouth curved into an infectious grin.

"I'll remember," she smiled as a tint of color washed over her.

Cade pushed up onto his arm and slowly began to unfasten the buttons on her blouse, sliding his fingers intimately beneath the fabric to graze the velvet skin below.

"You're mine, Erin," he said as he opened the first fastening. "I'll take care of you as long as you need me." His fingers continued their task purposefully, causing her toes to curl with delicious anticipation as she wriggled her feet from her sandals. "When I first saw you, I thought to myself, I want to marry a woman like this, but I knew you were way out of my league. Then your grandmother sent you home with me like a lovely present, and I knew I wanted—you—to be my wife." He began work on another button. "From the time I brought you here, I didn't need Lydia's 'no entanglement clause' to remind me it was an impossible dream."

"You taught me so much." She smiled. "You taught me to trust you, but you couldn't bring yourself to believe me when I said I loved you." She swallowed hard, her captured right hand nestled in his palm. "I thought I would die when you left. You were so angry. I was afraid I'd lost you, betrayed you."

179

He gave a grunt of self-disdain. "I made a fool of myself then, just like today. All I knew was that you were leaving me. God, I couldn't bear that. The thought of your going back to Washington was splitting my skull, and I think I imagined the pain would be less if I hurt you."

"We ended up hurting each other." She nodded.

"I wanted you to stay, but I was afraid you'd grow tired of this life so far from everything you've ever known. If I felt the magic we share was dwindling away or saw that trapped look reappear in your eyes . . ." Erin was coming to realize her warrior god was susceptible to human frailties, that he too was plagued with doubts and loneliness in this mortal world. He needed her to be complete as badly as she needed him. And she experienced what she felt was impossible; she loved him even more.

"I thought I wanted to be free, but I was wrong." She spoke strongly, tears of joy glistening in her eyes. "I can't be whole unless I can spend the rest of my life with you. I had to learn to share, to give, to trust, so I could be truly free. You've given me all these things. I love you. That you can always believe, always." She reached up with her arm and pulled her mighty eagleman down to her waiting lips. The tenderness of his answering caress swept waves of desire through every nerve of her body. He moaned but lifted his head a moment, his breathing irregular.

"Why didn't you tell me about your inheritance?"

"I didn't want you to know my own grandmother didn't think I was adult enough to handle my own affairs. But I should have realized you already knew what a fool I am," she admitted sheepishly. "I've spent the last two days thinking about what a big and lonely responsibility it will be to handle the Wentworth estate. I don't know . . ."

"You're a fighter, Erin. You can handle anything that comes your way. But the job doesn't have to be a lonely one," he reminded her, pecking her lightly on the nose. "Please don't ever keep anything else from me," he whispered. "I'll understand anything if you explain it to me; don't let me imagine what you're thinking. Trust me." His lips were gliding across her cheek to nibble at her earlobe. "I've had a lot of experience accounting for large sums of other people's money, so if you need me I'll be here to help."

"All I have to do is whistle," she whispered, trying to keep her mind on the conversation. "Mitch, I've known for weeks I can count on your honesty and strength. And now I know I can trust your love." She kissed him lightly. "I love you so much," she said, eyes bright with emotion, but calm like a perfect cloudless sky. She pulled him back down to her with seductive intent, avidly caressing his wide mouth with her strawberry lips. Her captivating tongue flicked over his jaw, tasting his spicy skin as she nibbled along the column of his throat, completely disarming her golden warrior. His breathing was sporadic as he raised up and leaned his weight on his arms, releasing her wrist.

"Erin . . . ?" He seemed unable to finish his question. She carefully pursed her lips and blew out a long whistling tone, as she curled her arms around his neck.

"I've been practicing," she confessed, answering his arched brow with a sexy bedroom smile. "I love you and I need you for the rest of my life."

"You need me?"

"Absolutely." She nodded seriously, returning his silent regard. She didn't require his words. She could already feel his hardness swell and press against her, matching her own inner drawing beat. She slowly unbuttoned his shirt and freed it from the waistband of his cutoffs, sliding it over his broad shoulders. His fingers made quick work of the remaining buttons of her blouse, and he laid back the fabric, admiring her breasts still contained by her lacy bra.

Erin's hands tugged at the snap of his denims and lowered the zipper as he lifted her slightly to flick open the hook of her bra revealing her symmetrical beauty to his deliberate study and undisguised pleasure. Her clothes joined his on the floor, and she lay very still as his longing gaze blazed over her skin with tantalizing sensations. His palm smoothed over the flat plane of her abdomen, effecting a quivering wake in its path as it moved up to cup a curving globe. Her nipples were dark and round as his palm brushed over them, sending shuddering waves of desire through her as they involuntarily tightened into sensitive buds. Her hands roamed over his back in adventurous circles, as her fingers slipped inside the waistbands of his denims and briefs, sliding them provocatively low on his muscled buttocks.

The fevered passion of their night on the river was gone, replaced by a grateful awe. They fondled each other with tender patience and with the loving freedom of forever as they rediscovered ecstasy. Paradise nearly lost was paradise found. His hand moved to capture a shaded nipple between his thumb and finger, tugging gently to signal the erotic sparking of her passion. She arched her hips against his in subtle invitation, lifting closer to him as her breast brushed against his cheek. His beard was rough against the tender peaks, drawing a tiny cry from her. Erin closed her eyes against the sweet torture until his lips and tongue replaced his cheek and flirted possessively over the velvet rise, soothing and suckling the pointed tips, transforming pain into heated waves of shuddering pleasure. His hand slipped across her belly, tugging her jogging shorts over her hips, pushing them down her thighs. He stopped abruptly, lifted from her, and stood beside the bed.

"Mitch, please," she breathed. He smiled down at her as he slipped from his loosened pants and briefs, stepping out of them and pulling off his shoes with impatient hands. No longer encumbered by his clothes, he leaned over to divest her of her clinging briefs and she flagrantly studied his male form, intrigued by his every move, eager to learn each glorious golden detail of his body.

"You're beautiful," she whispered, her eyes scanning his bronzed torso and sturdy thighs as she raised her hands to welcome the powerful arms reaching for her.

"That's supposed to be my line." He chuckled.

"Uh-uh," she murmured, shaking her head. Her lips parted in anticipation of his kiss as he lowered next to her, and when his mouth closed with hers, she let her fingers trail upwards to bury themselves in his golden hair.

"I love you, Erin," he said against her lips. "I'll never let you go. Never." His words matched his passion as his hungry mouth left hers spreading fire across her sensitized skin to fasten on a responsive nipple, pulling it into the warm moistness of his mouth. His hand strayed and began a gentle stroking along the velvet line of her inner thighs. She moved with unconscious sexuality to accommodate the seeking caress, the loving exploration melting her into fluid, molten pools of desire. She lifted up, and their lips met to intensify the mounting tension and promise. She moaned softly under the searing pressure of his lips and the continued stroking of his fingertip. Her own hand slipped along his ribs over a jutting hip to boldly caress his manhood, lovingly returning the joy he was giving her.

With a groan he shifted his position covering her slender form with the weight of his body. She opened to him naturally with no hesitation, welcoming the probing entrance of his virility. His mouth covered hers with a heated passion as their tongues intertwined in exquisite coupling. He thrust deeper, aching to soar high with his life-mate. He pushed his chest up, his weight on extended arms, pressing deeper into his love as her fingers brushed through the tangled hair of his chest, snagging his flat nipple with her nail. She moved with sweet compliance to the rhythm of his body in hers, following his lead, urging him to greater heights with the seductive movements of her hips and hands. They scaled the pinnacle of delight in unison, as they descended wing to wing, mated, loved, collapsing in the embers of their own pleasurable inferno.

EPILOGUE

Primary colors flamed from the birch and maple that stretched along the shoreline as Erin stood on the suspended bridge over the Big Two-Hearted River. The autumn-tinted beauty was richly counterpointed by the conical pines, their black trunks reaching down the river bank and their verdant branches stretching toward the pristine blue sky. Ahead of her the red-brown river merged into the restless sparkling blue of Lake Superior, and a cold wind whipped at her as she made her way carefully onto the spit of sand dunes that separated the last stretch of river from the encroaching lake.

"Hurry up, Erin," her husband urged from the top of a dune. He was standing by the hack box that held the caged eagle. The box had been placed here several days ago so Cindy would have a chance to get her bearings and become more familiar with these new surroundings. Hopefully she would make this area her new home. They were returning the bird to the wilderness today, but they would continue to leave food on the hack box for several more days until she was hunting adequately for herself. Erin watched Mitch for a moment as he shrugged off his knapsack before turning to help her up the last slope of shifting sand.

"Would you like to do the honors?" he asked, grinning at her as she caught her breath from the climb. "After all your money paid for the radio transmitter."

"Are you making fun of my wedding gift?" she pouted, but her eyes were shining with merriment. "I thought it was perfect."

"It was, and if we ever get this bird released, I'll show you again just how much I appreciate your thoughtfulness." His eyes traveled over her with lazy regard, and her heart and breath

184

quickened in pleasurable response. Her new red and black wool jacket matched his, and now her cheeks had a rosy glow and her tousled curls glistened in the sun.

"Out here? We'll freeze to death! You'll really have to start showing some regard for my delicate condition," she reminded him, patting her still annoyingly flat stomach.

"That's the best wedding present of all. But I warned you about being a pregnant bride, Erin," he said with mock severity as he pulled her close for a long heady kiss that sent her senses winging skyward. "You were the one that insisted the wedding wait until the banding was finished." Erin nodded, beaming into his proud, loving face.

She had never been so happy. They were alone for the first time since their marriage a month earlier. Tex had left a few days ago, heading for warmer weather, but he would return with the eagles in the spring. Mitch and Erin would pack up soon for a quick visit to Washington and a move into a comfortable house near Cornell. There Mitch would be close to the reference materials he needed to complete the research for his book, and Erin would be near expert medical facilities, a fact he considered more important. "Imagine trying to get you fifty miles to the hospital in that jeep through the snow," he had growled when Erin had protested the proposed move. "And no," he interrupted her next words before they left her mouth. "You're not buying me a new jeep, at least not this year," he amended with a wicked grin. It was going to be a happy, busy winter, and she was looking forward to every day of it as she watched Mitch unpack the radio receiver and don heavy gloves. While she knelt to release the hasp of the cage, Mitch lifted the rehabilitated eagle from its confinement and checked her over one last time.

"Everything looks fine," he said as Erin unwrapped the special binder that protected the healed wings from contact with the box. "Ready?"

"Let her fly," Erin called happily as he launched the eagle skyward. The healthy raptor surged into the air with whipping strokes of giant wings, slicing her way steadily upward. She turned into the wind, glided over the river, and landed with reaching talons in the branch of a dead tree as though to mull over this sudden return to her own world. "Is she all right?" Erin questioned from the haven of her husband's embrace.

"I think so; she's just testing things. The transmitter is working fine," he affirmed, glancing at the directional finder by the box tuned into Cindy's designated frequency. "We'll be able to track her until she leaves the area in a few weeks."

"And we'll know for sure when she returns in the spring," Erin added with quiet satisfaction. "Do you think she'll set up housekeeping in the abandoned nest near the Big Two-Hearted?" Mitch started his answer, but at that moment Cindy took flight, rising with powerful beats to meet the warm currents of air above the water. Strong wings held her aloft as she spiraled higher, her head and tail gleaming snowy white in the sun. Erin used a hand to shield her eyes as she followed the flight to freedom, and Mitch kept a protective arm around his wife, giving her a reassuring squeeze. Would he ever really know the freedom she felt in the shower of his constant love? Erin's true independence could be marked from the moment she knew he wanted her to stay with him forever, free from loneliness at last. Her pleasure was even more complete now that it was confirmed that she was pregnant. A family to cherish and her own proud eagleman to love and protect her. She smiled in the splendor of her own paradise gained. Erin tugged at his hand, pulling Mitch down with her onto the sand to stretch out and watch the raptor from the wind-sheltered slope. "I can't wait for her to return next spring to see if she's found a mate."

"You're going to be too busy caring our baby by then to be tramping through the forest."

"Oh, no you don't!" She spoke with characteristic rebellion. "We'll bring our child along with us. We refuse," she said, tapping her belly, "to be separated from you for a whole banding season. We'll manage everything—together?" She ended her speech on an inquisitive note.

"Together," he affirmed, pressing her gently back into the sun-warmed sand. Before his face blotted out the sky, she saw the freed eagle pass over them once again in an upward spiral. "Are you sure as I am that we should be together for the rest of our lives?"

"Absolutely," she whispered, pulling his head down to meet hers. His mouth gently tasted her lips, before the kiss deepened and he gathered her into his arms. As their lips met and mingled, their love lifted them to join the soaring eagle—together.

LOOK FOR NEXT MONTH'S
CANDLELIGHT ECSTASY ROMANCES ®

162   VIDEO VIXEN, *Elaine Raco Chase*
163   BRIAN'S CAPTIVE, *Alexis Hill Jordan*
164   ILLUSIVE LOVER, *Jo Calloway*
165   A PASSIONATE VENTURE, *Julia Howard*
166   NO PROMISE GIVEN, *Donna Kimel Vitek*
167   BENEATH THE WILLOW TREE, *Emma Bennett*
168   CHAMPAGNE FLIGHT, *Prudence Martin*
169   INTERLUDE OF LOVE, *Beverly Sommers*

COMING
IN
AUGUST—

Beginning this August, you can read a romance series unlike all the others — CANDLELIGHT ECSTASY SUPREMES! Ecstasy Supremes are the stories you've been waiting for—longer, and more exciting, filled with more passion, adventure and intrigue. Breathtaking and unforgettable. Love, the way you always imagined it could be. Look for CANDLELIGHT ECSTASY SUPREMES, four new titles every other month.

NEW DELL

CANDLELIGHT
Ecstasy Supreme

TEMPESTUOUS EDEN,
by Heather Graham.
$2.50

Blair Morgan—daughter of a powerful man, widow of a famous senator—sacrifices a world of wealth to work among the needy in the Central American jungle and meets Craig Taylor, a man she can deny nothing.

EMERALD FIRE,
by Barbara Andrews
$2.50

She was stranded on a deserted island with a handsome millionaire—what more could Kelly want? Love.

NEW DELL

CANDLELIGHT
Ecstasy Supreme

LOVERS AND PRETENDERS,
by Prudence Martin
$2.50

Christine and Paul—looking for new lives on a cross-country jaunt, were bound by lies and a passion that grew more dangerously honest with each passing day. Would the truth destroy their love?

WARMED BY THE FIRE,
by Donna Kimel Vitek
$2.50

When malicious gossip forces Juliet to switch jobs from one television network to another, she swears an office romance will never threaten her career again—until she meets superstar anchorman Marc Tyner.